# NIGHTMARE

## S. K. EPPERSON

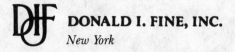

**DONALD I. FINE, INC.**
*New York*

ISBN 1-55611-338-2

Manufactured in the United States of America

Designed by Irving Perkins Associates

*This novel is dedicated to
my wonderful mother, Nelda, and
my sister Donna—words can't express
what you mean to me.*

# 1

## Thursday, May 5, 3:30 a.m.

To Cilla's thinking, the best place on the ranch to hide would be in the trees by the lake. No one would come to look for her there. Everyone was afraid of the lake at night, afraid of the sounds made by the mischievous gods of wind and water. Afraid of their own miserable souls in the powerful shadow of the wolf.

Cilla had no fear. The wolf was her guardian. Its bristling hairs were the tiny ripples on the surface of the water; its eyes were the moon and the sun. The vast, fluid torso of her protector was invulnerable to attack. She would feel safe in the shroud of the wolf. Its rumbling voice assured her of sanctuary in the high limbs of the cottonwood trees that lined the banks. All she had to do was reach those limbs.

Small cuts and gashes painted her way with blood as the greedy bark of the tallest tree sliced and gnawed at Cilla's flesh. She felt no pain. Even as the nails of her hand splintered and broke away during the climb, Cilla was urged on by the silvery eye of the wolf. There were no thoughts of the others, no thoughts of a life beyond this moment, when all that mattered was reaching the highest branch.

At the top of the tree, Cilla paused. With blood-smeared

hands and a heaving chest, she turned to look back. The house was visible from her position. There were lights glowing in a few of the windows. The sounds of men shouting to one another were carried to her by the wind. The wolf growled deep in its chest and tossed a fierce, petulant gust against the leaves of the trees.

They had discovered her empty bed.

Any moment they would begin the search.

Cilla smiled and perched herself on a sturdy limb. The eye of the wolf peered at her through the leafy canopy of the tree. Her chest bubbled with the sudden urge to laugh. They would never find her here. Never.

She opened her mouth and gave freedom to the laughter as another gust shook the tree limb. The sound amazed her; it was wild and throaty, full of victory. And her guardian was pleased, she knew, as she heard a high, answering whine. She looked out over the body of the wolf and spread her arms wide. Below the tree, the ripples on the surface of the water danced and swirled. Cilla ached to join the dance, to celebrate her freedom. . . .

"Jump," a voice said.

Startled, Cilla grabbed a branch and looked around herself. She could see no one.

"Jump," the voice repeated.

"Where are you?" Cilla breathed.

"Right here. Right here with you. Now jump."

"Oh . . ." said Cilla. "It's you again. You won't tell them where I am, will you?"

"No. Come on. I'll go down with you."

"I don't want them to know I'm here." Cilla looked toward the house again.

"No one will know. Come on, Cilla. It'll be fun."

"I'd rather play a game," Cilla said to the voice. "The wolf will protect us while they're out looking." She pointed to the moon. "See. It's watching over us."

"I don't want to play a game. I want to jump from the top of the tree into the water."

Cilla sighed in annoyance at the insistent voice. "You're not like the others," she said. "You want to be boss all the time."

There was no reply.

"Are you still there?"

"Let's jump."

Cilla's chin jutted. "I said no. I don't want to jump." She leaned back and began to fidget with a tiny branch above her. "I just wanted to go for a walk. They said none of us could come here, but I did."

"And you climbed all the way up the tree. There's nowhere to go but down, Cilla."

She blew air through her nose in frustration. "I'll show you the wolf if you like. Just look down." She leaned out on the limb and pointed to the dancing waters of the lake. Her torn and bleeding hands were beginning to hurt, but she didn't mind. The breath of the wolf tossed her hair and lifted her gown to tickle her legs.

"Everyone else is afraid to come here at night," she said. "They won't go to the boathouse either, because he said it might be dangerous. Animals come here to drink, he says. Coyotes mostly, and sometimes even bobcats. It's dangerous where we are now, but we'll be all right. Can you see the wolf? Look through the branches."

The voice was silent.

Sulking, Cilla thought. "I don't think the wolf would like it if I jumped. It might not be able to protect me that way."

"I'll protect you, Cilla."

"You can't," Cilla said. "How can you?"

"Let's go."

"No," Cilla said as she felt her thighs begin to slip from the branch. She reached out with her hands and grabbed a limb, but something inside was pulling. The voice inside was pulling at her legs.

Just one of the many voices inside of her, not real like her, but she was falling anyway.

Her arms scooped at the wind and crashed against spiked

branches as her legs left her perch. Her mouth opened to scream, but the air was already being sucked from her lungs as she plummeted toward the lake. Beneath the rush of wind in her ears, Cilla could hear the wolf snarling. There was a loud snapping sound as her neck connected with a thick, unyielding branch. There was a ripping sound and the tearing of flesh, followed by unbearable pain. Then she was in the water.

# 2

## Thursday, May 5, 3:30 p.m.

DAVID PEERED THROUGH the therapy room window and was surprised at what he saw: six women, several of them very attractive, sitting on the floor like children and drawing with crayons on large pads of paper. He looked for his brother and saw Bryan standing beside a desk beneath the windows on the other side of the room. He was going over some papers. David turned to reach for the door when he saw one of the women on the floor sneak a purple crayon into her mouth. He grimaced as he watched her begin to chew and spit out paper. Judging by the red flakes around her mouth, he thought she must have already eaten a red crayon. He looked to see if Bryan had noticed and saw him arbitrating a squabble that had erupted between two of the other patients.

David had second thoughts about going inside. He stood outside the window and watched as a woman with whitish-blond hair and incredibly white skin moved to stand over the crayon-eater. She bent over the patient with her hand extended, and David had time to eye a pair of long, slender legs before she stumbled back and jerked her hand away. The crayon-eater had bitten her. David could see the teethmarks in her hand filling up with blood. It spilled in thick red drops onto her straight brown skirt and spattered the carpet beneath her feet.

Bryan finally separated his dueling duo and looked up to see what had happened. He cursed to himself and whipped out his handkerchief. A pretty, petite brunette emerged from somewhere, and David could hear her strident voice through the glass as she spied the blood.

"All right. Who did it? Which one of you little brats took a bite out of Katie?"

Bryan snapped at her, and the woman snarled something right back. This, evidently, was Mel Kierkes. David had heard all about her some months ago. He didn't recognize the blonde from any description given to him by his brother, so maybe she was new. She was porcelain-pretty with her white skin, and David looked closer as he noticed how she backed away from Bryan and his handkerchief. This in itself was strange, since most women clamored to do exactly the opposite to Bryan Raleigh, noted psychiatrist and humanitarian.

He was older, forty-one to David's thirty-eight, but he was taller, suntan-handsome, and had the body of a seasoned athlete. His hair was blond, his eyes were blue, and David had seen him work his magic on countless women. These two who worked for him were obviously aware of the real Bryan, the bullying, manipulating, egoistic jerk.

David smiled to himself as he watched Mel Kierkes herd the group into some chairs around a table. Some of the women appeared to be grownups again; the crayon-eater was wiping the blood and crayon from her mouth with a quizzical expression. The embarrassed and uncomfortable looks on their faces caused David's smile to slowly fade. Working with multiples was no walk in the park, he concluded, and after a glance at his watch he turned away from the window and headed for the building's exit. Bryan's clinic was close to the famed K.U. Med Center, but good bars weren't far away, and he drove his rental car to the tavern where he had agreed to meet his brother for a drink.

The ad in the *Kansas City Star* personals had sounded just

desperate enough to intrigue him: *Proposition for you, David. Please contact me, L.B.*

The word *please* was a first in David's memory.

*L.B.* stood for little brother.

The combination of the two had been irresistible.

He wouldn't tell Bryan about his brief look at the therapy session or what he had witnessed. He had simply been curious about what his brother was up to these days.

Bryan was exactly twelve minutes late for their meeting. He made no excuses as he slid into David's booth.

"It took you long enough to get in touch with me," he complained to David. "Do you know how much those personal ads cost?"

David lifted a shoulder. "I don't read the personals on a regular basis."

"My mistake. You're happy to be single again, aren't you?"

David only looked at him.

Bryan smiled before turning to bark a drink order at a passing waitress. The girl jerked around with a go-to-hell expression that immediately melted upon sight of Bryan. David shook his head. Some things never changed.

"Bring me Glenfiddich," Bryan ordered. "And give him another of whatever he's having."

"Budweiser," said David.

The waitress smiled sweetly and made her way to the bar. Bryan watched her before turning back to David.

"Where have you been hiding for the last ten months?"

"I haven't been hiding," David answered. "I just haven't been in contact with you."

"Why? After I put myself on the line, the least you could have done was thank me."

"I didn't ask for any favors," David reminded him. "You did that all on your own."

Bryan snorted. "I should have let you go to prison, you ungrateful bastard. And you would have, believe me. The police would have laughed their asses off at the story you told me."

"It was the truth."

"So you say."

The waitress returned with their drinks, and David watched her hands linger over Bryan's as he gave her money. If he felt the urge, Bryan could have her up against the wall in the ladies room within the hour.

Bryan looked at him and curled the corner of his mouth as the waitress departed.

"Let's talk," he suggested.

"Yes, doctor," replied David.

"I'm serious. I want to hear what you have to say for yourself."

David leaned back. "I've said everything I have to say on the subject. I didn't kill her."

"But you have the money, don't you?"

"No."

"Liar. You must have it. You haven't written anything in months. I've been watching for your byline."

David looked away from his brother's blue stare. "What did you give him, anyway?"

"Who?"

"The medical examiner."

"Let's just say I helped his financial future considerably. He knew what he was doing when he called me. He's Frieda's cousin's brother-in-law, if that makes any sense."

"A dozen blank prescription pads?" David guessed.

"Forget it," said Bryan. "Where are you living? And when's the last time you had a haircut? You look like hell, David."

"Thanks."

"You want me to lie and say you look great?"

"No. I didn't come to talk about my appearance. And if you asked me here just to talk about Julia's money, then the reunion is over."

Bryan caught him by the arm as he made to slide out of the booth. "Relax, little brother. I do have a proposition for you. One that could mean a lot to both of us."

David hesitated, then he sat back again. "All right. I'm listening."

"Good," said Bryan. "For the last nine months I've been running a group therapy program for patients with a disorder known as—"

"Multiple personalities," David interrupted. "I've read about it."

Bryan's nostrils flared. He disliked being interrupted. "Two weeks ago I received a phone call from Dr. Russell Guerin. He's been working with multiples for more than a decade, even before it was recognized in the diagnostic journals as a distinct disorder. He's what you might call a pioneer in the treatment of multiples. And he's impressed with my work. So much so that he's invited me to join him and co-author a paper to be presented at the next International Conference on Multiple Personality, Dissociative States. He would like you to come as well."

"For treatment?" David inquired, and he had the pleasure of seeing his brother's nostrils flare again.

"To write a book on multiples for public consumption," Bryan said in a flat voice. "Nothing like *Sybil,* or any of those television movie-type dramas. Just good, readable documentation. The disorder is pathetically misunderstood, even by doctors. And it's far more common than anyone realizes."

"Why doesn't Guerin write the book himself?" David asked.

"Lack of objectivity. Not to mention the style the public seems to favor. He enjoyed the series you did on urban cults, and he seems to think you have a rare understanding, journalistically speaking, of human nature."

David smiled. "Right. It's been a great pitch, but I'm not interested."

"He already has a publisher, David. The advance could be in your pocket within the month."

"I don't need it."

Bryan's mouth twitched. "So you do have the money. What was she worth, anyway?"

"Goodbye, Bryan."

Bryan's hand shot out again, and this time his grip was un-yielding. "I'm not above blackmailing you on this, David. Ask for it or not, I took a hell of a risk for you. You owe me."

"If I go down, we'll go together," David replied.

His brother snorted. "I'm smarter than that and you know it. Frieda's cousin's brother-in-law is no longer a resident of this city. In fact, I don't think anyone knows exactly where he is."

"Have they checked your dumpster?" David jerked his arm out of Bryan's grasp. "What the hell is this? Does Guerin want a package deal? Both of us or neither?"

"*This* is important to me," said Bryan. "I've worked all my life for this sort of recognition, and if he wants you there too, then I'm going to do everything and anything to see that you come. You can even bring her along if you like."

"Who?"

"You know who. The girl Julia had her fatal fit about."

David's tone was bitter. "Bryan, there is no girl. There never was."

Bryan's expression said he didn't believe him.

Julia hadn't either.

"All right, David. Let's talk future. You're not doing anything now, are you? When was the last time you had an article pub-lished?"

David sighed and took a drink of his beer. Bryan was persis-tent as ever. And David had lied about not needing the money. He was almost broke. The lease on his apartment was up for renewal on Saturday, and the cable people were coming to shut him down tomorrow. No more ESPN for Frank.

"Where is Guerin working?" he asked.

"South," Bryan responded. "On a ranch in the Flint Hills. It's quiet and secluded. I understand his patients are made up of old money and new, so some amount of anonymity is going to be—"

David began to shake his head.

"I understand how you feel," said Bryan. "But Guerin doesn't pamper them in any way. There are amenities, of course, but these people are patients, after all."

"Are you taking Frieda?"

"No," Bryan said shortly. "She's busy with her photography class."

"What about Frank? Can I take him?"

"If you must," Bryan said, and his distaste was evident. "Does this mean you'll come?"

David sipped at his beer. "How do we get there?"

"By plane. Guerin has everything arranged. My bags have been packed for a week. All I had to do was find you."

"I'm not making any promises about a book," David told him. "How long will we be there?"

"It depends." Bryan slid out of the booth and stood. The waitress at the bar gave a little wave, and Bryan smiled at her before turning to David. "I'll expect you at my place by seven tomorrow morning. Try not to be late. And don't worry about bringing any equipment along with you. There's a word processor at the ranch."

David opened his mouth to ask what kind, but Bryan was already on his way out of the bar. He finished his beer and signaled the waitress, but she ignored him. Soon he grew tired of waiting and left.

The Flint Hills sounded inviting. He had been in the area once, years ago on a fishing trip. He wouldn't mind going back. There was only one element that disturbed him: old money and new.

It was a shame no one believed him about Julia's money. The house on Lake Quivira, the Jaguar, and the BMW had all been sold months ago. David hadn't received a cent. Julia had seen to that.

If anyone cared enough to check, they would find that everything of Julia's had gone back to where it had come from: her father's magazine. And if anyone cared enough to ask, they would find that David lived on his own meager savings, drove a rental car when he needed to go somewhere, and drank any beer on sale. But there was no story there. No scandal. People

preferred to believe he was hidden away in some uptown pent-
house, cackling as he counted his late wife's money.

He stopped at a supermarket just outside of Westport and
picked up extra shaving cream and toothpaste for the trip. He
thought about getting a quick haircut, then decided to hell with
it.

Frank screamed at him when he turned the key in his apartment door. David immediately placed a finger to his lips to
shush the blue-feathered parrot.

"Oprah!" Frank shrieked.

David kicked himself. He had forgotten to turn on the television when he left. Frank had missed Oprah.

"Sorry, Frank. My fault."

"Oprah!" the parrot insisted.

"Too late. I'm sorry. We'll watch Oprah tomorrow."

Frank knew what tomorrow meant. He glared balefully as
David passed the cage and carried his sack into the bedroom.

David had taken the parrot from a shop clerk while on assignment in Mississippi one hot summer. The clerk had told him
that the bird's foul tongue had angered God Most Holy, and so
he must be taken to the church and killed. David offered to pay
for the parrot, which had promptly labeled him "Whitey" the
moment he entered the shop, but the clerk refused his money.
David went to the owner of the shop, a snake-kissing preacher,
and explained that he would like to have the bird. The preacher
asked him for his watch and then called the store clerk. The next
day David had the bird, and God Most Holy had a Seiko.

Through frequent stays at various animal hostels, Frank's vo-
cabulary had expanded. David would come home from out-of-
town assignments and find himself subjected to a shrieking
chorus of the latest hostel lingo. It took him months to break
Frank of calling every dog he saw a "rabid little mongrel." All
cats were still "pussyboots."

Julia had hated Frank. The parrot had more than a dozen
names for her.

Frank squawked loudly several times before David realized he heard someone knocking. He left the bedroom and made a fist to shush the bird as he passed the cage. Frank rolled his eyes and tried to look helpless. David hoped it wasn't one of his neighbors. Frank was at the top of the apartment pet hit list. He ranked right up there with the yapping schnauzer three doors down.

David's visitor was the apartment manager. The hired gun of the neighbors. She said, "Mr. Raleigh, we need to talk."

"Maybe not," he said. "My lease is up in two days, and I've decided not to renew."

The manager's smile was weak. "Fine. We'll—"

"I'll be vacating tomorrow. I'll call to have the rental company pick up the furniture before Saturday."

"Good. Then we won't find it necessary to—"

"No, I'm sure we won't. Goodnight." David shut the door.

"Witch," said Frank.

David looked at the bobbing blue head and wondered if it would be possible to muzzle his pet. The ranch wouldn't be quiet for long if the parrot gave vent to his birdly frustrations every time something displeased him.

He walked to the cage and thrummed the bars with his fingers. "What do you think, Frank? Are you ready for something new?"

"Live at Five," Frank replied proudly. "News, weather, sports."

David stared at the bird, then he shook his head and went to his room to pack.

The moment David was out of sight, Frank began to scream for his nightly cup of beer.

# 3

## Friday, May 6, 9:05 a.m.

KATE BERQUIST CLOSED her eyes as the Beechjet began to lift. She wasn't afraid to fly, but her head was feeling strangely thick, and her ears and throat felt clogged. After a moment she opened her eyes and forced herself to swallow. She glanced over her shoulder to the left and saw Dr. Raleigh smiling at her. She smiled back and shifted her glance to the man in the seat directly across from her. He had been introduced as Dr. Raleigh's brother, David. A journalist.

"Gum, anyone?" asked Mel from the seat behind Kate.

"None for me, thanks," Kate answered.

"It helps. Better than popping your jaw."

"I'm fine, Mel." Kate looked down to the book in her lap and then glanced up again as a shriek sounded throughout the cabin. Two seats in the rear had been removed to accommodate the noisy parrot's cage, leaving only four of the jet's eight seats occupied with people going to the Guerin ranch. Kate still couldn't believe she was going. It was the only time she had ever considered herself lucky to be single and unattached. Mel had left a lover behind, but her lovers were always purposely forgettable. Lesbians lived dangerously, she claimed.

Mel was a social worker, Kate was an occupational therapist, and both had been with Dr. Raleigh from the birth of his group therapy program. There were other therapists, but all of them were married and none had been available for an extended trip away from home.

Lucky me, Kate thought. In thirty-one years she had never been more than a hundred miles away from the Kansas City area. A trip to the Flint Hills would be a definite change of pace for her. And a welcome one.

She glanced out the window and found herself entranced by the view. The ride was going to be a short one in the fast-moving jet. Already the land was mostly green, largely treeless, and seemed to roll along beneath them with a life of its own. The shadow of the jet was an amorphous gray ghost that twisted and writhed as it sped across the low hills and . . . She paused.

"Dr. Raleigh?" She twisted around to see him. "Not that I'm worried or anything, but how is this jet going to land in those hills?"

His smile was warm as always. "Only a mile or so is necessary. Guerin said the strip is close to the house, so I assume the land there is relatively level. He said it takes half an hour to—"

An ear-shattering scream from the parrot drowned out the rest of his words. He angrily thumped the seat in front of him. "Can't you keep that thing quiet?"

"It's his first time on a jet," his brother David said mildly. "He's excited."

"He's going to be dead if he doesn't shut up."

Kate cleared her throat. "Tell us about the ranch, Dr. Raleigh. How long has Dr. Guerin owned it?"

Bryan seemed relieved to have his attention diverted. "Actually, his wife is the owner. Augusta Arnette Guerin. Arnette as in the Houston Arnettes, which doubtlessly means oil. I didn't ask. It seems her father bought the ranch many years ago and willed it to her when he died. Guerin's son handles the ranch business and takes care of the livestock end of things."

"Livestock?" Kate repeated.

"Cattle," said Bryan. "The Flint Hills has some of the best grazing land in the country. There's only eight to ten inches of topsoil, but it's prime Bluestem grass. Other states ship cattle in to feed here."

"This is before they go to the slaughterhouses," said Mel. "That's where they have their brains caved in by an air gun, which is supposedly a much more merciful way to kill them than simply hitting them over the head with a sledgehammer and then slitting their throats."

"Thank you, Mel," Bryan said in disgust.

"Don't mention it," said the vegetarian Mel.

Kate cleared her throat again. "What about the ranch itself, Dr. Raleigh? How many acres?"

"Four thousand. With a pool, a stable, a lake, and lighted tennis courts."

Mel's face brightened. "A lake?"

"Several acres worth. It's a watershed built by the government in one of their efforts for water control. Most of the ponds in the Flint Hills are said to be spring-fed. Very clear. Hardly any silt."

Mel nodded and her look turned dreamy. "And a stable, too. I've always wanted to meet a horse up close and personal."

Kate looked out the window. "What other kinds of animals are there?"

"The usual. Prairie chickens. Rabbits. Coyotes. Maybe a few snakes."

"No," said Kate.

David looked up from his magazine.

"It is a ranch, Kate," Bryan said in a soothing voice. "I won't let anything happen to you. I promise."

"Where will we be staying?" she asked.

"In the big house."

Kate lifted her brows. "Everybody in one house?"

Bryan smiled. "I thought the same thing until Guerin told me the place has more rooms than the White House. He was probably exaggerating, but he assured me there's plenty of room for everyone. He said the first level contains his clinic and the patients' rooms. The second level is for guests, and the third level is used exclusively by the family. There's a separate dwelling for the ranch workers."

Mel was impressed. "I hope the food is good. If Mrs. Guerin is a Texan, then there's bound to be some strange combinations on the menu, like chili and fried chicken in one meal."

Kate wrinkled her nose. "Texans eat that?"

"And worse," Mel assured her. "Much worse. Ask me to tell you about a restaurant in Lubbock sometime. It was harrowing, Kate."

Kate grinned and twisted around to see her. "Tell me now."

"Later." Mel darted a warning glance to the men and dropped her voice. "I don't think the Brothers Grim would appreciate the details, since all the entrees turned out to be the fried testicles of one species or another."

"Ugh." Kate made a face and looked to see the hint of a smile on David Raleigh's mouth. He had heard.

She sat back in her seat and turned her head just enough so she could study him through her lashes. He didn't look much like Dr. Raleigh. His hair was brown and his eyes were a different blue. He wasn't as tall and his shoulders weren't as broad. Still, Kate thought he had his own appeal. It was probably in his expression, a look he wore that said nothing you did would surprise him.

Kate knew a little bit about him. His wife, the daughter of a wealthy magazine publisher, had committed suicide last summer. Kate read about it in the paper. The woman had been several years older than David, and wealthy in her own right. Dr. Raleigh had been in fits about her suicide when it happened, not so much distraught as distressed. Kate looked at David Raleigh and wondered how he had dealt with his wife's death.

He didn't appear to be the jet-setting type. She couldn't see him in the tuxedo or the tails he had surely worn when accompanying his late wife to various social functions. She couldn't see him in anything but what he wore: a white cotton shirt, baggy khaki cargo pants, and scruffy brown loafers with white socks.

On his jaw was a dark strip that he had missed while shaving, and he occasionally lifted a hand to rub at the spot while he read.

Kate allowed her eyes to close. According to Bryan Raleigh, his brother David didn't give a damn about anyone but himself.

With the possible exception of the parrot that was now repeatedly calling his name. Kate opened her eyes and looked openly at David.

"What does he want?"

David put aside his magazine. "My attention."

Kate smiled. "How old is he?"

"Twelve. Just a kid."

"Is that right? How long have you had him?"

"Six years."

"I can see it," Bryan interrupted. "We're almost there. It's even bigger than I thought."

Kate and Mel strained in their seats to see their destination, but Bryan and David had the best view.

"There's the lake," Bryan said in excitement. Then his voice abruptly changed. "David . . . is that what I think it is? Did you see it?"

"Yes," said David.

"What?" Mel was unbuckling her seat belt. "What did you see?"

Bryan had to swallow before he spoke. "A body. A body facedown in the middle of the lake. It looked like a woman."

Kate blinked and looked to David for confirmation. He met her glance for only an instant before turning back to the window. She would swear she had seen a flicker of excitement in his face.

"A body?" Mel said. "A dead body? A floating dead body? Are you joking?"

Bryan didn't answer.

"Are you sure it was dead?" Mel continued. "It could have been someone swimming."

"It wasn't a swimmer," said Bryan.

"Well, if you think I'm getting off this plane now, you're crazy. Forget the Multiple Personality Ponderosa, I've seen enough hack-and-splat movies to know the setting when I see one."

"Shut up and fasten your seat belt," Bryan told her. "We're landing."

Mel stared at him. "Shut up? Dead bodies floating around, and you want me to shut up?"

"Mel, your seat belt," said Kate.

"My seat belt." Mel's hands moved to fasten the buckle. "You calmly, rationally ask me to worry about my seat belt when we're about to land at friendly Camp Hackaway."

Kate swallowed repeatedly as the jet descended. Mel went on grumbling, joined by the parrot, and between the bumpy landing and the discordant noise, Kate was sure she was going to be sick.

"Okay, let's go," said a level voice, and Kate looked over to see David unfastening his seat belt. He went directly to the front of the plane, where she assumed he would speak to the pilot, a surly fellow named Grant. Kate unbuckled her own belt and gathered her purse and her book. When she stood she turned to look at Mel, who hadn't moved.

"You're getting off?" Mel asked in disbelief.

"We don't know what happened," Kate told her. "It could have been an accident."

"Not likely," Mel replied.

"Come on, Kierkes." Bryan stood. "Let's find out what the hell is going on."

"Okay." Mel threw her hands up. "All right. But don't anyone give me any lip when I say I told you so. This place has already been crossed off my list of vacation hideaways. Me and Robin Leach. 'Would you care for a body with that vintage, sir? Oh no, serve it with the Grey Poupon, Charles. And make sure it's chilled in the lake first.' Fine. Just wonderful. No one believes in intuition anymore."

Kate left her and followed Bryan to the exit. When they reached the ground she turned back to see David coming after them with the parrot's cage in one hand and Mel's arm in the other.

"Let go of me," Mel snarled at him.

"Look," Bryan said suddenly, and three heads turned to follow his gaze. "Guerin said it was close to the strip, but I didn't think it would be this close."

Less than three hundred yards away, behind a sparse growth of cottonwoods, Kate saw a large brick mansion looming over the tops of the trees. The house was huge, seeming to take up two or three acres worth of the level ground. She didn't count the windows across the third story, but she decided there couldn't be less than a dozen. The dark red brick monstrosity seemed to intimidate the landscape, shrinking the distant surrounding hills with its immensity.

"Looks like a criminal institution," observed Mel. "Big Daddy definitely lacked taste in architecture."

Kate silently agreed.

"I'll lay odds right now there's a room with stuffed dead things inside," Mel went on. "And maybe a gargoyle or two. Any takers?"

Bryan looked at her in annoyance. "Mel, do us all a big favor and keep it to yourself, all right?"

"Our welcoming party," David said with a nod.

Kate looked and saw a man dressed in denim leaving the cover of the trees. His spine was ramrod-stiff as he approached them. His hair was black, his skin darkly tanned. He didn't smile as he greeted them. His dark eyes flickered briefly over the small party and lingered on Kate before he extended a hand to Bryan.

"I'm Jay Guerin. My father is waiting for you in the house. He would have met you himself, but there's been a small crisis. One of his patients is missing."

"Not anymore," said Mel.

Jay Guerin looked at her. "Excuse me?"

"We have some bad news," Bryan explained. "Let's go in and see your father."

# 4

## FRIDAY, MAY 6, 10:25 A.M.

THE FIRST FLOOR reminded David of a certain hotel lobby in Santa Fe, New Mexico. White stucco walls with wooden beams and red tiled floors, Indian rugs, pottery and sculpture; large over-stuffed sofas and chairs arranged around a huge fireplace; a bar against one wall, French doors that opened onto a patio, and a large, ornate elevator.

Women whom David assumed to be patients were every-where. They wore shorts and swimsuits and a few held tennis rackets as they sat on stools at the bar and eyed the newcomers. He looked around and saw hallways on opposite sides of the room. He guessed that one hallway led to the patients' rooms, while the other doubtlessly led to a dining and kitchen area.

He was impressed with what he had seen thus far of the house. He was less impressed with Dr. Guerin, a paler, grayer version of his son, who seemed less disturbed than annoyed with the news of the body in the lake. He ran a thick-knuckled hand through his hair and looked impatiently at his son. "Go down and try to get her with the outboard."

Jay nodded. "I'll take Tim and Grant with me."

"Be careful with her, Jay," Guerin ordered.

Jay turned his back on his father and quickly exited the room. David watched his retreat and decided that father and son were not the best of friends. It was in the way they looked at each other.

"Would you mind telling us what happened?" Bryan asked.

Guerin turned to him. "Her name was Sheila Muehler. She was twenty-eight, healthy, but a problem patient from the very beginning. Her host personality was very weak and easily dominated by an eleven-year-old named Cilla. Cilla was a chronic runaway, sometimes on a daily basis. She loved to play hide-and-seek on the ranch, always claiming that her wolf would protect—"

"Wolf?" Mel looked at Bryan. "I thought you said there were only coyotes here."

"A fictional wolf, Miss Kierkes," Guerin assured her. "Sheila came from Hollywood. Her mother is an actress, and her father was an animal trainer. Unfortunately, he was also a very cruel man. When he lost his temper he would beat Sheila along with his animals, until the day he found himself locked in one of his cages with a newly acquired and unusually aggressive wolf. Sheila's mother was convinced that her daughter had something to do with her father's death, but nothing was ever proved."

"So the wolf symbolically became Sheila's protector from harm," Bryan guessed. "Or rather, Cilla's."

"Exactly," said Guerin. "She claimed it watched over her always."

"How old was Sheila when her father died?" asked Bryan.

"Eight years old."

Mel was frowning. "None of that explains what she was doing in the lake."

Guerin's tone became defensive. "Cilla was very willful and resented any form of authority. I couldn't control her. She probably decided to defy the rules and go for a moonlight swim. She must have gone in the water, suffered a cramp, and drowned."

"Well, I know *I* feel better," Mel said in a dry voice.

Guerin looked at her in angry surprise. Then his shoulders

sagged and lines previously hidden appeared in his face. "I realize this wasn't the best of welcomes. I'm sorry you had to be involved, believe me. I'll get someone to show you to your rooms and we can talk later. All but you, Mr. Raleigh. My wife is anxious to meet you."

David lifted a brow as he realized Guerin was talking to him. He opened his mouth to ask why, but the doctor had already left his chair to disappear down the hall to the right.

"Hi, there," Mel said to the women lining the bar, most of whom had been staring. "Never seen such a vibrant beauty before?"

"Mel," Bryan said in warning.

"I was talking about you, Raleigh."

Guerin returned with a small Mexican woman in tow. "This is Juana. Maps of the house and the grounds will be given to each of you. If anyone has a question or a problem with the room, just see Juana. Meals are informal here. Breakfast is served from seven to nine, lunch from twelve to two, and dinner from six to ten." His shoulders lifted at the group reaction to his announcement.

"Everyone has a different body clock," he explained. "I find it easier to accommodate personal habit than to enforce any ridiculous rules of etiquette. Now, if you'll excuse me, I need to call Sheila's mother."

"And the police," Mel said pointedly. "They'll want to know, won't they?"

"Yes, of course," said Guerin. "Mr. Raleigh, would you come with me?"

David glanced at Frank. The bird had been ominously quiet since their arrival.

Guerin laid a hand on his arm. "Don't worry. Juana will have someone take your pet up to your room."

As if on cue, Juana guided the small group across the floor and into the elevator. David followed Guerin down the hall to the left and into a room that presumably served as the doctor's office. Once inside, Guerin closed the door and walked to a tiny intercom on the wall behind a massive mahogany desk. He placed a hand over the speaker.

"There's one of these in nearly every room of the house—excluding the guest rooms, of course. My wife is bedridden, Mr. Raleigh. She hasn't been out of her rooms for several years now, but she still likes to know what's going on in the house. I wanted to prepare you for your meeting with her. She's quite obese, and, well, you might say she's an imperious sort. She's also very keen. If she senses disgust, no matter how well disguised you think it is, it will upset her. Do you understand?"

"Why does she want to meet me?" David asked.

"I don't know," Guerin said frankly. "I've been married to her for thirty years and I still can't guess her motives."

"You're saying it was actually her idea that I come here?" David asked. "Not yours?"

Guerin glanced down at his desk. "When I told her I was going to ask your brother to come here, she immediately requested that you join him." He looked up then. "But don't get the wrong idea, Mr. Raleigh. I do want a book, and I'd like it very much if you agreed to write it."

David rubbed his neck. "We'll see. You lost me back there with the host-personality business. Why don't you make your calls so we can get this over with?"

Guerin nodded and took his hand from the intercom speaker. He moved to flip through a Rolodex beside the phone on his desk. When he started to punch in the number, David let his gaze wander around the office. All the right certificates were on the walls. No pictures on the desk. Maybe three tons worth of file cabinets and bookshelves against the walls. The man was obviously serious about his work.

"Hello. This is Dr. Russell Guerin."

David looked back to the doctor. The name of the woman Guerin asked to speak with took him by surprise. But it explained why Sheila was here. The further away from Los Angeles, the better. Guerin's voice lowered then, but David heard enough to guess that Sheila's mother was on location and couldn't be reached until later. Guerin went on speaking and mentioned transporting the body back to California. He told the other party he would put Sheila on a plane as soon as he received the go-ahead from the local authorities.

The second phone conversation was not as cordial.

The local authorities appeared to be less than happy to hear from the harried Dr. Guerin.

"Investigate all you like," the doctor snapped before hanging up the phone.

"Why do I get the feeling this isn't the first trouble you've had?" David said.

Guerin looked at him and frowned before pulling at his collar. "Are you ready?"

David nodded. He followed Guerin into the hall again and through the lobby to the elevator. The trip up was a short one. When the doors opened he immediately noticed the change in the lighting. The third floor appeared to be dimmer than the rest of the house.

Purposely? David wondered. Here, as on the first floor, there were whirling ceiling fans every twenty feet. David guessed the electric bills in the summer were in the headache range. Migraine, if the pool was heated.

"This way," Guerin said. Another large, lobbylike room, ostensibly a living area. Another hall and another door, outside of which sat an incredibly robust woman. A nurse, David guessed. She looked up and nodded as they approached. David eyed the huge female and suddenly wished he had asked Guerin if the woman in the bedroom had some sort of contagious or dangerous disease.

"Just here for a short visit, Rosalie," Guerin said to the muscular maid.

"She's awake," Rosalie responded.

"Good." Guerin opened the door and poked his head inside. "I've brought Mr. Raleigh to meet you, Augusta."

David heard a sound of assent, then he was pulled inside the room.

Dark. Dark and cool. The only light seemed to come from some kind of control panel beside a monstrous bed.

And on the bed was a monstrous woman.

*Obese?* David thought in the first wild seconds after his eyes had adjusted. Had Guerin said obese? Surely he had meant to say *leviathan.*

Like a kid in church, David had the sudden hysterical urge to laugh. Elephantiasis? he thought, torturing himself as he bit the inside of his cheek to keep from bursting out and spraying the silk coverlet of the bed.

The poor woman appeared to be wearing about a size-eight slip, which barely covered a pair of massive breasts with huge nipples. Her hair, indeterminate in color, was splayed fanlike across the highest of a row of pillows behind her head. Her swollen fingers were adorned with rings: large chunks of gems that perched on settings buried in flesh. When her mouth opened, David saw a shifting and resettling of the folds of skin that made up her chin and neck.

"Welcome to my home, Mr. Raleigh. I'm so pleased you could come."

The voice was smooth and sexy and completely incongruous with the rest of her.

"There's a chair at the foot of the bed. Won't you come and sit down? Russell, you can leave now. I'll ask Rosalie to show Mr. Raleigh to his room when we've had our chat."

No yellow rose from Texas here, David told himself while still biting the inside of one cheek. More like a slip-covered Twinkie. The hostess with the mostest.

His mouth threatened to twitch again—it was ridiculous, he knew, but he couldn't seem to stop—and he hid his face as he moved to the chair.

"I'll see you later, Mr. Raleigh." Guerin backed out of the room, and David could sense the doctor's relief as he escaped into the hall and closed the door. It was a pretty safe assumption that Mr. and Mrs. Guerin hadn't shared a bed for a few years.

There wasn't room in this one. Anywhere.

David took a deep breath and made himself look at the control panel. Intercom switches for each room, he guessed. And probably controls for the television screen and stereo system on the wall behind him . . . and maybe a ninety-eight-decibel dinner gong.

The bad jokes flew into his mind in rapid succession. And all the while she was looking at him, studying him with a pair of tiny glistening eyes that reminded David of two chocolate M&M's stuck in a glob of rising bread dough.

Finally she smiled at him. "Amusement is a very human reaction, Mr. Raleigh."

No anger in her voice. An almost regal tolerance, but no anger.

"I'm nothing if not human," David managed.

"You look just like I thought you would," she said sweetly. "Bookish, but still very masculine. What have you been doing with yourself?"

He stared at her. "What do you mean?"

"In the months that you haven't been writing. What have you been doing with your life, David?"

*Frankly, Augusta, it's none of your business.*

He wanted to say that. He resented her familiar tone, and it was, after all, a fairly personal inquiry. At the risk of displeasing the queen and being decapitated before lunch, he decided to remain silent.

"Forgive me," she said when he didn't answer. "I'm a big fan of yours, and I was disappointed when you stopped writing. I was so very impressed with you."

David had no doubt that she was his *biggest* fan.

"Is that why you wanted to meet me?" he asked.

"Oh, yes. Your interest in the unusual has been evident throughout your career. Has that interest waned?"

"I don't know. Maybe it has." He decided to play it safe. He didn't know where she was going.

"I see," Augusta said with a frown. "Your failed marriage had something to do with this, no doubt."

David angrily opened his mouth, but she apparently wasn't interested in a debate. She extended one large fleshy arm and pushed a button on her panel. Only then did David see and smell the baby powder. She was covered with it.

"Rosalie, please show Mr. Raleigh to his room. I've finished with him for now."

He was dismissed. Not only had he displeased the queen, but David felt certain he had disappointed her as well. In what way he had no idea, but her sudden coolness was not in his imagination.

"Mr. Raleigh?" Rosalie was waiting for him at the door.

David stood and left the room without another glance at the woman on the bed. He couldn't say he was happy to have met her, because he wasn't. Four minutes with the matriarch and he felt like covering his privates and checking his back for the hilt of a bloody dagger.

Creepy, he thought as he entered the long, dark hall. She was definitely creepy. There was no other word to describe the fat woman with the control panel and the M&M eyes. David felt as if he had just been through some kind of interview. One that found him lacking.

While waiting for the elevator with Rosalie he glanced toward the living area again. The furniture on this floor was more plush, the decor more feminine. He wasn't surprised at the lavender and purple; Augusta doubtlessly imagined herself to be royalty of some sort. But if the woman hadn't been out of her bed in several years, then she never saw the decor.

Rosalie, he decided, was perfect for her job. Anyone who attended Augusta would need the arms and thighs of a wrestler, and perhaps the disposition, as well. She led him out of the elevator on the second floor and then paused as a beeper attached to the pocket of her smock sounded.

"You'll have to excuse me, Mr. Raleigh. Just go to your left here. I believe your room is the third door on the right. I'm sure everything will be satisfactory."

She was gone before he could move. The beep was a summons

from her royal thighness, no doubt. The moment the elevator doors closed he moved down the hall to his right. No lobby-living area here; it was more like a rumpus room, complete with a large screen TV and VCR, a stereo system with a CD player, a long sofa with matching chairs, a card table, a video game machine, and a ping-pong table. Beyond this mammoth room he found a library and more bedrooms, each one containing a queen-sized bed, a vanity, a chest of drawers, a walk-in closet, and a small bathroom.

David let out a low whistle and went back in the direction he had come, counting doors from the elevator. He saw Bryan unpacking some books in the second room on the right. Directly across the hall from Bryan's room, he heard Mel Kierkes muttering to herself behind a closed door. He stopped in front of the third room on the right and saw Frank's cage resting on a table by a window. The parrot's feathers were ruffled up around his neck. He was upset about the move, David guessed.

The door across the hall from his room was slightly ajar. He peered through the crack and saw Kate standing before a window, both hands clamped over her mouth.

He pushed open the door. "What's wrong? Are you all right?"

She turned and looked relieved when she saw him. She pointed out the window. "I don't think that woman drowned, Mr. Raleigh."

"What?" He moved beside her and looked out the glass. On the ground below he saw four men standing over a body on a tarpaulin. The pasty white flesh of the corpse was marred by numerous gouges and long scratches. One of the men knelt down and attempted to straighten the impossibly twisted neck of the corpse. When he succeeded, Kate fell abruptly away from the window. David had the same impulse, but his feet remained rooted. He was helpless to do anything but stare at the stringy red mess that had once been a face. One eye was missing and most of the chin and nose appeared to have been eaten away by whatever lived in the lake.

Jay Guerin spun on his booted heel and walked away from the

other men. Jay's stiff spine was in a definite slump now, David noted, and he found himself feeling around in his pockets for a pad and a pencil. A woman was dead, mutilated, and his journalist's instincts said to record every morbid moment.

Then he caught himself. This was no ordinary woman. This was a patient with a mental disorder and a history of pain in her short, tragic life.

David didn't know what was wrong with him. He shook his head and dropped his hands.

"Mr. Raleigh? Did you hear me?"

"What?" he said brusquely. Then he blinked and turned around. "I'm sorry . . . Kate, is it? Call me David."

Her skin was so pale it appeared translucent. For the first time he noticed her eyes, round and china blue. She picked nervously at the bandage on her hand.

"What do you think happened to her? I mean . . . her neck."

"I don't know," David said. "But I'll be interested to hear what the police have to say."

# 5

## FRIDAY, MAY 6, 1:00 P.M.

THE POLICE WERE two young deputies from the sheriff's department, accompanied by two men from the coroner. David made sure he was downstairs when the body was bagged. As one deputy went into Guerin's office for more questioning, David approached the other man outside.

"Is this the first time you've been out here?" he asked.

"Who are you?" the deputy replied without looking at David. His eyes were following the body into the coroner's van.

"A guest," David told him. "Just arrived today. We spotted her from the jet."

"Oh."

"So what's your guess, Deputy Waltman?" David asked after looking at the name above the deputy's badge.

Waltman shrugged. "I couldn't say. I think maybe she was in a tree and fell out. There was a leaf stuck in the collar of her nightgown. Twigs in her hair. There are cottonwood trees all around that lake, and they're thick with limbs. Probably how she got all cut up."

David was impressed. "How long have you been with the sheriff's department?"

"About a year. I was out here last time, too. During the Russian thistle harvest."

"What's that?"

"It's where they burn off all the thistle and the ragweed so the grass can grow in. They do it around March or April every year."

"And the fire got out of control?" David guessed.

"No—hell, no." The deputy was comfortable now. "Jay knows what he's doing. Some lady just walked into the fire. Burned the hide right off her. She was a charred-up mess before anyone got to her. Probably still in a hospital somewhere. Another one of the kooks, I guess."

"Why was the sheriff called?"

"The Guerins didn't call us. The gal's folks did. Say, what was your name again?"

David stuck out his hand. "David Raleigh. I'm here to write a book about the kooks."

Waltman grinned. "A writer, huh? Are you famous?"

"Yeah, sure," David lied, matching the deputy's grin.

"Well, hey, if you get bored or anything just come in to Marwell and we'll drink a beer or something. Jay knows where I live."

"I'll do it," David said. "See you later, Waltman."

" 'Bye, now."

David walked inside and took his house map out of his hip pocket to find the dining area. He took a right into the hall by the fireplace and passed up five or six rooms until he came to another hallway. He made a left and found himself entering what the map called the dining hall.

Bryan sat alone at one of more than ten tables. Mel and Kate were making lunch choices from a cook-monitored food bar, behind which was a cut-out in the wall where he could see through into a steamy, industrial-sized kitchen.

The White House version of a cafeteria, David imagined, with large oak tables and chairs and sink-to-the-ankle carpet.

"Is this something?" Bryan asked, and showed David his plate. "Trout Almondine."

"Augusta must be rolling in something besides baby powder," David murmured as he sat down.

"What?"

"Never mind. I'll tell you later." He had suddenly remembered the intercoms. He couldn't see one, but he assumed there was one somewhere in the room. He lowered his voice. "I just talked to one of the deputies outside. Sheila Muehler's accident was not an isolated incident. A month or so ago another patient walked into the fire at the yearly weed burn-off. Deputy Waltman said her parents called—"

Bryan dropped his fork with a loud clatter. "Just what the hell are you doing?"

David looked at him. "What do you think?"

"I think you're trying to figure out a way to screw this up for me. We're here to help Guerin, not investigate him. Damn you, David, why does everything have to become complicated when you're involved?"

"Whoa," said Mel as she approached with her tray. "I don't think we want to sit at this table, Katie. The blood is running thicker than the gravy."

David stood. "Have a seat, ladies. I won't be joining you."

He left the dining hall and made his way back to the bar in the front room. He removed two beers from a chest-high cooler and walked to the elevator. It was in use, so he looked for some stairs to climb. He found them in an alcove by the French doors. He paused in front of the doors and looked out onto the house-length patio. Two women were doing lazy laps in the pool; two more were sunning themselves on redwood chaise lounges.

Were there any male multiples? he wondered.

"Did you bring a suit?" a female voice asked, and David turned to see a smiling, slender brunette eyeing him. She wore a red bikini. Barely.

"No, as a matter of fact, I didn't," he said.

"I'm sure Jay has something that will fit you. You look about the same size." The woman stepped forward and put a hand to his crotch, causing David to jump, swear, and nearly drop both beers.

"Maybe not," the woman said, smiling. "You may have to swim without one."

A patient, David reminded himself as he backed toward the stairs. The woman was a patient here.

The patient slowly lowered one strap from her shoulder to show David a pale, coral-nippled breast.

His feet struggled to find purchase on the stairs behind him. Finally he made himself turn to see where he was going.

Behind him he could hear the woman laughing.

In his room he opened one beer and filled up the beer cup in Frank's cage. The parrot came to immediate attention. "Bud."

"No, it's Miller," said David. "But it'll do." He took a long swallow and looked out the window to the pool for a moment before taking out his map again.

"This is a strange place, Frank. But you already knew that, didn't you?"

Frank was too busy slurping to answer.

David took a drink of his beer and stared unseeing at the map while he thought of what Bryan had said to him in the dining hall.

When the first beer was finished he opened the second. Frank looked up hopefully, but David shook his head. "You've had your limit."

He concentrated on the map again and saw that the stables and the house for the ranch workers lay on the other side of the pool cabana. He could see only the roofs from his window. The tennis courts were on the southeast side of the house, fairly close to the pool, and the lake appeared to be less than a quarter of a mile away, due south.

"Eyeballing the bathing beauties?" Mel sauntered into the room and looked over his shoulder. "What a nice view. I hope I'm not interrupting anything."

"No," David said with a smile.

Mel put a finger to Frank's cage and immediately snatched it back as the parrot lunged.

"He bites," David told her. Then he turned to look at her. "Didn't I just leave you in the dining hall?"

"I wasn't that hungry. I was more curious about your spat with Golden Boy."

"Why?"

"Anyone who can make him lose his cool as easily as you can has got to be worth knowing."

"Why do you work for him?" David asked.

"Because he's good."

"But you don't like him."

"I respect him."

David nodded. "What about Kate? Is there something going on between them?"

Mel shrugged. "Nothing romantic. You ask me, he babies her too much. Kate doesn't like it. But she respects him, just like I do."

"Why does he baby her?"

"I don't know. Probably because of the way she looks, like she'd shatter if you played the right Memorex tape. The original china doll."

David finished his beer and stood up. "Come on. Let's take a tour of the ranch."

"Anywhere but the lake," Mel told him.

"Too bad. That's my first stop."

"Seriously? Why?"

"Put on your walking shoes and meet me downstairs," David said, and Mel lifted her eyes to the ceiling.

"I knew you were trouble the minute I laid eyes on you. You didn't buy that drowning business, did you?"

"No, and you wouldn't either if you'd seen the way her neck was broken. I want to check out the deputy's tree theory. Coming?"

"Yes. I can't stand not knowing, and you won't tell me if I don't come. Can we take horses?"

"Have you ever ridden?"

"Not horses," she said with a sly grin.

"Horses can make you sore," David warned.

Mel winked at him. "So can anything else if you stay on long enough. I'll meet you at the stables."

Twenty minutes later they had secured two mounts from a watchful stable hand and were riding south away from the ranch. Mel grinned and bounced in her saddle. "I could learn to like this. My Levis are rubbing in all the right places."

"Tart," David teased.

"You wish. Am I holding the reins too loose?"

He looked. "Don't change a thing. You're doing fine."

"Your horse is bigger than mine," Mel observed. "Where did you learn to ride?"

"Argentina."

"No kidding? On assignment?"

David nodded. "In my youth I covered all the important issues. I wrote a documentary of a rock group on their first world tour. When they wanted to ride the pampas, we all rode the pampas."

Mel laughed. "You lie like a rug."

"I'm serious," he said. "I also learned how to throw a bola and say a few words in Portuguese."

"All around the world, huh? Which country was your favorite?"

"This one. You can drink the water."

"Speaking of which, can you smell that?" Mel asked.

David could. The wind was blowing from the south, and the scent of the lake grew stronger with each plodding step of the horses hooves. In minutes they were approaching the high bank. The deputy had been right: there were large, thick-limbed trees all around the shimmering lake.

"What's that?" Mel hissed suddenly.

David followed her dark gaze. He smiled. "You know what that is?"

"Why would I ask if I knew what it was?"

"It's an antelope," he said.

"You're joking. As in 'where the deer and the antelope play'?"

"That's right. It must not be able to smell us. The wind is in the wrong direction. I didn't know there were any antelope left out here."

"Don't tell Kate," Mel warned. "That girl is weird about animals."

David watched the antelope's ears flick as it drank from the lake. From less than a hundred yards away, the white markings on its body looked pure as new snow.

"Why?" he asked.

"Why what?"

"Why is she weird about animals?"

"I don't know. Oh, look, it sees us."

It did, but the antelope clearly didn't know what to do about it. It lifted one tiny hoof in indecision, then seemed to opt for flight as the best precaution. David was sad to see it go. His horse whinnied and strained its head toward the water, as if the scent were pulling it forward. David dismounted and walked the rest of the way up the bank and down to the water's edge. Mel followed suit.

"It looks so peaceful. It's hard to believe that a woman actually died here last night," Mel said as she watched the horses plunge their noses into the clear water.

David ignored the statement and looked at each of the trees around him. "If you were a runaway, which tree would you choose to climb?"

Mel looked up. "The tallest, probably." She pointed. "That one."

"Let's take a look."

"You take a look. I'll wait right here. When you come back, let's check out that little boathouse."

David handed her his reins and followed the bank until he

reached the trunk of the tallest tree. Once underneath, he looked up. The tree was perfect for climbing, with most of the heavier branches reaching out over the water. Many limbs were broken, he noticed. Halfway up, he spied a scrap of fabric clinging to a branch. He lifted himself into the tree and climbed up to the scrap . . . then he climbed back down. It wasn't fabric, it was skin. The inhabitants of the lake were innocent. The bark of the tree had ripped Sheila Muehler's face away.

"Well, Inspector?" Mel said when he returned to her.

David exhaled. "She must have fallen out of the tree and broken her neck on one of the bigger branches. The deputy was right."

"You sound disappointed," Mel remarked.

David said nothing.

They remained silent a moment, both lost in their own thoughts as they stared out over the glittering surface of the lake. Finally, Mel handed him the reins and made a move toward the small boathouse. As David turned to follow her, she held up a hand to stop him. "Don't come yet. I have to pee."

"Hold it and we'll go back to the house."

"I can't. Do you have a tissue or anything on you?"

"Sorry."

Mel grumbled and disappeared around the side of the boathouse. David held the reins and waited. He turned back to look at the tree again, and the hair on his neck suddenly bristled as a low, sonorous wail sounded across the water. He jerked his head in the direction of the cry, but the wind foiled him. Mel came wobbling around the side of the boathouse, still pulling up her jeans.

"Very funny. I peed all over my shoe."

"That wasn't me," David told her.

"Oh, sure. If you—"

The cry sounded again, louder this time. David locked gazes with Mel.

"I'm ready to go anytime," Mel said.

"Maybe a bobcat," David suggested, just for something to say.

Bobcats were mostly nocturnal animals, but he didn't think Mel would know that.

"Yeah, a bobcat. Wouldn't be the ghost of that dead lady or anything, now would it?"

"Did you look in the boathouse?"

"I saw a boat through the window. Let's go before this turns into a Tobe Hooper movie."

David walked away from her and headed for the boathouse. The last cry he heard had seemed to come from that direction. A few yards away from the boathouse, the horses stopped and refused to go any farther. David dropped both sets of reins and went on, leaving Mel to catch up the horses.

The interior of the boathouse was dim. David felt along the wall beside the door until his fingers found a switch. The moment he flicked on the light, a high screech assaulted his ears. In the corner of the boathouse, sitting beside a row of gasoline cans, was the source of the sound.

The noise she was making didn't bother David nearly as much as the sight of the screwdriver the woman was using to stab herself in the head.

He shouted for Mel and rushed toward the injured woman. Her light brown hair and most of her face were soaked in blood. David grabbed the wrist with the screwdriver and tried to yank the tool away. The strength of the woman amazed him. She held on and aimed for her eyes while she screamed at him over and over again to get out and leave her alone. "I won't do what you ask!" she shouted. "I can't! Please don't ask me!"

Mel came to the door and wasted no time in joining the struggle. She rushed over and held back the woman's left arm while David wrenched the screwdriver from her right hand. The woman was still screaming. Over the noise, David asked Mel if she could ride back to the ranch and get help.

The woman went stiff suddenly and froze. Her eyes focused on neither David nor Mel but on something beyond them.

"I can't hurt anyone," she whispered.

Mel and David looked at each other.

"Can you go for help?" David asked Mel again.

"You'd better do it," Mel answered. "I can handle her better than I can handle a horse."

"Are you sure?"

"I'd stake my career on it. You go on." Mel gathered the woman to her and held on tight, trying hard not to look at the dark, seeping wounds in the blood-matted scalp. Mel had seen a few head wounds in her time, but this was her first glimpse of actual, living brain tissue. She closed her eyes and tightened her arms as her stomach gave a threatening heave.

"I don't know about you, Raleigh, but I'm ready to blow this place. Go back to work for SRS and nag people on welfare. I don't need this."

David was already running for the horses.

# 6

## FRIDAY, MAY 6, 6:00 P.M.

THE MEETING WAS informally held at the bar. Guerin served drinks to his four guests, then sat wearily on a stool, looking even paler than he had that morning.

"I cannot explain these events," he said. "It may be a chain reaction of some kind. I've worked at the ranch for three years without a single incident. Now I have three in one month. I can apologize to all of you, but I can't explain it. If you wish to leave, I understand."

Bryan put his glass down hard on the bar. "No one is leaving. We came here to demonstrate how our program works and that's exactly what we're going to do."

Mel and David traded a glance.

"Chain reaction may be exactly what you're dealing with here," Bryan continued. "At the risk of sounding archaic, I firmly believe that violence begets violence. The best course, as I see it, would be to make certain none of the other patients hear about this latest incident. If you tell them Miss Martin simply discontinued her therapy, their host personalities will have to accept that as fact. It's the other personas, in my opinion, who react to the trauma and begin to grow unwitting seeds of their own."

Kate sighed inwardly as she listened. Dr. Raleigh obviously didn't intend to have his plans thwarted by a few troubled patients. She glanced at Mel, who had told her what happened at the lake, and then she looked at David, who had forced Dr. Guerin to acknowledge the first in these series of accidents. A woman who walked into a fire, another who broke her neck in a fall from a tree, and a third who attacked herself with a screwdriver. Kate eyed the tension in David Raleigh's hands and the strange light in his eyes and wondered why he appeared to be excited in some odd way by these events.

"It shouldn't be difficult," Guerin said finally. "I'll instruct Jay to keep everyone quiet about the real reason for Miss Martin's departure."

"Did you contact her relatives?" asked Mel.

"She has none, Miss Kierkes. Melanie Martin placed herself in my care." The doctor's face changed then and became more animated. "Now, if you're all staying, then we should talk about a schedule. As you know, most of my days have been filled with individual sessions. I see each patient for three hours, once a week. With fourteen patients—well, twelve now—I'm not sure exactly how we should fit in your group therapy sessions."

Bryan nodded. "At home we have one group that meets twice a week for four hours, and another that meets only once a week, usually in the afternoon, for the same amount of time. It's up to you."

"I think mornings would be best," Guerin said. "Then I can still conduct my individual sessions in the afternoon, and the ladies can enjoy their leisure activities during the warmest part of the day. We can split them up into groups of four. There'll be less argument that way. A few of them—"

"No men?" David interrupted.

"Most multiples are women," Guerin explained. "And a fact that might shed light on the reason is that nearly ninety-five percent of multiples were abused as children, with seventy-five percent of that number suffering some form of sexual abuse."

Mel added, "Many little boys who are sexually abused become abusers themselves. They aggressively act out their pain, while little girls withdraw and internalize."

Guerin looked at her in disapproval. "You are, of course, generalizing." He turned his attention to David then. "I meant to ask where you would like the word processor to be placed. Would you like it in your room, or perhaps the second-floor library?"

"There's no desk in my room," David pointed out.

"I can fix that," Guerin said with a smile. "You'll have free access to all my notes and most of my files. I thought we could use the video equipment to record the group sessions for you. I'm afraid your presence in the room would be too disruptive. I understand you met Natalie today."

"Red swimsuit?"

"Yes."

"She met me."

Guerin waved a hand. "It wasn't really Natalie, you understand. It was Cindy, a fourteen-year-old exhibitionist. Natalie was mortified at Cindy's behavior with you. She's asked me to apologize."

"She knows about Cindy?"

"Yes. It's the other four personas she doesn't know anything about. But I'm working on it." Guerin looked at his watch then. "I hate to leave you, but I usually eat my supper at this time. Would anyone care to join me?"

Bryan and Mel immediately stood, leaving Kate and David sitting at the bar.

"You didn't have any lunch," Mel reminded David.

"Not hungry yet," he told her. "I'll see you later."

Kate felt a small spark of envy at the wink shared between them. Mel was friendly and gregarious and made friends so easily with people. Kate wished she were more like her. She wished people felt more comfortable with her. When the others had gone, she turned to David and said, "Do you think she'll be all right?"

He paused with his beer halfway to his lips. "Who?"

"Melanie Martin."

"Oh. I don't know. It was pretty bad."

"Where did they send her?"

"K.U. Med Center. Bryan plays golf with the chief of staff." David put down his beer. "Did you agree with his idea of not telling the other patients?"

"I have no choice but to agree," Kate said. "I work for him."

David's smile was crooked. "At least you're honest." He studied her a moment, then said, "Mind if I ask you a personal question?"

Kate's voice was cautious. "What?"

"Is that white hair natural?"

"Yes," she said coolly.

"Don't be offended," he said. "I told you it was personal."

"My turn," she said.

He looked at her, waiting.

"Why do you dislike your brother so much?"

David winced. "No fair. I asked you a yes or no question."

"I thought there might be a simple explanation for the animosity between you."

"Do you have any siblings?"

"No."

"Then you wouldn't understand if I told you. My turn again."

"You didn't answer mine yet," she protested.

"It wasn't a yes or no question," he reminded her.

"All right. Go ahead."

"Are you involved with Bryan?"

"What?" Kate was shocked. "Of course not. What made you think I was?"

"His proprietary air."

"Oh. No, Dr. Raleigh is like a father or a brother to me," she explained. "Besides that, he's married."

David's beer went down the wrong way. He twisted away as he coughed the liquid from his lungs.

"Did I say something funny?" Kate looked at the droplets of beer on her white blouse. "Are you jealous of him? Of the way he looks?"

David wiped his mouth and tossed her a napkin. "No, sweetheart. He doesn't have anything I want. Sorry I sprayed you."

Kate felt twin spots of heat in her cheeks as she dabbed at her blouse with the napkin. She wished he hadn't called her sweetheart in such a reckless, offhand manner. It felt somehow demeaning.

"How did your meeting with Mrs. Guerin go today?" she asked. "What was she like?"

"Unusual," David said loudly. Then he slid over next to Kate and put his mouth close to her ear to tell her about the intercoms. His whispering tickled; she ran her hands over the goosebumps on her arms and frowned when she heard about the control panel.

"Really?"

He nodded and moved away again. Before he could reach for his beer, a buzzing sound from above made both of them start.

"Mr. Raleigh, this is Rosalie. Would you please take the elevator to the third floor?"

David looked upward. The speaker was in the ceiling directly above him. He shook his head and smiled at Kate.

"Can I come with you?" she asked in a whisper.

"No," a voice said behind them, and Kate turned to see Jay Guerin approach. "When my mother wants to meet you, she'll ask for you. Mr. Raleigh, please don't keep her waiting."

David inclined his head and got off his stool. Kate was tempted to follow him anyway, but Jay Guerin was standing beside her and watching her with an enigmatic expression in his black eyes. Only when David reached the elevator and went inside did Jay speak.

"I haven't had a chance to talk to you . . . may I call you Kate?"

She nodded.

"How's your room? Did you get settled in all right?"

"Just fine, thank you. Everything is beautiful. You must be very grateful to your grandfather for buying this place."

"Yes and no." Jay's teeth were a brilliant white against his tanned skin. "It's a lot of work. But there is something he left me that's worth gloating over. Would you care to come and see it?"

"Where is it?" Kate asked uncertainly. His black gaze was unreadable.

"The third floor. It's a rare gun collection."

"Guns?"

"Rare guns. It was his hobby, and now it's mine. I show them off every chance I get."

The pride in his voice persuaded her. She nodded and allowed him to guide her to the elevator. Once inside, she stepped discreetly away from him and wondered how to voice her question. Finally she took a breath and said, "Jay, is your mother ill?"

"No," he said. "She just stays in her room."

Kate opened her mouth to ask why, but the elevator was already stopping on the third floor. Jay led her out and walked her past an opulent purple and lavender living area into a corridor with several closed doors. Kate wondered if David was behind one of those doors.

Jay stopped before one and took a key ring out of his pocket. "The patients," he explained. "Occasionally they like to wander where they don't belong."

"Are the guns loaded?" Kate asked.

"No." Jay smiled as he twisted the knob and opened the door. "But they are priceless. Come in."

Kate entered the room and saw wood-framed cabinets with glass doors covering every wall. Track lights suspended from the ceiling illuminated the gleaming metal and polished furniture of the dozens of handguns hanging in display behind the glass. The smell of oil filled her nostrils as she moved to the center of the room.

"So many . . ." she breathed.

Jay pulled her back to the door and guided her to the left. He was beaming now. "We'll start here. Do you know anything about the history of guns?"

"Not really," Kate admitted. "The Chinese were the first with gunpowder, right?"

"No," he said. "That hasn't been proved. They had pyrotechnic substances, along with the Greeks, but it wasn't gunpowder. It had no explosive properties. They can't prove who had gunpowder first, but the first documented evidence occurred in the writings of a thirteenth-century Franciscan friar."

"A friar?"

"Yes."

Jay Guerin resembled his father when he was animated, Kate noticed. She wondered what his mother looked like.

"What was the first gun?" she asked, hoping he would take his hand from her elbow to illustrate.

He did. "It was a cannon, actually. Big, awkward things. But by the thirteen fifties they came up with what amounted to a portable, under-the-arm cannon about three feet long with a one- to three-foot iron barrel. Imagine the recoil on that sucker," he said with a grin.

Kate's smile was weak. "Um, who was doing this?"

"You name it," he replied. "Anyone with brains could put together saltpeter, charcoal, and sulphur and come up with gunpowder. I could bore you and go on to tell you about matchlocks and wheel-locks, which worked like your average cigarette lighter, and then the percussion principle."

"Don't," Kate said with a smile.

He didn't hear her. "And then there were flintlocks, breechloading, and eventually the revolver, Ted the Red's big love."

"Ted the Red?"

"Theodore Arnette. My grandfather."

"Ted the Red?" Kate repeated. "Did he have red hair?"

"No, he was a hemophiliac."

Kate looked to see if he was serious. He was.

"Ted was big on Sam Colt. He devoted half of his free time to reading about the man."

"Colt, as in Colt revolvers."

"Yes. One legend says the idea for Colt's first gun came from the wheel of a ship where he served as a cabin boy. After his sea days were over he supposedly went ashore and became one Dr. Coult"—he paused to spell it for her—"with his own traveling medicine show. Can you imagine that? The man who practically perfected death by hand and made killers out of cowards was a practicing con artist.

"I'll tell you what else he was," Jay quickly continued. "He was a sharp businessman with an idea of industrializing the making of his guns. Eli Whitney helped him. Mr. Cotton Gin had his own arms-manufacturing business, you know."

"No, I didn't know." Kate was fascinated by Jay's story, but something wasn't right. There was something in the cracking of his voice and the rigidity of his body.

"Whitney took on Colt's order for a thousand revolvers because Colt didn't have the equipment to do it. Colt's company went broke in the same year he blew up the Tombs prison trying to get his brother out of jail. Well, they never proved it was old Sam, but he *was* working on some new explosive at the time. The prison was blown all to hell, but John Colt didn't get out. He married his sweetheart in jail and killed himself with a knife she smuggled in to him. He was going to hang for murder, anyway."

Kate let her gaze fall from her escort's face long enough to realize what was wrong with Jay Guerin. He had become sexually aroused in talking about his guns, and his state of arousal was now quite obvious.

"Now this," he was saying, "is what Mr. Colt and Mr. Whitney produced after General Zach Taylor sent Captain Sam Walker to see our boy. This is a Colt Walker. Only two thousand were manufactured, so I don't have to tell you how rare this gun is. Fifteen-and-a-half inches long and a handful at seventy-three ounces, this big awkward monster was the first six-shooter.

Walker was a soldier, remember, and he knew what he wanted out there on the field . . ."

"Jay, I think—"

". . . and Colt listened to him. But after those first two thousand, Colt's own wheels were spinning again, and he came up with this, the Colt Dragoon. And here, of course, is the legendary Colt Peacemaker, the gun to have in the Old West. Ted used to—"

"Excuse me," Kate said, and she stopped where she was. "I should be going now, Jay. This has all been wonderfully fascinating, and I'd love to come back and continue another time, but I haven't had any supper yet and I'm feeling a little tired. Would you mind if we did this later?"

Jay's face fell. "I'm sorry. I didn't even think to ask if you had eaten. It's so rare that I have company, I can be an idiot about bending someone's ear. Forgive me?"

"Of course." Kate was ashamed. The man lived on a secluded ranch with parents, patients, and people who worked for him. It couldn't be easy.

"I've already eaten, otherwise I'd join you," Jay said as he steered her toward the door. "Perhaps tomorrow you'll let me show you around the ranch."

Kate didn't know what to say. She gave a half nod.

"Can you find the elevator?" he asked. "I'm going to stay up here for a while."

"I'm sure I'll be able to find my way back," Kate told him. "Thank you for showing me your collection."

"My pleasure," he said. "It's one of the best in the country. I'm very proud of it." He touched her arm then. "I'll see you tomorrow. Goodnight, Kate."

His eyes were flat black and unreadable again. Kate smiled at him and exited the room. In the hall she let out the breath she had been holding and raced for the elevator.

# 7

"THIS HAS BEEN a very long day, Mrs. Guerin," David said for the third time.

"Just one more game, please," she said in her most alluring voice. "I promise not to Yahtzee more than once this time. You start."

David heaved a sigh and picked up the dice from the box on her bed. He threw three fives and two fours.

"My full house," he said.

"Wise decision," Augusta told him. The scent of baby powder came off her in waves as she scooped up the dice and took her turn at throwing them.

"My ones. I always like to get those out of the way. You can never throw them when you need them. Your turn."

Crazy, David thought as he scooped up the dice and tossed them. This is crazy.

"You should take your threes, David. Really."

"Fine." He rolled twice more, adding one more three to his score. He thought he would feel better if he could roll a Yahtzee. In five games he hadn't even come close.

"Are you such a poor loser?" Augusta asked. She had changed

her gown, or perhaps she had somehow added material to the other one. David couldn't tell in the dimness.

"I'm tired," he said. "And hungry."

One pillowy arm reached for the control panel. "I can send Rosalie to fetch you a sandwich."

"No, don't. I'll get something later. Roll the dice."

"You don't have to be so abrupt with me," Augusta complained. "You are a poor loser."

"Roll the dice," he repeated. Everything he had felt earlier in the day had been replaced by pity and the disgust Dr. Guerin had warned him about earlier. Augusta was a lonely lady, starved for attention and desperate for even the most unwilling company.

"No," she said. "I don't want to play anymore. We'll talk now. I've been watching you, and I think I did the right thing in bringing you here." Her voice dropped to a conspiratorial tone then. "Tell me, David, where did you acquire your taste for the macabre? Was it in war?"

David stood. "I never fought in one. If we're not going to play anymore, I'd like to go. I've got a date with a parrot and a tape of today's Oprah show."

"Sit," Augusta said, and her voice was no longer low and feminine. The simple command shook the skin of her jowls with its fierceness.

David remained standing. "I said I'd like to go."

"You are a guest in my home, David. I expect you to show me some respect. Now sit down and listen to what I have to say to you."

"Mrs. Guerin, I don't—"

"SIT!" she roared, and puffs of baby powder leapt into the air as one chunky fist struck the mattress.

Reluctantly, David sat. He didn't want to be held responsible for a heart attack. If the drool on Augusta's row of chins meant anything, one would be coming along any minute now. Her massive breasts were heaving.

"Is everything all right?" Rosalie's face was grim as she peered into the room.

"Get out of here," Augusta snapped.

The door closed.

David waited for the queen to calm herself. When she did, the seductive voice returned, honeyed as ever. The M&M eyes were fixed on him as she placed one thick finger to her temple. "I know what you must be thinking by now. But I want to tell you why I asked Russell to bring you here. He laughs at me, but I know I'm right about this."

"About what?"

Augusta dropped her hand to smooth the silk coverlet. "Something is going on around here, David. Something very wrong."

"What do you mean?"

"I can't say. I just know it's happening. I can feel it. The day that woman walked into the fire the feeling was very real. And Russell lied to you people. There have been other incidents, all very minor in comparison to what's been happening lately, but incidents nonetheless."

"Why would your husband lie to us?" David asked.

"To save face. His work means everything to him. And I'm sure he doesn't want to alarm anyone."

"Can you be more specific about these feelings of yours?" David asked.

"You're ridiculing me," Augusta said.

"I'm not. I just want to understand what you mean."

"I mean it's something foul, is what I mean. I don't trust anyone anymore. And no matter what they've told you, I'm a prisoner here. Rosalie is my guard."

"I see," said David.

"Do you think any sane woman would allow herself to come to this state? They have forced me to become what I am."

David lifted a hand to rub the back of his neck. He was tired. And hungry. "Just what do you want from me?" he asked.

"I want you to find out what's going on. I know you can do it."

"I'm a journalist, not a private investigator."

"You're a bloodhound," Augusta replied. "And you enjoy it. I've read your work and I know you, David Raleigh." She paused then. "Julia tried to ruin you, didn't she? She tried to change you and make you into a different kind of man. Don't tell me she succeeded, David."

He was out of the chair and crossing the floor before she could call him back. Rosalie was startled out of her eavesdropping as he jerked open the door. The nurse fell back and away as he pushed past her and strode down the hall.

For a moment he could see Julia's face as she lay on the steel table in the morgue. He could see the tiny curve of her lips, the triumphant jut of her jaw. Even as she died, she believed she had won.

He punched the elevator button with his fist and willed the vision away. She had won nothing. He was still here and he was still standing.

Women with wealth were a breed unto themselves, he thought as the doors sealed him inside the elevator. At some point in their lofty lives, they lost touch with reality. Whatever interest he'd had in Augusta's fears of wrongdoing at the ranch had been strangled by her manipulative remarks. He would stay out of it. He needed operating capital, and if he could squeeze out a few hundred manuscript pages for Guerin and Bryan, then everything would be fine. But that was it. There was no sense in getting sucked into the paranoid delusions of a rich, crazy fat woman. And she was crazy. David was convinced of that. If he had been cooped up in the same room for several years he thought he might be foaming at the mouth, too. But that didn't excuse her remarks about his personal life. About his dead wife.

He went directly to the bar and grabbed a beer before heading to the dining hall. The place was empty, but there was still food available. He put together a plate of sliced turkey breast, macaroni salad, baked potato, and two sourdough rolls and carried it out of the dining hall. No one stopped him.

On his way past the bar he grabbed another beer.

Upstairs, he expected to hear Frank screaming. He wouldn't have been surprised to see feathers trailing from Bryan's room, the threat to kill turned fact.

The hall was quiet. Frank's cage was missing from his room. David carried his plate to Bryan's door and lifted a hand to knock. Then he heard noises from the activity room. He treaded in that direction and saw Kate curled up on the long sofa. Frank's cage sat in front of the television monitor, where the "Oprah Winfrey Show" was in progress. David moved to a chair and sat down with his plate in his lap.

"He was upset," Kate explained. "I came in here and saw the tape and finally figured out what he wanted."

"Thanks," David said. He was surprised the parrot had let her near the cage. "Where is everyone?"

"Dr. Raleigh is in the library. I think Mel went to take a bath."

David noticed that her gaze kept dropping to his plate of food. "Didn't you eat?" he asked.

"No," she told him. "I was going to, but . . ."

He tore one of his sourdough rolls apart and stuffed sliced turkey between the halves. "Here."

Kate leaned forward to take it. "Thank you. It was so quiet down there I couldn't make myself stay. I guess they turn in early around here."

"Guess so," David said. "I didn't see anyone when I was downstairs."

Kate took a bite of her sandwich and chewed for a moment before speaking again. "I know this isn't a very nice thing to say, but do the Guerins seem strange to you in any way?"

David swallowed and wiped his mouth. "Just your average, wholesome, Republican American family."

"You're being facetious, aren't you?"

"Yes," he assured her. "I am."

"Good," she said, relieved. "I thought I might be the only one to notice."

"What have you noticed?"

Kate waved a hand. "Just little things. Like the way Dr. Guerin and his son behave with each other. Jay showed me his rare gun collection after you went to see his mother. He was very eager to show it to me. In fact, he was a completely different person from the man who met us on the airstrip today."

"And that worries you?"

"No. But he . . ." Her mouth worked and her cheeks began to pinken as she searched for the right words.

"What?" David said.

She lifted her hands. "Forget I said anything. It was nothing. I was probably spooked by Mel's ramblings."

"Did he make advances toward you?"

"No. He was a perfect gentleman."

David took a bite of macaroni salad. Whatever was bothering her, she wasn't going to tell him. She was either too embarrassed or too uncertain of him. He eyed the delicate fingers holding the sandwich and watched as she nibbled at the bread. He was beginning to understand why Bryan treated her the way he did. There was something about Kate, a fragile quality that begged for protection.

"The tape is over." She was looking at the snow on the screen. "Does he want to watch it again?"

"No. He's had his daily fix. He'll be fine now."

Kate turned off the VCR, and the parrot made only minor protest as she removed the tape. David watched in surprise as the bird allowed her to reach through the bars of his cage and touch his blue head.

"Watch your fingers, sweetheart. He doesn't know what petting is."

"I like him," she said. "He's noisy, but I like him." She turned from the cage then. "I like you, too, David. After listening to Dr. Raleigh, I didn't think I would, but I do."

Something in her expression set off a warning bell in David's head. "Don't," he said shortly. "I'm just being friendly. It doesn't mean anything."

Kate blinked at his brusque tone. Her blue eyes darkened. "I was only being friendly myself. And I would appreciate it if you stopped calling me sweetheart. Goodnight."

Her departure was swift. David dropped his fork and rubbed hard at the tension in his neck. He put his plate away and sat back to stare at the blank television screen.

And he had accused Augusta Guerin of being the paranoid one.

"What did you say to Kate?" Bryan asked as he entered the room. He was carrying an armful of books.

"I didn't say anything."

Bryan snorted. "I'm sure. Do me a favor and stay away from her. Kate is miles out of your league."

"Thanks," said David. "I'll remember that."

# 8

MEL LOVED THE feel of the sun on her skin. The warming rays made her feel clean and somehow pure. The lapping and splashing sounds of the pool lulled her into a semidaze as she lay stretched out on a padded chaise lounge. Kate was nearby, applying a sunscreen to her porcelain skin.

Things had calmed down considerably since their first day on the ranch. The group therapy sessions had gone relatively smoothly so far, and Guerin seemed pleased with everything and everyone. Still, a nagging sense of unease prevented Mel from dropping her guard completely. She slept with a blade under her pillow, but that was more habit than fear. The last few nights she had dreamed of Melanie Martin and the horrible screwdriver holes in her head. That wasn't bad. The bad part was when Melanie somehow turned into Mel's brother Duane.

Duane was the reason for the blade under the pillow. Duane, with his drug-induced, alcohol-aided rages. Duane, with his rolling eyes and sinewy arms, coming into her room with a hatchet dripping blood and saying that he had just killed Aunt Caroline because she wouldn't give him her Social Security check and he *needed* it. Did Mel have any money? He had to give them something. Anything.

Mel never found out the exact identity of "them." It was either the Crips or the Jamaicans, two of the gangs battling for control of the KC drug trade. Small-time independents like Duane were recruited or killed. Duane had probably resisted, right up until someone wrapped his intestines around his neck and hanged him from a street sign.

Mel hadn't cried for her brother. She had cried for her Aunt Caroline, and for the home she had lost, but there were no tears for Duane. He had made his choice.

And she had made hers. No headworks, no smoke, and no dripping hatchets. Being born poor didn't make you worthless —you did that all on your own.

The dreams had reminded Mel of who she was and just what kind of fire she had come through to be where she was today. Duane was gone. That life was gone. Aunt Caroline's funeral had been ten years ago next week.

And that was probably the reason for her state of mind, Mel told herself. She had the anniversary blues. Her unease had nothing to do with the ranch, or the people. It was in her own head. Her own past. Her dreams.

"Mel, can you put some sunscreen on my back?"

"Huh?" She turned her head. "Oh, sure."

Kate smiled at her. "What were you thinking about? You looked awfully serious."

"Turn over, Katie. Actually, I was patting myself on the back for rising above my white trash past and becoming such a model person. I do that a lot."

"You should," Kate said. "I don't know anyone who doesn't like and respect you."

"Thank you." Mel looked at her then. "Was it my imagination, or did I hear a little envy in that statement?"

"You did," Kate said honestly. "People never warm up to me the way they do to you."

"Kate, people respect me because I'm honest and I don't take any bull. They like me because I have a great sense of humor. Or haven't you noticed?"

"Ouch," Kate said at the pinch to her arm.

"You're going to fry like an egg," Mel said as she rubbed in the lotion. "You shouldn't even be out here."

"I thought maybe if I started slow and built up, I could get some color. You look so attractive when you get some sun."

"Aren't we full of compliments today? Thank you, but there's fair skin, and then there's white, and I'm telling you right now that sunscreen or no, you're going to burn. Why don't you move to the shade?"

"Don't you start," Kate said, her tone irritated. "Dr. Raleigh is bad enough. I'll be all right for a while, Mel. Really."

"Suit yourself. Don't come crying to me to pop your blisters. The real reason you're out here is so you won't run into Dastardly David in the house. Don't think I haven't noticed the way you've been avoiding him all week."

Kate scowled. "He's callous and rude. Dr. Raleigh was right about him."

"Oh, please," Mel said with a groan. "If he was half the jerk Raleigh makes him out to be someone would have shortened his odds a long time ago."

"You like him?"

"I do. And I'd give a week's pay to see him out here in a suit."

Kate sat up and looked at Mel in surprise.

"Don't look so shocked, Kate. I've still got eyes in my head, not to mention an everlasting admiration for the finer points of the male physique. Dr. Raleigh is pretty obvious about his assets, but I'll wager old David has a body worth howling over under those baggy clothes. He's just a little more modest is all."

"So . . . you still like men?" Kate asked.

"Of course I do. I love men. I love to look at them and talk to them and be one of the boys with them. It's everything else I have a problem with. They screw you and they think they own you. Then they go out and screw someone else and act pissed when they get caught. They might even go so far as to do a little headbashing if they catch you down at the lawyer's office filing for a divorce."

"You?" Kate said.

"Me," Mel confirmed. "Only I didn't learn my lesson the first time. When the second one came home with a dripping STD, I said forget it. And I did."

Kate stretched out on her stomach again. Mel watched her and knew she was dying to ask. It was only a matter of time and courage with timid Kate. It didn't take long.

"Mel, can I ask you something?"

"Only if you're sure you want to hear the answer."

"I do. How did you become a . . . you know."

Mel shook her head. "You can't even say it and you want me to tell you."

"I'm curious."

"Okay." Mel wiped her hands and returned to a reclining position on her lounge. "It's a long sad story about what we call self-esteem. I had none. I believed I was a failure as a woman because I couldn't hold a man. Of course it had nothing to do with me—I wasn't the one with the problem—but you don't think about that when you're alone in bed at night with no hairy-legged man to keep you warm. You blame yourself. You go over each memory with a magnifying glass to see if you can find just where and how you messed up."

"But it wasn't—"

"I know, Katie. I'm just telling you how it feels. You pick out the little things and add them up and pretty soon you're thinking it was all your fault. You didn't do this, you didn't do that, and on and on, until you're ranking yourself right below dog doo in worth. No one is ever going to care about you again, and why should they? You're a failure. In my case, I reached out in desperation and took love and affection from the first person to offer any. That person just happened to be a woman."

Kate's eyes were round with attention. Mel looked at her and gave an inward sigh. There was one more question coming. The big one. Mel could feel it.

"What's it like, Mel?"

"What?" No sense making it easy on her.

"You know. Being with a woman."

Mel shrugged. "Comfortable. You're a woman and you know the things women think about. The way they feel. And the sex is just as good, if not better, because we know exactly what feels good and where. On an emotional level it can be nice, too. Closer."

Kate was frowning. "If that's true, why haven't you made a commitment to anyone?"

Mel said, "I've yet to see one that's worked. My father beat the hell out of my mother and left. My husbands couldn't keep their putters in their pants, and poor Aunt Caroline got stood up every Friday night for three years at the local retirees' dance. If Prince Charles and Princess Di get a divorce I'll probably commit suicide."

She laughed then and made her voice gentle.

"Or maybe I'm just biding my time until I meet my true love. On paper I'd be labeled bisexual, because I still haven't ruled men out of my life. But in reality I'm just taking love and affection where I find it. That may not be the Moral Majority's idea of right, but it's hard to care about right when you need to be held. I feel sorry for the people who keep passing up chances while they're still looking. Know what I mean?"

"I think so." Kate lowered her gaze then. "Why act the stereotype then, Mel?"

Mel smiled. "People feel comfortable with stereotypes. I want them to be comfortable with me."

Kate looked at her. "Thanks for telling me. I mean, we've never really talked before."

"We've never had the chance. Tomorrow you can tell me about *your* love life."

Kate's mouth twisted. "That'll be a short conversation. My nickname should be One-Date Kate. They never call back."

"Why?" Mel was surprised.

"I wish I knew. One date told me I was too polite for him. He said he would feel guilty if he ever cursed or passed gas in front of me."

Mel laughed. "Sounds like Ice Princess Syndrome to me. Most guys don't have the courage to ask you out because you look so angelic, and the ones who do ask you out are afraid they'll never be able to live up to you."

"That's ridiculous," Kate said.

"Maybe. Is there someone you've been overlooking? Someone who's gotten past your appearance and knows the real you?"

"Not really. Wait . . . are you talking about men?"

"I'm talking about anyone. Whether you're attracted to a midget with a tin nose, an eight-foot amazon with a shaved head, or that blue-eyed, beer-drinking bola thrower, just go for it. Love is love, Katie. Corny or not, that's how I feel."

"It *is* corny," Kate said with a grin.

"We'll, we're in Kansas, so that's cool. You can be corny in Kansas, you know. It's allowed."

"What's a bola, Mel?"

"It's something they throw in South America. A cord with two balls attached."

"David Raleigh is a bola thrower?"

"One of his many talents, I'm sure. Oh, looky, looky here. Speaking of things with two balls attached, it's Golden Boy in the flesh, and my, oh my, just look at all that flesh. Am I drooling, Kate? Do I need to wipe my chin?"

"Shut up, Mel," said Bryan.

Mel and Kate exchanged a smile as he approached. His swimsuit was a small splash of white against the golden bronze of his tan. He moved to stand beside Kate.

"You need some sunscreen on your back. Where is it? I'll put it on for you."

"Mel put some on me."

He nodded. "All right."

"Nice try," said Mel.

Bryan ignored her and turned away to dive into the water. Within minutes, patients began to appear around the pool. Two went into the water and three others set up camp around the edge, watching as Bryan swam his laps.

"Desperate little darlings," Mel murmured.

"Mel," Kate scolded.

"Well, look at them, Kate. Like mares lining up for stud service. See the one with her tail in the air? She hasn't had any in a while."

Kate looked. "She's the architect."

"Right. And she's . . . uh-oh, Cindy the Nympho is making her move. Would you look at that? Not a safe leg in the house when that little hound is in heat. Come out of the water, Raleigh, and let's see what all the attention is doing for you."

Kate was laughing now. "You're terrible, Mel."

"I know." Mel frowned then. "I wonder if Jay misses the attention. I figure it was him before Golden Boy arrived."

"I don't know," said Kate. "I don't think so."

"Why?" Mel asked.

"He told me he usually avoids interaction with the patients."

"This was during your grand tour?"

"Yes. He said his father asked that he and the ranch employees keep their distance."

"I can see why," said Mel. "But that's probably a dung-ridden dose of duplicity on Jay's part. I'll bet he roots around the sexually active ones on the sly."

Kate shook her head. "I don't know. He's different."

"Different how?"

"I'm not . . ." After a long intake of breath, Kate told Mel what had happened in the gun room.

"I've heard about guys like that," Mel told her.

"You have?"

"Yeah. Guns turn them on. Or death, I can't remember which. But that's pretty weird. Are you sure he wasn't turned on by you?"

"On fifteen minutes' acquaintance?"

"He likes you, Kate. I knew that the day we arrived."

"I know, but it wasn't like that. The guns excited him, not me."

"Bizarre. I'm surprised you went out in the Jeep with him the next day."

"I didn't have a choice. He was waiting for me after the session."

"Has he been bothering you?"

"Not really. He wants me to come up and see the rest of his collection, but I keep making excuses."

"Good thing the cows keep him busy." Mel's eyes rounded then. "Speaking of cows, look at that shameless heifer. I'm surprised at Raleigh. He wouldn't get away with this at home."

"He is enjoying himself, isn't he?" Kate observed.

"Guerin might have to put his foot down on someone besides Jay," Mel said. She turned to look at the house and saw a shade fall in a window on the third floor. For just an instant she had glimpsed a face behind the glass. A white, impossibly large face with two small dark eyes.

Mel felt the hair on her nape begin to prickle. Was that the reclusive Mrs. Guerin?

"I think I'll go in now," she said to Kate. "Are you coming?"

"No. Not yet. I'm comfortable where I am."

"Don't stay out here too long. You're already turning pinkish."

"Yes, Mother," said Kate.

"I mean it." Mel put on her robe and took off her sunglasses. She looked up to the window again and saw nothing. "Kate, have you met Guerin's wife yet?"

"No. Have you?"

"Not officially," Mel breathed. But she had a feeling that would soon change.

# 9

## THURSDAY, MAY 12, 2:00 P.M.

DAVID REVERSED THE tape to the spot he wanted and sat back again, not to take notes this time, but simply to watch. Mel was great with the patients. Her aid to Bryan in the discussion part of the sessions was obviously invaluable. She handled the various personas that emerged with a surprising show of equanimity. Surprising because some of the patients had initially displayed open contempt and dislike for her. Now it was different. David could see the women responding to and growing comfortable with her firm tone. A few were still preening around Bryan, but that was understandable. They were females.

Kate found it harder to command respect, so she relied upon friendliness instead. David was watching her now as she instructed the women in sculpting with clay. She had a particular problem with Natalie, whose Tammy persona wanted to do nothing but poke holes in the clay with her fingers. Guerin's file mentioned that Natalie had sometimes been used as a living dartboard as a child, so the holes she put in the smooth surface of the clay were not insignificant.

Another patient created a face with a wide, yawning mouth, a mashed nose, and only one ear. David thought nothing of this until he saw Kate move behind the woman and push the long brown curtain of her hair away from her face. The hair fell immediately forward again, because there was no ear to hold it back. Kate gave the patient's shoulder a tender squeeze and whispered some words of encouragement to her before moving on.

It was hard to believe these women were all capable of carrying on normal lives under the control of their host personalities. The host was generally the keeper through trips to the grocery store, the paying of bills, and the making of lunch. All the mundane things normal women did in a normal life. But these women weren't normal. There were others inside, each one on call for the moment he or she would be needed to come out and deal with something the host was unprepared to negotiate. Anger, pain, fear—there was a persona for every form of trauma.

Even more amazing was the fact that over half of these women had been misdiagnosed as schizophrenics or hysterics before coming to Dr. Guerin. A quick scan of the doctor's notes told him that 1980 had been the breakthrough year for the disorder. Before that, only two hundred cases had made it to the psychiatric annals as legitimate. Today, by Dr. Guerin's estimate, there were close to ten thousand multiples in the country. David had to wonder about those who had gone untreated before the disorder was officially recognized. In some ways, he thought, civilization was still operating in the Dark Ages.

Natalie's family believed she was faking her illness. They didn't buy her stories about what kind old Grandpa, a former state supreme justice, had done to her.

The injustice disgusted David. Everything came back to money. Grandpa would never have to watch Natalie poke holes in clay and drool all over herself. He had sent her away to be made well again. *Put her back together, Doc, and I'll donate some money to a hospital or a clinic.*

Put her back together. The fusion of personalities would send them all home again. Co-awareness was the name of the game here on the ranch-spa-retreat. Co-awareness was the goal.

David rubbed his eyes and leaned back against the cushions. He was too aware. Aware of Bryan's watchful stare, Rosalie's heavy tread on the carpet, and Kate Berquist's careful avoidance of him. He hadn't meant to be so rude in his warning to her, or to make her angry. His own avoidance of women had become instinctive after Julia's death. Better to avoid and be avoided than to be caught in such a tangled mess again.

If Bryan hadn't told him to stay away, and if Kate didn't turn and walk in the opposite direction each time she saw him coming, he knew he wouldn't be spending so much of the day thinking about her. He wouldn't be doing what he was doing right now, watching her on tape and thinking how unself-consciously pretty she was, and how purely innocent she could sometimes appear.

How could anyone past the age of thirty seem so completely guileless? It was impossible. Perhaps it was an act of hers, something for Bryan to mope over because he was married and couldn't touch her. Perhaps she enjoyed torturing him, telling him how he was like a father to her, knowing that it would make him grit his teeth and do those twenty extra sit-ups at the gym.

David shook his head at his imaginings and got up to turn off the machine. It was time to bring Frank in to watch Oprah. He carried his notebooks back to his room and lifted the parrot's cage from the table. "Ready for Oprah?" he asked.

"Sweetheart," Frank replied.

David frowned. "What?"

"Sweetheart," the parrot clearly repeated.

"Quiet," David said. "We're not supposed to say that around here, remember?"

"Sweetheart," Frank croaked.

David ignored the noises that followed and carried the bird into the activity room. He thought it strange that Frank had picked up the word so quickly. David wasn't in the habit of calling women sweetheart. His use of the word had been unconscious until it had been so coolly brought to his attention.

Frank's grumbling stopped the moment he saw Oprah on the

screen. David left the bird to his love and went to pass the hour in the library.

Small, well-lighted, and cozy, the library was a place to spend rainy days. The mahogany shelves were built in, leaving plenty of space for the black leather upholstered sofa and recliner. The room held a smell that had attracted David for as long as he could remember: the smell of books. Paper and binding and that slightly musty odor that no one was supposed to like. No one but writers, scholars, and constant readers.

At the beginning of the week he had scanned the shelves, but now he took his time looking over the selection. When he found an entire section devoted to mysticism, he paused to study each title. There were books on palm reading, the tarot, runes, hypnotism, reincarnation, past-life regression, witchcraft, astral projection, numerology, and astrology, as well as other arcane subjects.

He wasn't surprised to find Augusta's name penned inside the cover of the first book he removed. All Yahtzee players were big on fate and destiny. Everyone knew that.

He sat down with the book, a four-inch-thick tome on astrology and the ancients, and opened it to find many of the pages scribbled on in ink, not just in the margins, but across the entire page. The complete chapter on persons born in the house of Scorpio was missing from the book. David thought he might be safe in assuming Augusta was born under the sign of Scorpio. That, or she hated Scorpios.

She probably hated David by now. Three summons to her chambers had been ignored. Each time Rosalie came to fetch him he made certain he was too busy with his work to be troubled. The nurse was on to him, but she obviously didn't think she could best him in a wrestling match. David wasn't so sure—he figured she had at least twenty pounds on his meager one-seventy—but he was glad she didn't force the issue.

He placed the book back on the shelf and was reaching for another when he heard Frank begin to squawk. He left the library and was surprised to see Oprah still lifting eyebrows on the screen.

"It's not over yet, Frank."

Down the hall he heard a door close.

The parrot shrieked something unintelligible and fluttered his feathers. David put a finger to the cage and promptly had it nipped. "Hey," he said angrily.

"Sweetheart."

David turned off the TV and picked up the cage. Frank immediately set about making him deaf, screaming at the top of his tiny lungs and causing David to swear loudly as the sharp beak went for his fingers again.

"What the hell is wrong with you, Frank?"

Outside his door, the noise abruptly stopped. David looked at the bird and saw Frank looking at Kate's door.

David exhaled through his nose and started to move when he heard something that made him pause. He waited and soon heard it again. A whimper.

He took Frank into his room and hesitated only a moment before returning to stand outside Kate's door.

"Go away," a thick voice said to his knock.

Definite pain there, David thought, and he twisted the knob and opened the door. It was dim inside the room, but his eyes quickly adjusted. When he saw Kate, he took an automatic step back. "Oh, *shit*."

She covered up her face, but not before he saw the huge blisters on her cheeks. Her shoulders were even worse.

"Get out of here." She tried to cover up the blisters on her shoulders and winced in pain. Her pink two-piece suit wasn't revealing, but its color paled in comparison to her red, swollen skin.

"Are you that dumb?" David asked her. "Why did you stay out there so long?"

"Get out," she repeated.

"Get in the tub," he told her.

"No. It hurts to even move. I'm going to stay right here on the edge of the bed."

David walked into her bathroom and threw every towel he could find in the bathtub. Then he turned on the cold water. She glared at him when he carried the wet, sopping bundle out and dumped it on the bed.

"Slide this way," he said.

"I fell asleep," she explained. "I fell asleep and no one noticed. Dr. Raleigh was busy talking to—"

"Kate, slide over here."

"What are you going to do?"

"What do you think? I'm going to wrap you."

Slowly, carefully, she moved toward him. "I'm not dumb," she said. "Don't call me dumb."

"I'm sorry. Lie down if you can."

"I started to go downstairs to see if they had any burn cream, but it hurts so awfully to move. And I didn't want Mel to see me. She told me not to stay out too long and I told her I wouldn't and I'm embarrassed enough as it is without you treating me like some witless child."

She was talking unusually fast, David thought.

"Do you feel dizzy?"

"No, I feel sick." Her eyes squeezed shut as she tried to lower herself onto the mattress. "David, I can't. It hurts too much."

"Let's try the tub, Kate. I promise it will help."

"How long do I have to stay there?"

"Until you don't feel sick. Come on."

With painstakingly slow movements, she got off the bed. By the time she reached the bathroom, tears of pain were running down her face. "I think I'm going to throw up," she said, and David steered her to the toilet before moving to turn on the bath water. The tub began to fill, and he looked to see if she was still over the toilet. He stood back in what felt like shock when he saw her begin to remove her suit in front of him. It was so completely unexpected, so out of sync with his image of her, that he found himself staring in dismay rather than appreciation at her small white breasts and slender hips.

"Do you do that often?"

"What?"

"Strip in front of strange men."

Comprehension rounded her eyes, and the tears flowed anew as she attempted to cover herself. Her shoulders began to quiver.

"I'm sorry," David said.

"Get out," she mumbled.

He reached for the door. "I'll go downstairs and see if they have anything that will help."

She refused to look at him. "Don't tell anyone."

"They'll find out sooner or later. Just get in the tub and try to relax. I'll be back as soon as I find something."

Her intake of breath was loud as she slipped into the cool water. David watched her only a moment before leaving the room. His disappointment was ridiculously irrational. For some reason he had expected those rounded breasts and ivory thighs to remain a mystery to him, a hidden secret of the timid, ethereal being he had created while viewing the tapes.

She had shattered his image by revealing herself to him without ceremony, without grace, with nothing but careless human haste. And he had lashed out at her for it. For having pain and being conscious of nothing but the need to stop that pain. For having blisters and burns and a birthmark below her navel that marred what otherwise would have been porcelain perfection. He had lashed out at her for being real after all.

He felt like a jerk.

There wasn't a tube of burn cream in the house, he was informed in the kitchen. Someone had used the last of it a month ago and it hadn't been restocked. David started for the stairs again, then he stopped and went back to inquire about a car. Reluctantly, the cook handed over her keys and gave him directions to Marwell, the nearest town. He saw Mel at the bar, but David didn't stop to chat, merely waved at her as he strode out the door.

The cook's car was an ancient blue Volvo wagon with a dozen bumper stickers on the rear bumper. One David remembered quite well was: *Eat beans and rabbit stew, Beat Nixon in '72.*

David's mouth curved as he got behind the wheel.

He drove the twelve miles and passed through Marwell once before he realized it was in fact the town. He went back and saw a familiar figure standing in front of a gas pump, putting gas into a green, late-model Chevy pickup.

"Hey, Waltman," he called out the window as he braked to a stop beside the truck.

Waltman looked up with a frown.

"David Raleigh, from the Guerin place," David said.

"Oh yeah. I didn't recognize you." Waltman looked around himself before deciding to smile. "Sandy loan you her car?"

Out of his uniform Waltman looked even younger. Just a kid.

"Yeah, she loaned it to me. Do you know where I can buy some burn cream around here?"

"Burn cream?"

"For skin burns," David clarified.

"Oh. I think Wally's got some in the shop. He's the closest thing we have to a convenience store. About three shelves' worth. Somebody else stroll into a fire?"

"No. This is just a bad sunburn."

Waltman nodded and David got out of the car.

"So how's the book coming?"

"Still in the outline stage. You off duty today?"

"What? Me? Oh, yeah. Thought I'd go over to Fox Lake and do a little fishing."

"Good luck." David frowned as he entered the small shop called Wally's. The deputy had certainly acted different.

"Help you?" A short, potbellied man with round cheeks and a pouch of Redman chewing tobacco in his hand appeared behind the dust-covered counter. This was Wally, no doubt. David looked at the shelves behind the man. "Do you have any burn cream?"

"Burn cream?"

"For skin burns. Sunburn."

Wally turned to look. "Nothin' but the big tubes."

"That'll be fine. I'll take two."

"Two?" Wally was suddenly suspicious.

"Two."

"Haven't seen you around here before, have I?"

"I'm staying at the Guerin place."

"A visitor, huh?"

David smiled. "No, a patient."

Wally's face reddened. A stream of tobacco juice escaped from the corner of his mouth as he told David the total for two tubes of burn cream.

David intended to tell the man he was joking, but the effect on Wally was far too amusing. David felt like rolling his eyes and waggling his eyebrows just to see what happened, but he decided against it. Wally probably had a shotgun around the place somewhere.

He paid for the burn cream and returned to the Volvo. On the drive back to the ranch he passed Waltman's truck on the county road. Waltman pretended not to see him when David waved. The deputy's eyes remained directly ahead.

"Strange," David muttered to himself, and he pressed down on the accelerator.

# 10

## Thursday, May 12, 5:00 p.m.

MEL WAS UNPREPARED when Rosalie tapped on her shoulder. Mel
turned from the bar and nearly dropped her beer when she got
her first good look at the large nurse.

"Mrs. Guerin would like to meet you, Miss Kierkes. Would
you come with me, please?"

What happens if I say no? Mel wondered.

"Just for a brief chat," Rosalie added.

"Sure," said Mel. "No problem. Can I bring this with me?"
She held up her beer.

"I'm sorry, no. Mrs. Guerin doesn't approve of alcohol."

"Really? Tut, tut." Mel downed the contents while Rosalie
watched. When the beer was empty, she said, "I don't like to
waste anything myself. It's just the way I was raised. Eat what
you take, drink what you open, and never forget those less fortu-
nate than yourself."

Rosalie was less than moved. "She's waiting, Miss Kierkes."

"We're all waiting for something," Mel replied. Then she
lifted a hand. "Okay, okay, I'm coming."

In the elevator, Mel gave a nervous laugh. "This woman never

leaves her room, right? So what does she do in there all day—
besides peek out the window?"

Rosalie's eyelids fluttered, but she remained silent.

Steroids can do that, Mel thought to herself as the elevator
stopped.

"This way, please." Rosalie extended one large hand.

Mel went ahead and allowed herself to be guided by firm fingertips as she took in the surroundings.

"Why is it so dark up here?"

No answer. The only sound was the whirring of the ceiling
fans.

Goosebumps began to appear on Mel's flesh.

They stopped in front of a door and Rosalie knocked. A moment later she twisted the knob and gave Mel a push. Mel stood
just inside the door and blinked, waiting for her eyes to adjust.
For a fleeting instant she wished she had her blade with her.
This was just too weird.

"Come in and sit down, Miss Kierkes."

Mel stared at the source of the voice. She swallowed while
searching for something to say.

David hadn't been kidding about her weight. The poor thing
was padded with fat, a human with a marshmallow coating. The
control panel was there, too, with its little row of lights, switches,
and dials. Amazing.

"Are you enjoying your stay in my home, Miss Kierkes? Besides the work, I mean."

Mel took note of the stress on the word *my.* "Yes, I am, thank
you. I saw you at the window earlier."

"I know. Please sit down."

Mel found a chair and sat. "Is that why you sent for me?
Because I saw you at the window?"

"No. I've heard a lot about you. I wanted to meet you for
myself. Russell says you can be very amusing."

"Did he." Mel didn't know what to think about that.

"Say something funny."

"Excuse me?"

The tiny dark eyes glittered. "Make me laugh. Say something funny."

Mel stood. "I'll be going now. Thanks for having me up."

Augusta's demeanor immediately changed. "I'm sorry. Did I sound demanding? I didn't mean to, Miss Kierkes. It's just that I laugh so little. And as you can see, I really have nothing to laugh about. Won't you please sit down and talk awhile? I'm sorry. Really I am."

Pitiful, Mel thought as she reluctantly took her seat once more. The woman was pathetic.

"Has David told you anything about me?" Augusta asked.

"A little."

Augusta smiled. "I like David. He's such an extraordinary man."

"I don't know him that well," Mel said.

"Don't you?"

"We met just last week."

This seemed to please the fat woman. "I see. Well, I've known him for years. Mostly through his work, you understand. I'm very good at judging people, and he has the most incredible inner resilience. And do you know why? Do you know what gives him his strength?"

Mel only lifted a brow. She knew the answer wouldn't be what the big boys eat.

"He believes in nothing but himself," Augusta informed her. "He has no faith but faith in himself. He trusts and relies on no one but David. Don't you find that intriguing? And admirable. I admire him very much."

In a sense, so did Mel. But she didn't believe all of it. David Raleigh could be had. Any man could be had. She felt like saying so, but she didn't want to interfere with Augusta's idol worship. She wondered if David knew about the fat woman's obvious infatuation with him.

"He is definitely a challenge for me," Augusta went on. "Imagine what it must have been like growing up in his brother's shadow. It made him tough, I suspect. Did you know their parents were killed in a house fire?"

"No, I didn't know that."

"Everything was destroyed. Bryan was still in school, and David came home from a world tour to find his life in ashes. No clothes, no pictures, no childhood mementos, and no mother and father. Tragic."

Mel agreed. But life was full of tragedies. Like the woman on the bed in front of her. Now there was a full-blown tragedy. Mel smiled and said, "Not to change the subject or anything, but why don't you leave this room, Mrs. Guerin? If you can get out of bed to look out the window, you can surely make it out to the elevator. The exercise certainly wouldn't hurt."

Immediately, Mel knew she had said the wrong thing. Powdered white flesh jiggled and swayed as Augusta began to shake her head. Her fleshy mouth trembled in anger.

"You come in here and tell me how to live? You, with your unnatural sexual proclivities and your wasted life? None of you seems to understand that I am a *prisoner* in this room. I will *die* if I leave this room. Do you know what it's like for me to lie here and *listen* to all of you? Laughing and talking and going about your merry way while I'm stuck—where are you going?"

"Out. Our visit is over, Mrs. Guerin. Do yourself a favor and cut out the sweets."

"Come back here, *Melvina*. I'm warning you . . ."

"Warn away. I don't have to stay here and listen to you."

Mel opened the door to see a tight-mouthed Rosalie blocking her way.

"Move it," Mel warned, "or I'll take skin and hair with me when I come out."

Augusta, surprisingly, began to laugh. "That's good. Oh, that's wonderful. Russell was right. Let her go, Rosalie. Oh my goodness, she *is* funny."

Mel knew she looked as incredulous as she felt. When Rosalie stepped aside, Mel turned to look back. The bed was shaking with Augusta's mirth. Her laughter sounded like a series of shrieks, hiccoughs, and insane giggles.

"Sick," Mel whispered, and she strode out of the room. She could still hear the laughter as she stepped into the elevator.

Playing me, she thought as she pushed the button. From the moment Mel had walked into the room. Just a little bored, so she thought she would send for one of the guests to liven things up for her.

When the elevator stopped, Mel got off and began a search for Dr. Guerin. She wanted some answers. She wanted to know if he was aware that his wife was a ranting, raving looney-tuner of the Petunia Pig ilk, and if so, what kind of medication he was giving her to make her little button eyes look so weird. She also wanted to know why Augusta claimed to be a prisoner. Why Rosalie stood guard outside the door. Why the third floor was all dim lights and spooky purple.

She found Guerin in his office, a smiling Natalie bouncing in his lap.

Mel backed up ten steps and started over again. "Dr. Guerin?" she said from the hall. "Dr. Guerin, it's Mel. Are you back here somewhere?"

In just over five seconds, Guerin's head appeared through the open door.

"I'm in here. What is it, Miss Kierkes?"

"Are you busy? I wanted to talk to you about your wife."

His brows met. "Cindy, would you excuse us?"

Natalie/Cindy flounced out of the office, her face in an adolescent pout.

"Hope I didn't disturb anything," Mel said.

"Not at all. Cindy's craving for attention doesn't limit itself to office hours. Come in and sit down."

Mel chose the chair in front of the desk. "I've just met your wife. She sent for me. Not to be rude or anything, but just what is her problem?"

"Problem?"

"Mania. Psychosis. Illness. What the hell is wrong with her?"

Guerin smoothed his collar and sat down behind his desk. His salt-and-pepper hair was slightly tousled.

"Aside from agoraphobia, Augusta has no problems that I'm aware of."

Mel's eyes rounded. "Have you looked at her lately? Talked to her?"

"She is just a shade eccentric," Guerin admitted.

"And you're just a shade obtuse," Mel said in annoyance. "I'm asking you how she got this way."

The doctor stiffened. "Miss Kierkes, I respect your work, but I don't think this is any of your business."

Mel smiled and pointed to the thick piece of foam taped over the intercom speaker behind his desk.

"Cindy's oohing and aahing too loud for comfort?"

Guerin's eyes turned black. "It wasn't what you're thinking."

"Then I'm disappointed," Mel said. "I'd hate to think of a good-looking guy like you rolling around on top of that thing upstairs."

"You're talking about my wife."

"I know, but I'm not getting anywhere. I want you to talk about her. She insulted me and then started cackling like a soul full of belly. I got the feeling you told her to send for me."

"I didn't," Guerin said immediately. "And I'm sorry if she offended you. She isn't used to having guests. The presence of Dr. Raleigh's brother has excited her."

"Do tell," said Mel. "Pardon the pun, but she has a big thing for him."

"For now," Guerin responded. "Augusta's interests are sporadic. Her preoccupation with David Raleigh seemed to intensify when she read the news of his wife's suicide. It won't last much longer, I'm sure. They never do."

"Huh," Mel said thoughtfully. She was sure David would be glad to hear the news. "So talk to me, Doctor. Has she always been big? Is it a gland thing?"

Guerin sighed and opened a drawer in his desk. He sifted through the contents and finally withdrew a tattered photograph. "Here. This was taken a year or so after we were married."

"Wow," Mel said. The woman in the picture had a perfect hourglass figure. Her hair was a thick, healthy shade of auburn, and the face was astonishingly beautiful. It was hard to reconcile this image with the woman upstairs.

"What happened? Did she start gaining weight after Jay was born?"

"No." Guerin took back the photograph and placed it in the drawer again. "She didn't gain the weight until after her father died. That was three and a half years ago. His passing affected her very deeply—and frightened her. Ted was a hemophiliac. He went out riding one day and received a serious head injury when his horse spooked at something and threw him. When the horse came back to the ranch without him, Augusta went out to look. She found him too late."

"He bled to death from the head wound," Mel guessed.

"Yes. Augusta arrived in time to see him die. There was nothing she could do. For days afterward she moved about in a stupor, rambling about the life draining out of him and staining the ground. She had two of the ranch hands dig up the earth and blood-soaked grass where he died and haul it upstairs to her bedroom. Then she began to powder herself. One day I found her lying on the dirt and grass-covered bed with completely white, bloodless features. Only then did I realize she was trying to re-create her father's death."

Mel stared. "To try and change the facts?"

Guerin lifted a shoulder. "I never discovered the reason. Fearing the worst, I had the dirt and grass removed from the room. Augusta flew into a rage and refused to come out. She said her own life was in danger of draining away."

"So she stays in her room," Mel said. *And eats,* she silently added. Probably to build up reserves in case of the big drain. "Is she a hemophiliac, too?"

"No, it doesn't work that way. Females are generally carriers. Augusta herself is safe."

"Jay is a hemophiliac?" Mel asked.

"Yes, unfortunately. And very much like his late grandfather in every other respect as well. Augusta is very fearful for his life. If she could, she would protect his every move. Jay won't allow it, thank God."

"What about treatment?" asked Mel. "For Augusta, I mean."

"I haven't been able to help her," Guerin admitted. "Which is laughable, I suppose, considering my professional reputation." He wiped at his face then and tried to smile. "She really is harmless, you know. Her only pleasure comes from eavesdropping on the activities of others. And, too, she enjoys the idea of being a reclusive, somewhat frightening figure. She loves to bully Rosalie, and for some reason she's fond of telling complete strangers that she is being held prisoner. It can be a bit embarrassing at times. Two years ago the interior designer she hired to do the work on the third floor bought her story. The woman went so far as to bring in the police. They took Augusta with them and were later sued by her lawyers. She was livid at being taken out of her room against her will and being exposed to the public. She hasn't been out of the house since."

"Well, she's telling the story again," Mel said, eyeing him. "She told me the prisoner bit not half an hour ago."

Guerin smiled. "Surely you don't believe her?"

"I don't know. I don't know *what* to believe about you people. I'm still regretting getting off the jet to begin with. Broken necks, screwdriver suicidals, and a powdered fat woman with a console that has more buttons than NASA." Mel leaned forward then. "I appreciate everything you've told me, but I want you to know I'll be keeping my eyes open and my back covered."

"Don't you think you're exaggerating things?" Guerin asked in a mild tone. "You're in no danger here, I can assure you. I apologize for Augusta's upsetting you, but we are doing some valuable work where the patients are concerned. I'd hate to see that come to an end."

"I'll bet you would," Mel said. "Then you'd have to live off

Augusta's bankroll, and my oh my, she'd have fun with you then, wouldn't she?"

Guerin stood. "I think we're finished."

"She probably supported you through school and the first five or ten years of your career, right?"

The doctor walked pointedly to the door.

"Okay," Mel said. "That was a cheap shot. Just a little payback for telling your wife how *amusing* I am."

"Goodnight, Miss Kierkes."

Mel stood and walked to the door. "I like the way you call me 'Miss.' No one ever calls me that anymore."

Guerin looked past her. "If my wife sends for you again, just tell Rosalie you're busy. You're not obligated to go up there."

"Thank you," Mel told him. "But Rosalie and four of your horses couldn't get me in that room again."

She moved past him and walked briskly down the hall. When an irresistible urge made her glance over her shoulder, she saw him still standing in the doorway, his black eyes fastened on her.

Mel's flesh prickled all over again.

# 11

## Thursday, May 12, 5:45 p.m.

Augusta adjusted the volume level several times, but she still couldn't make out the conversation in Russell's office. He had covered the speaker again, she finally deduced. So clever of him. She pushed another button and Rosalie immediately opened the door.

"Go downstairs and find out what Russell's doing. He's got something over the speaker."

Rosalie nodded and withdrew. Augusta settled back against the pillows and reached for her baby powder. She held the container over her face and hummed as the cool sprinkles dusted her skin. The kitchen people were talking about Sandy loaning her car to a guest. Augusta adjusted the volume control for the kitchen and heard Sandy grumble about not being offered any money for gas.

"I wouldn't have trusted him," someone else said. "He looks mean to me. My first husband looked like that, like he'd just as soon hit you as speak to you."

David, Augusta thought. They were talking about David.

Where had he gone in Sandy's car?

She flicked a switch. "Sandy, this is Mrs. Guerin. I think I'd like to have something Italian for dinner this evening. Some manicotti, I think."

Augusta pictured Sandy grimacing and wiping her hands on a towel before reaching for the intercom switch.

"It'll be an hour, Mrs. Guerin," came the answer.

"That's fine. Make sure there's plenty of garlic bread. Oh, and Sandy, who borrowed your car?"

A pause. "The younger Mr. Raleigh. He drove into town to buy some burn cream."

"I see," said Augusta. "Check with me next time, Sandy. Mr. Raleigh could have used one of my cars. We can't have him troubling you people."

"I will. Thank you, Mrs. Guerin."

"You're welcome, Sandy. Don't forget the garlic bread."

"No, ma'am."

Augusta smiled to herself and turned down the volume.

"Mrs. Guerin?" Rosalie was back already.

"Come in. What was he doing?"

"Working at his desk," Rosalie reported. "The speaker was uncovered. I did see Mel Kierkes come from that direction, though."

"Figures. She probably ran right to him. And he doubtlessly told her all sorts of outlandish tales about me. He does that, you know. He likes to cover up the real reason why I'm up here."

"Yes, ma'am," said Rosalie.

"He can't let anyone know it's his fault. Not the famous doctor. Are you sure he was alone?"

"He was alone."

Augusta sneered. "Not for long, I'm sure. Don't think I'm a fool, Rosalie. I'm not. Things go on here that would shock you, I know. I wish David would believe me. Did you happen to see him anywhere?"

"No, ma'am."

"I wonder who he bought the burn cream for? Surely not for himself. He's not the type to burn. I imagine it's for that Kate woman. She was out by the pool today, and she must be a stupid little thing, really. Skin like hers just doesn't take sun. Do you think David likes her?"

"I wouldn't know, Mrs. Guerin."

"Well, find out. If he's avoiding me because of her we'll have to do something about it. Jay likes her, you know. Don't ask me why, but he does. I can tell."

Rosalie shifted her feet but said nothing. Augusta wasn't finished yet.

"And she really isn't the sort of woman David needs. Not in my opinion, anyway. He doesn't need some frail, cringing thing straight out of a fairy tale, he needs someone to complement himself. He should have learned that after his mistake with Julia. I'll never forget the first time I saw him in that picture with her. The one in the *Kansas City Star*, taken at that campaign fundraiser. He looked so ridiculously uncomfortable in his evening clothes. I knew right away they weren't suited for one another. She was my age, you know. But she was a phony. Real pearls on a faux woman. She wanted David for a showpiece. Don't you think so, Rosalie?"

Rosalie nodded. "Are you ready for a snack?"

"No, I . . . What have you got?"

"A loaf of banana nut bread."

"Butter?"

"Of course."

"Go ahead and slice it then. Banana nut bread isn't my favorite, but I do need something to tide me over until dinner. Now, where was I?"

"A showpiece."

"Yes. A showpiece." Augusta's eyes glazed over as she watched Rosalie slice the bread. "I used to feel like that with Russell, only I don't suppose it matters now. He got what he wanted. He has always gotten what he wanted. Don't you think it's my turn now, Rosalie? Shouldn't it be my turn to get what I want?"

"Yes, Mrs. Guerin."

"Well, aren't you going to ask me what I want?"

Rosalie barely hid a sigh. "What is it you want?"

Augusta smiled and reached for a piece of buttered bread. "Revenge, of course. Some well-deserved renown of my own. And something very precious that belongs to David Raleigh." She chuckled then and crammed the bread into her mouth.

# 12

## Thursday, May 12, 6:00 p.m.

Kate closed her eyes to the blue tiles above the tub and wondered if the blisters would leave scars on her face. She didn't think so. The burns were painful, but not deep enough to do lasting damage. She couldn't believe she had been so stupid as to fall asleep outside. Mel was going to have a great time saying I told you so.

"Shit," Kate whispered, and the sound of the word coming from her lips made her laugh, promptly followed by a cry of pain as the blisters on her lower lip popped open and began to run. She moaned and lowered her head into the cool water until only her nose was above the surface.

Mel had only been using common sense. It wasn't overprotectiveness that had made her suggest Kate move to the shade. Mel was the only person Kate knew who didn't treat her like some fragile, brainless child.

Then again, the patients didn't. The teethmarks in her hand proved that. But everyone else did.

It was a form of discrimination, Kate thought. She was too white. Being too white placed her with all the other minorities. People treated her differently, either by looking at her eyes to see if they were pink, or by acting as if she were some fading winter flower that needed delicate care. It was embarrassing. Almost as embarrassing as the sly winks men gave her when they asked if her hair color was natural.

David Raleigh hadn't winked. But he had asked.

Nudity had been the last thing on her mind when she took her swimsuit off in front of him. She hadn't even been aware of the apparent sin until the electric-blue surprise in his eyes told her that yes, she was standing naked in front of him, and no, the look on his face was not at all complimentary. It hurt. It hurt worse than the sunburn.

She didn't care if he came back. She didn't want him to come back. He could leave the burn cream on her nightstand and spare himself the trauma of being subjected to her nudity.

Did he think he was someone to swoon over? He wasn't. Compared to Dr. Raleigh, David's looks were average. His nose was too thick at the bridge, his brows were too heavy, his hair never stayed combed, and he missed the same spot shaving every day. He walked like he was in the woods, he talked like he was in front of a senate committee, and he was flirting with alcoholism.

Besides all of that, he had a questionable past. Kate had known Dr. Raleigh a long time, and David seemed to be the source of many a misery to her employer.

Knowing what she did, and having been exposed to his *charm* herself, she had no idea why she was still intrigued by the man. Why she still thought about him even while avoiding him. Why she was thinking of him now.

She immersed herself completely and opened her eyes to see a watery image leaning over the edge of the tub. Kate sucked in water and came up coughing, opening the blisters on her cheeks and splitting her lower lip even deeper.

"That looks painful," Jay said. "Your door was open. I guess you didn't hear me knocking."

"Out," Kate spluttered. "Please . . . get out."

Jay smiled at her and took a lingering look at the parts she couldn't cover up. "Do you have anything to put on those blisters?"

"It's taken care of." David appeared at the door. He glanced at Kate. "You okay?"

She was still coughing, but she managed to nod her head. She lifted one arm and tried to wave them out.

Jay didn't move. "Is there anything I can do?"

"You can excuse us." David stood back and away from the door. In his tone was a challenge.

Jay gave a curt nod and smiled once more at Kate before departing. David shook his head in wonder and moved to sit on the edge of the tub. "He just walked right in, didn't he?"

Kate kept one arm over her breasts. "So did you."

He ignored her. "Sorry it took so long. I had to borrow a car and drive into town."

Kate's mouth was open to tell him to leave, but she closed it without uttering a sound. She was surprised at his efforts on her behalf.

He put a finger under her chin and lifted her head. "Your lip's split. Hurt?"

"Mmmm."

"Still feel sick?"

"Not so bad," she mumbled. The cool water had reduced the fiery pain and lessened the nausea somewhat.

"Your blisters opened." He poked at her left cheek. "I don't think it'll scar. Why don't you get out now and try to lie down. I brought some aspirin."

Kate nodded, then she hesitated. "What I did before . . . I didn't realize. Would you mind not looking at me?"

He stood. "I deserve that. Do you have a glass around here somewhere?"

"On the sink." Kate rose from the water and realized there was no towel in sight. "David, my towels."

He glanced into the bedroom, where the sopping bundle still lay on the bed. "No dry ones. You want one from my room?"

"No, just get one of mine, please. I don't think I'll be able to stand drying off, anyway. I want it to cover up."

David turned. "That's enough, Kate. I said I was sorry, so stop rubbing my nose in it. Just walk over to the damned bed and lie down."

Kate got stiffly out of the tub and went past him into the bedroom. She was all too aware of her backside as he followed her to the bed.

"Here." He handed her a glass of water. "The aspirin bottle is on the nightstand. Let me move those towels."

Kate took three aspirin and drank all the water before turning back the bed. The sheets were cool and damp where the wet towels had been.

"On your stomach," David said as he emerged from the bathroom. The tube of burn cream was in his hand.

"I can do it," Kate told him.

"No, you can't. Lie down on your stomach."

"You're going to hurt me."

His voice was dry. "I'll try not to, but I'm sure it's going to hurt a little."

Kate didn't think that was what she meant. She gave herself a mental shake and slowly eased down on the mattress. Her skin immediately protested the contact.

"Ouch."

"I haven't even started," he said.

"I know." She winced as the mattress sagged under his weight. "I should have stayed in the tub. Even the linen hurts me. Can you move over just a—" Kate nearly bit off her tongue as he smoothed the cream onto her left shoulder. "No, no. I changed my mind. I don't want to do this. We can do it tomorrow, David. Please. It *hurts*."

"Hush. I know it does."

"I mean it. Please stop." Hot tears sprang to her eyes as the pain worsened. She turned her face away from him and felt his fingers move her hair from her neck.

"David . . ."

"Stop holding your breath, Kate. Breathe in deep, hold it for a count of seven, then breathe out to a count of eight."

Kate filled her lungs with air, counted, and exhaled with a loud hiss as he moved to the other shoulder.

"Talk," she begged. "Say something. Talk about anything to take my mind off—" She finished with a sharp cry as a blister gave way beneath his fingers.

David gritted his teeth and lightened his touch. "I don't know what you were thinking about out there. You ought to know better. I've seen fire victims with less damage."

Kate clenched her own teeth. "Talk about something else. Tell me about the last article you wrote. Or your favorite sport. Or what kind of movies you like to watch and why, and please just say something while you're doing this to me so I don't have to think about how much it hurts."

Out of the corner of her eye she saw his hand lift and she squeezed her eyes shut in anticipation of the pain. Her lids fluttered open again when she felt him flick a tear from the tip of her nose.

"My last story was a grisly one, about an occult priest in India who was caught sacrificing small children. My favorite sport is anything with a ball. I like Gene Hackman movies and most kinds of music."

He was touching her shoulder again, smoothing in the cream as gently as possible.

"What kind of music don't you like?"

"I don't know until I hear it."

"Keep talking," she urged. "Why was the priest sacrificing children?"

"To serve his gods."

"Was he crazy?"

"No more than anyone else in a world of animal patents, television religion, and Christ's face in a cupcake."

Kate wanted to smile, but her lip prevented it. "Why was that your last story?"

"Julia died the day after it was printed."

"Your wife?"

"Yes. I didn't take any more assignments after that. In fact, I quit."

Kate chanced a look at him. He was intent on watching his fingers. "Why?" she asked.

"I don't know. Suddenly my specialty was too close to home."

"Your specialty?"

"Human motivation in relation to bloodshed and death."

"I see." Kate thought about this. "Does that really interest you?"

"It fascinates me. It always has."

"Are you morbid?"

His chuckle was mirthless. "Maybe."

Kate winced again as he shifted on the mattress. "David, can I ask you something?"

"Get ready, I'm on your hips now," he replied. "And the backs of your thighs are next, so don't squirm."

"I won't," she said. He wasn't going to let her ask. She closed her eyes and gave an involuntary shiver as he drew a line across her back with the cream.

After a moment he said, "Don't ask me, Kate. I won't talk about it with you."

"Why?" she asked against the pillow.

"Because it's none of your business. And because I'm sure Bryan has already told you his own version of the story."

Kate was silent. At the time of Julia's death, Dr. Raleigh had called his brother a heartless, money-grubbing, unfeeling bastard. None of those names seemed to fit the David sitting beside her now. Slowly, she craned her head to look at him. His blue gaze was intent on what his hands were doing, never straying from the area under treatment.

"We can talk about something else," she suggested.

"Still hurting?"

"Not as bad as the area around the blisters." She paused then. "I wasn't trying to pry, David. I only—"

"Almost done," he said abruptly.

Kate jumped as the cold cream was squeezed onto the backs of her thighs. Moisture formed in her eyes as his fingers went to work with a pressure that made her earlier pain seem comfortable. Her face began to burn and she clutched instinctively at the sheet as he rubbed the cream into the deep red welts just below her buttocks.

"Stop," she croaked.

"You said you wouldn't squirm," he reminded her in a distant voice. His touch was agony now, his fingers like sandpaper on the burned skin.

Kate buried her face in the pillow and fought hard to keep her shoulders from shaking. She felt humiliated by the impersonal attack. The intimate parts of her body tensed and cringed away from his fingers. If she looked at him now she was certain his face would be different. He wouldn't be David anymore, he would be someone who took deliberate pleasure in causing pain. He would be the man Dr. Raleigh had spoken of so angrily.

Then he stopped. She heard him draw a long breath.

"I'm done now."

"*Good.*" She shuddered and wiped her eyes and nose against the fabric of the pillow. "Thank you for your help. Now please go."

He sat there and didn't move. Finally, Kate turned to look at him.

"I'm sorry if I hurt you," he said. "You can believe that if you want to. If you don't, then you don't."

Kate hesitated while she studied his face. Then she said, "I want to believe it."

He squeezed more cream out of the tube and dabbed some on her cheeks. "You look awful."

"Maybe you'll treat me better," she suggested.

His lips curved. "Now that you're ugly?"

"Yes."

"I don't know. You look pretty bad."

She smiled and then winced at the pain it caused. David put some cream on his finger and ran it lightly over her lips. They looked at each other a moment, then he handed her the tube of cream. "I'll let you do the rest. Should I bring you some dinner?"

"Am I really ugly?"

He lifted his brows, but said nothing.

"Thanks," she mumbled.

"What?"

"For going after the cream. I didn't expect you to do that."

"I'll ask again," he said. "Dinner?"

"No. I'm not hungry. Still a little queasy. Thank you for asking."

David left the bed and saw her face crease in pain as the mattress shifted. "I'll tell Bryan you won't be able to make the session tomorrow."

Kate grudgingly nodded. "Can you tell everyone I'm already asleep? I don't want them to come in and see me like this."

"Lock your door," David told her. "Jay might be tempted to slip back in and see how you're getting along." He took the water glass from the nightstand and went into the bathroom to refill it. When he brought it back, Kate said, "I wonder what he wanted."

"Jay?"

"Yes. He's never been to my room before."

"Who knows?" David moved to the door. "Yell if you need anything. I'll be up pretty late."

"I will. Thank you for all your help."

He left the room without acknowledging her gratitude. Kate made a face at his back and squeezed some of the cream onto her hands. After a moment she left the bed and took his advice about locking the door. She didn't want to wake up and find Jay hovering over her again.

# 13

## Sunday, May 15, 7:00 a.m.

In an effort to escape another gruesome nightmare, Mel left her bed and the house and was at the stables before the sun had cleared the hills. The stable hand, a lanky young blond, grinned with pleasure when he saw her.

"You're up early this morning."

Mel nodded and pointed to the horses. "Which one can I have? That big one looks nice."

The blond looked at the chestnut gelding and shook his tousled head. "Nope. He's got a tender frog. Pick another."

Mel didn't know what a tender frog was, and she wasn't about to ask. She pointed again. "Him?"

"Her. And her mouth is a bit tender. Why don't you try the bay mare today? Chelsea's easy to get along with."

Tender frogs and tender mouths. Mel felt like a real tenderfoot. "Okay," she said. "Chelsea's fine with me."

She stepped back and inhaled the smell of the stable, as the hand went about saddling the mare. She could see how people fell in love with this sort of life. There was something very wholesome about walking through dewy grass, smelling hay and horse doo, and riding over low hills and small, quiet pastures with nothing but birdsong and the wind in your ears. A person could get attached to the land, develop a bond with the earth and its nonhuman inhabitants.

Horses, especially. Mel's riding had improved, but she still wasn't comfortable unless she was talking to the animal carrying her around on its back. She knew they listened; she could tell by the way their ears moved when she spoke. Away from the ranch she could almost imagine herself as a lone horsewoman from another century. It was easy to do that with hardly any fences or telephone poles to mar the image. Just her, the horse, and miles of rolling green terrain.

Yesterday she had seen her first badger, and the sight of the animal, so alien to her everyday existence, had completely and utterly fascinated her. Little black eyes and a fat, furry body scuttling across her path. Amazing. The thing reminded her of Augusta Guerin.

The badger had left in what passed for a badger's hurry after spotting her, but Mel hoped to see it again today. An antelope or a deer would be nice, too, she thought. What she wanted most was to get away from the oppressiveness of the house and all that she had recently learned about the Guerin family.

"She's ready," said the stable hand.

Mel approached the horse and gave the soft muzzle a gentle pat. "Me friend, okay?"

Chelsea blew on her fingers and made a rumbling sound deep in her chest.

"Does that mean she likes me?" Mel asked.

"Chelsea likes everybody." The hand gave her the reins and proceeded to help her into the saddle.

"What's your name, anyway?" Mel asked as she swung her leg over. "I like to know the names of males whose hands come into contact with my derriere."

"Denny," said the blond with an embarrassed grin. "I'm just helping out. You're pretty small."

"You're pretty tall. I like my cowboys tall."

A teasing light entered his eyes. "I like my women small."

"Flirt," said Mel. "Come on, Chelsea. It's too early in the morning for such repartee." The sound of Denny's chuckle made her smile to herself as she rode out of the stable. It never hurt to be flattered by a male belonging to an age group whose standards were notoriously high.

"What a sweet kid," she said to Chelsea's flickering ears. Then she looked around herself. "Well, Chelsea, I'm willing to go anywhere but the lake. I don't even want to think about that place."

Mel hadn't been back to the lake since the first day with David. The rest of the ranch was fair game, so she decided to head west.

Not that she was suspicious or anything, she told herself. Though of course she was. Mel believed in luck. If more than one mishap occurred in a certain place, then that place was bad luck. And in Mel's opinion, the area around the Guerins' lake was serious bad luck. It had nothing to do with the hundreds of horror films Mel had seen, she just had a feeling about the place. It was the same feeling she'd had in the jet when they were about to land. Mel called it intuition, but it was more or less a by-product of the instinct for survival.

Her dreams were full of that instinct. They were getting worse now. Bloodier. Twice now she had awakened to find herself clutching her blade, certain she was about to be attacked by someone . . . or something. The fear usually dispersed with the morning light, but the feeling of being watched stayed with her. Mel had gone so far as to check her room for a hidden lens, wondering if Augusta wasn't satisfied with merely hearing the activities of others. Her search turned up nothing, no intercom, no camera, and no form of entry other than the window and the door.

Last night she had been tempted to slip in and sleep in Kate's room. She would have if Kate hadn't been so cranky about company lately. Mel had been careful not to say I told you so, but Kate's sensitivity was at an all-time high. Mel guessed she would be upset herself if she looked like a post-nuclear blast victim. But there was something else simmering beneath Kate's pink and flaky skin. Just what, it was difficult to say.

Mel thought it had something to do with David, though Kate never mentioned him. David was his usual stoic self, so there was nothing to discern from his behavior. Mel did discover that he swam in the pool after dark. In search of someone to watch the Friday night spook movie with her, she had gone to his room and spotted him from his own window. He had swum countless laps, never seeming to pause for air, and when he finally left the water, Mel had cursed the inky darkness and the dim blue lights around the pool. She was positive he had been swimming in the nude.

Mel settled herself in to wait and see, but by the time he came back to his room he was fully dressed.

David had ridden with her a few mornings, and Mel thought he was actually beginning to grow fond of her. That made her feel good, because she didn't think David was fond of many people. She was flattered that his distrustfulness seemed to abate under her constant jokes and teasing. She wished he would show the same laughing, smiling David to Kate and Bryan, but she supposed that was asking a little much. Everyone had different faces for different people. Emotions dictated the changes and sent messages to the attitude sector. The attitude sector gauged reaction and molded the proper mask. It was automatic.

Mel was about to pat herself on the back again for being so smart when she saw something ahead that made her frown. There was a figure in the distance. She rode closer and saw that it was a man, kneeling on the ground beside a horse and holding his right arm out in front of him.

Chelsea came to a stop on her own, and Mel sat in the saddle and squinted while she tried to see what was happening. Some kind of Sunday morning water divination? she wondered.

There was a lone tree several yards away from the man. A cottonwood, from the looks of it. The tree and the kneeling man made a desolate, strangely beautiful picture. He was in some kind of gully, she thought. A stream bed? Then he rose from the ground and she recognized him. It was Jay Guerin.

Mel urged her horse forward and observed him wrapping something around his wrist. A blue bandanna.

Maybe he was saying a cowboy prayer or something, she told herself as she neared him.

He whirled at the sound of her horse and his dark brows creased into a frown when he recognized her.

"What are you doing out here?" he asked.

Mel shrugged. "Just out for a little sightseeing."

"You're nearly a mile from the house," Jay said in irritation. "What if you'd gotten lost?"

A mile? Mel was surprised. She did a quick pan and realized she hadn't noted a single landmark.

"Uh, wouldn't Chelsea have known the way back?"

"Not necessarily."

"Oh," said Mel. The scenery was great, but she didn't know about spending the night. "In that case, I'm glad I ran into you. Are you going back right away?"

"No." He mounted his horse and turned suddenly to smile at her. "Want to see something?"

"What?" Mel asked with suspicion.

"Some of the herd. I'll have you back in time for breakfast. Come on."

Mel hesitated, but Chelsea was all too willing to follow Jay's mount, a golden palomino with a glistening white mane that was a shade darker than Kate's hair. The rest of the animal was all muscle and clean lines. Horse and rider made an impressive picture, Mel silently acknowledged. Jay Guerin was darkly handsome, the opposite of the fair-haired Dr. Raleigh, but equally striking. And younger. Maybe only thirty.

"What were you doing back there?" Mel asked as she rode up beside him.

Jay didn't look at her. "My grandfather died on that spot. I often go there just to think."

Mel decided to play dumb. "How did he die?"

"His horse threw him and he hit his head. Used to be a stream there. Lots of rocks and gravel."

"He hit his head on a rock?"

Jay nodded. "My mother found him." He looked at Mel then. "Believe it or not, my mother was once a beautiful woman. She's changed a lot in the last few years."

The understatement of the millennium, Mel thought. "What happened to her?"

Jay lifted a shoulder. "While she was mourning the death of my grandfather, my father became famous for his work with multiples. Mother's career was left in his dust."

This lifted Mel's head. "She had a . . . What was her career?"

"She's a psychiatrist, too. You didn't know that?"

"No." Mel was stunned.

Jay smiled. "I guess I should have said *was*."

Thank God, Mel silently responded. "What branch was she in?"

"She started out working with paraphiliacs—"

"Sexual perverts?"

"That's right. Then she became interested in the paranormal. My father blames that interest for her failure. He wanted her to join him in his own research, and later in his treatment program, but she wasn't interested. She wanted to blaze her own trail."

"In what?" Mel asked. "Parapsychology?"

"That was the trouble," Jay said with a wry twist of the mouth. "She knew there was little or no acceptance in the field, but she wouldn't give it up. Then my father's work made the journals. She saw red when he became famous overnight. When Ted died, she gave up her work completely. She's never been the same since."

"Ted was your grandfather."

"Yes. Theodore Manfred Arnette."

"Did you know him well?"

"He raised me," Jay told her, a hint of pride in his voice. "My parents were always occupied with books and patients, so Ted took over. I lived with him in Houston before he bought the ranch here. I visited my parents on weekends."

"So you lived here before they did. On the ranch, I mean," Mel said.

"That's right. Ted wanted my mother and father to move here right away, but my father didn't agree until Ted said he could do his work with multiples here. Ted missed my mother, so he turned the first floor of the house into a hotel for lunatics and opened the doors."

"Obviously you disapproved," said Mel.

"It's a ranch," Jay replied in a flat voice. "I hated to see it turned into a retreat for the rich just so my father could find some pride and stop living off Arnette money. Do you know how much he charges per month to stay here?"

"I haven't asked," Mel told him. And she wasn't going to ask Jay, because she saw something under another lonely cotton-wood tree that immediately snared her full attention. "What in the name of ugly is that?"

Jay laughed. "Don't tell me you've never seen a cow before?"

"I've seen plenty of cows," she assured him. "Never one that looked like that. That thing is—oh, my lord, there's a whole bunch of them."

They had topped a rise and were soon looking down on a herd of fifty or sixty of the ugliest cattle Mel had ever seen. In the near distance she saw hundreds more of the odd, multi-colored beasts. Only a few of the nearest cows paused in their grazing to take notice of them.

"Look at those floppy ears," Mel exclaimed. "What kind of cow are they?"

"Mexican steers," Jay answered. "A cross between Brahma, Hereford, and Charlois. It's a profitable breed. Right now they're gaining about two-point-seven pounds a day in weight."

"Eating grass?" Mel said in disbelief.

"Bluestem," Jay said. "Rains in April make it thick in May. The richest grass in the world."

"I remember. Dr. Raleigh told us about it on the jet. Other states ship cattle in to feed off this stuff, right?"

Jay nodded. "Mostly from Texas, Louisiana, and New Mexico. They're trucked in and out of Emporia. They stay about ninety days before going back to the feed lot."

Mel pulled a face as she thought of what happened to the cows afterward.

"How many do you own?" she asked. "Cattle."

"Right now, about three thousand head."

Mel looked around. "So where are they? Am I in danger of a stampede?"

Jay smiled and turned his horse. "We graze around four hundred head per section, which amounts to three acres per head. They don't go hungry . . . do they, Chelsea?"

Chelsea's ears pricked and she immediately turned to follow the palomino without any guidance from Mel.

Mel tightened the reins as she drew up alongside Jay again. She did a doubletake as she spied his right arm. A trickle of blood had escaped the tightly knotted bandanna.

She opened her mouth and made noise, but no more. She wouldn't ask. The man seemed normal, but hey. Nothing on the dude ranch of death was as it appeared. If that crazy fat lady was a psychiatrist, anything was possible.

She dragged her gaze away from the bandanna and searched for something to talk about. Jay saved her the trouble.

"How's Kate coming along? Is she healing up?"

"More or less," Mel answered. "Lots of itching and flaking going on. Not a pretty sight."

"Is she still hiding in her room?"

"Yes." How did he know? Mel wondered. "She'll probably come out tomorrow. Dr. Raleigh has commanded her presence at the session."

"The patients certainly seem to like him," Jay commented.

Mel studied him from the corner of her eye. Was he jealous? If he was, he hid it well.

"Girls will be girls," she said with an exaggerated sigh. "What about you? Got a girlfriend in town?"

Jay merely looked at her.

"I was curious to know what you do for fun," Mel explained.

His smile was cool. "I take particular delight in leading nosy guests to a secret cave and leaving them to find their way out again."

Mel quickly scanned the area around herself. She saw no cave and nothing that looked like a cave entrance.

"You're kidding me, right?"

"Are you afraid?"

"You bet I am. Of badgers and bobcats and bears, oh no."

"No bears," said Jay. "The badgers and the bobcats are on target." He was still smiling that chilly smile.

"Stop kidding around," Mel told him. "You're not going to leave me out here. Is there really a cave?"

His sparkling black eyes answered her.

Mel looked again. Nothing. "Uh . . . why don't you take me back to the ranch instead, and show me that gun collection Kate told me about."

Jay's smile widened and became genuine. "She told you about my collection?"

"A little." Great, Mel thought. Why did I say that? Now I'm going to have to go and watch him get turned on.

"Would you like to see it?" Jay asked.

"How about after breakfast?" Mel suggested. "We can start back right now. I'm starving to death."

The palomino halted suddenly and Mel looked back to see Jay frowning at her.

"You really are afraid, aren't you?" he said. "And you don't have the slightest interest in seeing the collection."

"My interest in breakfast is getting stronger by the minute," Mel hedged. "Can we please go now?"

Jay looked long at her. "I wouldn't leave you out here. And there is no cave. I was only teasing you for asking so many questions. I'm sorry if I frightened you."

He sounded serious. He looked serious. But there was blood running down his wrist and all Mel could think was that she had discovered him in the act of some strange hemophiliac ritual and he hadn't tied off his wound properly and this family was getting stranger by the minute.

"You're bleeding," she said.

Jay's glance at the bandanna was cursory. "I do that sometimes. Let's go."

Mel was only too happy to follow. She stared at his rigid spine and decided it was time to impart some of this burdensome knowledge of the Guerin family to David and see what he thought about this bunch of weirdos.

# 14

## SUNDAY, MAY 15, 10:00 P.M.

DAVID STEPPED OUT of Kate's room in time to see Mel coming from his room. The lift of her winged brows was almost comical.

"You sandbagger," she accused in a fierce whisper. "You sure had me fooled."

He shook his head and pointed her down the hall to the activity room. She went ahead of him and plopped down on one end of the long sofa. He sat down beside her and stretched his legs out in front of him.

"So tell me," Mel said. "What gives?"

"Nothing."

"I'm sure. You helping her peel, or what?"

"She hasn't had a decent meal in three days," he replied. "I took some food to her and made her eat it."

Mel's humor quickly changed to concern. "Why hasn't she been eating? Is she ill?"

David put both hands to his jaw and rubbed at the evening growth. "I don't know what's wrong with her. She turned her nose up at the food I offered and asked if I had some chocolate."

The frown on Mel's face dissolved. "Okay. Her period must be coming."

It was David's turn to arch a brow. "How do you know?"

"Because I know Kate. Women who work together usually fall into the same cycle, and I'm near, so she must be, too. Some researchers speculate that the reason we crave chocolate is because it replaces the magnesium we lose during our periods."

David was thoughtful. "Maybe I should try to find some for you."

"Ask Augusta," Mel said with a snort. "I'm sure she has a Mormon stockload around here somewhere. Which reminds me of why I was looking for you. Put on your listening ears, Mr. Journalist. I'm about to make your life interesting."

David let his head loll back against the sofa. "Get me a beer and I'll listen to your life story. Twice."

"If you take me swimming with you tonight I'll bring you a six-pack," Mel returned with a grin.

He winked at her. "Might turn your life around, Mel. I'd ruin you for any other woman."

Mel burst out laughing and hopped off the sofa. "Don't move. I could use a brew myself."

She was back within minutes, her arms full of cold, wet cans of Miller. She handed one to David and lined the others up on the cocktail table in front of the couch.

"I hate this stuff," David said as he lifted the can to his mouth.

"I noticed," Mel commented. "I could tell just how much by counting the empty cans in your room."

"Smartass," said David. "Stop sniping and start talking."

Mel needed no more prodding. She leaned back and told him everything she had learned about the Guerins in the last few days. David felt his brow pucker when she came to the part about Jay and his bandanna. When she finished, he had downed two beers and was opening a third. It was a struggle to keep his interest at a minimum. The story about Augusta was intriguing, but he was determined to keep a tight rein on himself where she was concerned. She would love to know he was interested in her life. He could almost see those monstrous white arms opening up to draw him in.

"So . . . what you do think?" Mel asked as she watched his fingers pry at the aluminum top.

"What am I supposed to think?"

She stared at him. "I hope you think it's as weird as I do. I keep expecting to see David Lynch behind a camera somewhere. Am I crazy in thinking that these people aren't normal?"

David finally looked at her. She had no idea how he was struggling. "What's normal, Mel? Are you normal? Am I normal?"

Mel's jaw dropped. "Compared to these prairie psychotics, *yes*. What's wrong with you, David?"

"Nothing." He looked hard at the blank screen of the television. "I'm just tired of being manipulated. I don't want to get involved. I'm here to write a book and make some money and that's all."

"Oh, like you need it," Mel said angrily.

David stared at her. "What?"

"You heard me. Your old lady was loaded. I read the papers."

His head began to shake even as the bitter laughter erupted from his throat. He wiped his face after a moment and looked at her in disappointment. "Now why did I think you'd be any different?"

Mel looked hurt. "I don't know. Why did you?"

"What did Bryan tell you?"

She shrugged. "Enough to cast suspicion. Not that I'm in the habit of believing everything he says."

"Enough to cast suspicion," David repeated. Then he looked at her. "I take it he didn't mention the cyanide found in Julia's stomach during the autopsy."

"Cyanide?" Mel made a pained face and slid back on the sofa. "Don't be one of those people who drink and start confessing to crimes. Are you telling me that you did in fact murder your wife?"

"No," David said. "But she wanted to make it look like I did. Only three people in the world knew she was dyspeptic, and that was me, Julia, and the doctor—now dead—who made the diagnosis. Julia knew the cyanide wouldn't have any effect on her.

She ate it before she swallowed that bottle of Percodan—the bottle with my fingerprints all over it. She wanted to cast suspicion on her suicide, make the police think I had murdered her. And it would have worked if Bryan hadn't been on the ball."

Mel's eyes were round. "What did he do?"

"He paid off the medical examiner who performed the autopsy. The doctor was somehow related to Bryan's wife. He called Bryan looking for a bribe, and he got one."

"So the medical examiner calls it a drug overdose—what all the papers said—and no one ever heard about the cyanide."

"Everyone, including Bryan, assumed I was living it up," David told her. "My rich wife must have left me very well off." He drew in a deep breath then. "Everyone was wrong. Julia changed all of the appropriate paperwork long before she killed herself. She was smart. She knew what she was doing every step of the way."

"You didn't get a dime," Mel said, and she looked at him in amazement. "What did you do to make her hate you so much?"

"I was leaving her," David said. "That was reason enough for Julia."

"Was there another woman?"

"No, but I couldn't convince her of that. For the last year of our marriage she had me followed everywhere I went, even on assignment. I grew sick of it. Sick of her."

Mel took a slow sip of her beer. "Can I ask why you married her to begin with?"

David smiled in derision. "You can ask, but I'm still wondering myself. She was intelligent, mature, and she didn't seem to mind that I wasn't the most demonstrative person in the world. I thought she would make a good companion. Someone to come home to after an assignment."

"Only she wasn't as mature as you thought," Mel guessed. "Not in terms of relationships."

"No," David admitted. "We played dress-up and went to a succession of dinner parties, where she made a habit of publicly berating me for looking at younger women. Soon she began to

demand that I turn down assignments to accommodate her social schedule. She tried to manipulate me, first with her money
and then her health. When her possessiveness reached the point
of obsession, I decided it was time to get out."

Mel nodded. "The old cling-free story."

"What?" David thought of fabric softener.

"The more she would cling, the more you struggled to be
free," Mel explained.

"Something like that," David agreed. "The day I told her I
was leaving, she tossed a book into my suitcase and called it a
going-away present. I didn't make any connection until after her
death. The book was about Rasputin."

"So?" Mel said. "What's he got to do with anything?"

"He was dyspeptic. His assassins fed him enough cyanide to
kill a dozen men, not knowing that his stomach didn't secrete
the hydrochloric acid necessary to activate the poison. Just another one of Julia's little games, a clue to what she was planning."

"You were the one to find her?"

"Of course. That was also part of her scheme. She gave the
maid the night off."

Mel looked at him. "She didn't want anyone else to have you if
she couldn't. Still, it's hard to believe a woman would go so far to
have revenge on a man."

"It's the truth," David told her.

Mel raised a hand. "I believe you. It's too crazy to be anything
but the truth. What I can't understand is why you don't
straighten out your brother. Have you told him any of this?"

"All of it. Bryan is in love with the idea of having risked his
career to save me from certain imprisonment. The truth takes
away some of the glamor, which is not to say that he ever believed me to begin with. Bryan's opinion of me has never been
what you would call laudatory."

"Why?" asked Mel. "What is it with you two?"

David took a drink of beer. "A lot of things. Bryan thought I
would need him when I came home from my tour. Our parents

were killed in a fire a few days before I arrived and he had his books out, ready to treat me for everything from depression to trauma. I didn't exactly rebuff his attempts to help me, but he took it that way."

"You didn't need him?" Mel asked quietly.

"Not as much as I needed his girlfriend."

"You're joking . . . right?"

"No. I hadn't had sex in a year. It was all I could think about or focus on."

"You're not joking." Mel sat back again. "You stole a girl from the Golden Boy?"

"More like borrowed. Bryan eventually married her."

Mel's voice rose to a delighted squeal. "Frieda? Are you talking about his wife, Frieda?"

David's nod was reluctant. "My judgment was clouded by my libido. Frieda had purposes of her own. She knew Bryan would go insane if her affair was with me."

"Bet you weren't invited to the wedding," Mel said, and David smiled.

"You're right. I wasn't."


In the hallway, standing just outside the door, Natalie stood watching David and Mel. She didn't want them to see her, but she liked hearing the two of them talk. She would have liked to stay and listen to what they were discussing, but a voice inside pushed her to go on down the hall. When she reached the door of Kate's room, she lifted a hand to knock softly on the door. There was no answer, so Natalie twisted the knob. The door was locked. She had known it would be. Someone told her. Quietly she removed a ring of keys from the pocket of her shorts and tried one after another until she found the key that fit. Then she opened the door and let herself into the room.

The urge to giggle was impossible to quell. This was going to be so much fun. No one ever let her have any fun, but tonight was going to be different. With careful fingers, she removed the pistol from her other pocket. She crept toward the bed and sat down as gently as possible on the mattress. Kate was asleep. Her breathing was slow and even. Her nostrils flared once, as if picking up the scent of her visitor. Natalie lifted the pistol and carefully placed the point against Kate's right nostril.

This was going to be so much fun.


In the activity room, David reached for yet another beer and Mel shook her head. "Don't you ever get drunk?"

"Often," was David's reply.

"Coward," said Mel, and he looked at her.

"What?"

"You heard me." Mel's mouth was open to continue, but something she heard made her pause. "Did you hear that?"

"What?"

Then they both heard it. Someone was screaming.

"Kate," they said together, and both left the sofa and rushed out of the room, Mel at David's heels. Bryan opened his door as they raced past him down the hall.

"What the—"

David twisted the knob of Kate's door and pushed open the door to find himself facing the barrel of a small pistol. Mel bumped into his back at the sudden halt.

Natalie held the pistol with both hands and smiled at the visitors. Her face was smeared with blood from a dozen scratches. She was wearing her red bikini top and tennis shorts. David looked past the gun for the briefest of seconds to find Kate. She was nowhere in sight.

"Kate?" he called, keeping his eyes on Natalie.

"I'm all right," she called from the bathroom.

"My God," said Bryan as he came in behind Mel. "She's got a gun."

"No kidding," said Mel. She stepped up beside David. "Cindy, is that you? What are you doing with that thing? Is it loaded?"

The pistol was immediately pointed at Mel. David swore and pushed her behind him again.

"Remember me, Cindy?" he said. "I still haven't found a suit to swim in."

"I know," she said. "You never come out to the pool."

Her slight pout was encouraging.

"We can go for a swim right now if you want to," David said. "Just the two of us."

Natalie tilted her head, as if listening to something. Suddenly she frowned in annoyance and said, "I wish you would leave me alone."

For some reason, David didn't think she was talking to him. He wanted to look at Mel for confirmation, but he was afraid to turn his back on that pistol.

Then he remembered what Mel had told him earlier, the bit about Natalie's bouncing around on Dr. Guerin's lap in his office. David looked at a point on the wall beyond Natalie and said, "Dr. Guerin, would it be all right if Cindy came swimming with me?"

Natalie's head swerved to look; David moved in and struck the side of her wrist. The pistol fell to the floor and discharged into the wall, answering the question of whether or not it had been loaded. Natalie/Cindy's bleeding face was the picture of betrayal as she glared at David.

"You tricked me. That was mean."

Mel stepped forward. "What's wrong with you? Get your wicked little Cindy-self over here."

"I'll listen next time," Natalie/Cindy said in a threatening voice. "I will."

"To who?" asked Mel. "You won't be listening to anyone but me when I take away your pool privileges."

"No. Don't do that. I'll be good. I promise."

"I know you will," Mel said as she took the woman's arm and pulled her out of the room.

Bryan went to pick up the pistol. As he turned to show it to

David, his look was curious. "I've never seen one like this before."

David started for the bathroom and Bryan hurried to catch his arm. His grip was firm.

"I'll check on Kate, David. You go on to bed."

David shook him off. "Is that an order?"

"If it has to be," Bryan said. "You smell like a damned brewery. Mel can hold her own with you, but I don't want you—"

"David?" Kate called.

David stepped forward and heard the sleeve of his shirt rip as Bryan snatched at his arm again.

"Dammit, David, did you hear me?"

Too much. Maybe too much beer that day, and maybe too many years of being pushed and grabbed and maligned by his older brother.

David let him have the elbow he wanted, hard in the ribs. Bryan sucked in his breath, cursed, and came back swinging with his right fist. David caught the fist and went around with it, twisting it behind his brother's back until he heard a low grunt of pain.

"You bastard," Bryan snarled.

"Don't ever touch me again," David said to him.

Bryan's face grew red. "You're making a *big* mistake."

"I don't think so." David released his hold and pushed his brother away. Bryan stumbled on the carpet and then quickly straightened to rub the circulation back into his arm. His mouth worked with fury, but no sound came forth. David turned away from him. As he left the room, he heard Kate call his name again.

# 15

## MONDAY, MAY 16, 7:30 A.M.

ALL EYES WERE on Jay as he entered the dining hall. He passed through the tables and paused briefly behind Kate's chair to touch her on the shoulder before moving on to where Bryan sat. "You wanted to see me?"

Bryan placed a pistol on the table. "Is this yours?"

Jay's brows knitted. "Where did you get that?"

"Natalie," Bryan told him. "She threatened to shoot Kate with it last night. What I'm interested in is where Natalie got it."

Jay turned to Kate. "Are you all right?"

"I'm fine," she assured him. "I'm not sure exactly who visited me last night. She certainly frightened me."

A mild understatement. Waking up to find cold metal prying her lips apart had terrified her. Kate had reacted by digging trenches in Natalie's face with her fingernails and screaming her lungs out.

After seeing Natalie's face that morning she regretted her panicked frenzy of aggression. Natalie couldn't be held responsible for her actions. Natalie wasn't at fault.

"I assume it's from your collection," Bryan said, bringing Jay's attention back to the pistol.

"Yes. It's a Baby Nambu."

"Come again?" said Mel.

"Baby Nambu. A Japanese service pistol, also known as the Officer's Model. It was used mostly by staff officers and aviators. I added it to the collection myself."

Bryan seemed impressed. "Rare?"

"Slightly. It was introduced in the twenties, and it's estimated that only three to four thousand were made."

"So they don't make ammunition for it anymore," Bryan guessed. "Which means you went to a gunsmith to get cartridges made. Why?"

Jay shrugged. "Sometimes I like to shoot targets." He put his hands on his hips then. "Look, I don't know how she gained access to my collection. I keep the room locked up tight. Ask Kate."

"I told them," she said. "Was the pistol in one of the glass cases?"

"No. I keep it in a drawer in the cabinets below."

"Who else has a key to the room?" asked Mel.

"Juana. But she goes in there only to clean. Maybe this . . . Who did you say it was?"

"Natalie Parks," Bryan answered.

"Maybe this Natalie got the key from Juana and decided to try a little snooping. I don't know."

Bryan sat back. "Relax, Jay. No one here is accusing you of anything. We're only trying to figure out what happened."

"Figure it out on your own time," Jay snapped. "My schedule doesn't allow for interrogations by *guests*."

His emphasis on the last word was missed by no one. He snatched the pistol from the table and gave it a quick examination. His black brows lifted.

"She fired it?"

"It discharged when David knocked it out of her hands," Bryan told him. "You didn't hear the shot?"

"No," Jay said. "But that shouldn't surprise you. The house is very well insulated."

The better to hear things through intercoms, Kate thought to herself.

"Where is David?" Mel asked.

Bryan looked away from Jay. "Sleeping off last night's drunk, no doubt. You're spending too much time with him, Mel. It's beginning to show in your attitude."

Mel looked at Kate and rolled her eyes. "He's such a bad influence."

"If you'll excuse me," Jay said in a dry voice. He turned and paused again beside Kate's chair. "You don't look as bad as Mel said you did. I'll see you later, all right?" He left without waiting for a reply.

"What did that mean?" Bryan asked Kate.

She looked at him. "I don't know. What did you say to him, Mel?"

"That your skin looked like soggy cornflakes floating in milk," Mel teased.

"I meant about seeing you later," Bryan said. "Has he been—"

"Is that any of your business?" Mel interrupted.

Bryan glared at her. "That's just the attitude I was talking about, Kierkes. I suggest you re-examine your priorities before you do too much more mouthing off."

Kate glanced at her watch. "We'd better go. Dr. Guerin will be waiting for us."

Bryan immediately left his chair and came to pull out Kate's. She frowned at the action even as she thanked him. Since his first sight of her splotchy skin he had been unusually attentive to her. She wished he would stop; he was making her acutely uncomfortable. There had always been protectiveness in his behavior toward her, but now she was beginning to wonder if there was something more.

The idea made her sigh to herself. Two incredibly attractive men were showing her all sorts of attention, and she wanted nothing to do with either of them. Instead, she found herself attracted to the man who showed not the slightest bit of romantic interest in her. The man who had slipped a chocolate bar under her door sometime between last night and this morning.

"Hey," Mel said as they entered the main room. "We should have asked Jay what he intends to *do* about the pistol theft. Putting an extra lock or two on that door wouldn't hurt. I don't want to wake up to a Baby Mambo one of these nights."

"Nambu," Bryan corrected. "And I don't think you have to worry. Jay covered well, but underneath he was mad as hell. Did you ever notice how adolescent he can appear at times?"

Bryan was looking at Kate, but she turned her face away rather than answer him. She saw Mel fighting a grin.

"I think we should talk to Natalie today," Mel said finally. "Maybe she'll tell us who she was listening to last night."

"That's a good idea," Bryan said.


"Tammy," Natalie/Cindy replied with a petulant frown. "She was the one who told me to do it. She wouldn't leave me alone."

Mel and Bryan looked at each other. Tammy was Natalie's youngest persona, the tortured girl who liked to poke holes in clay and draw pictures of people with spikes protruding from their skin. Dr. Guerin leaned forward in his chair. "How did you get the gun, Cindy?"

"I'm not supposed to tell."

"All right. May I please speak to Tammy?"

"She won't tell you."

"Let me speak to her. Tammy, can you hear me?"

Natalie/Cindy gave her head a vigorous shake. "I won't let you talk to her. I want to know if Mel took away my pool privileges."

"I'll give them back if you let us talk to Tammy," Mel told her.

"You have to promise. Swear, even. Russell, make her swear."

Mel and Bryan looked at Dr. Guerin in surprise. From across the room, Kate glanced up to see the older man shift uncomfortably.

"She called him Russell," one of Kate's three charges whispered. The others looked up from the poems they were attempting to write.

"Sssh," Kate said. She moved around the table and forced the three women to look at her. "We can't interrupt them right now. Please try to concentrate on your poems."

"I'm sorry," one woman answered with the voice of a cultured young gentleman. "Concentration is impossible when she is speaking so loudly. What exactly has Natalie done?"

"She's done nothing, Herbert. They only want to talk to her for a few minutes."

Kate glanced across the room again and saw everyone getting up. Bryan came to speak to Kate. "We're going into Guerin's office. Will you be all right, or should I ask Mel to stay with you?"

"We'll be fine," Kate assured him, and she smiled at her small group.

Bryan pulled her aside then and lowered his voice to explain. "Cindy's too conscious of the others. She's doing a lot of pouting and posturing. She may talk to us in the office."

Kate gently removed her arm from his grasp. "Don't frighten her. I'm sure she meant me no harm. It was just a game to her."

"Some game," Bryan said, his eyes glinting. "She could have killed you, Kate. I want to find out why she chose you and not someone else. You've never had any problems with her to speak of, so why bring a loaded gun to your room?" He lifted a hand to stroke Kate's hair. "Even if you're not interested in finding out the reason, I am. I might have lost you."

Kate stepped back and away. "I am interested in the why, Dr. Raleigh, but I'm afraid of what will happen if you pressure her. She's the most unstable patient in the group."

"I know. But don't worry. If Guerin agrees, I might try to hypnotize her today. If Tammy is upset about something we should discover the reason before she resorts to more violence."

Kate had to agree with that reasoning. She nodded and watched him go after the others. The three women at the table were all looking at her. After a moment, Kate smiled.

"Your discussion time may be delayed today. After you finish your poems, we can do some watercoloring."

"Cindy certainly loves male attention," Herbert observed.

She certainly does, Kate silently agreed. To an unusual degree. Abuse victims generally tended to be distrustful of men. Most hated their own bodies and had low self-esteem. Some had problems becoming sexually aroused, but a rare few craved sex constantly. Five of Guerin's patients had managed to have at least one relationship that included marriage and children. These were women who were now closest to coming to terms with their victimization. Three of them were divorced at present, but they were gradually winning the battle against the anxiety and guilt that had destroyed their intimate relationships.

Natalie, at thirty-two, was single and as free-spirited as a woman could be when Cindy was at the helm. Kate had to put her in the sexually compulsive category. Still, she could only be glad it was Cindy, and not the hole-poking Tammy, who had visited her last night. Tammy may well have decided to fire the gun and make a very meaningful hole.

"I wish we could play baseball." Margaret pushed her poem away and propped her chin on her hand while she looked longingly out the window. Kate guessed it was Randy, a timid seven-year-old, now doing Margaret's wishing for her. From the first, Margaret had done very well in letting everyone out during group sessions.

"I've never played baseball," Kate told her. "Why don't you write down the rules of the game and explain how it's done?"

Margaret stretched her arms over her head. "Playing would be better. But okay."

Kate walked around to look at what the others were doing before settling down in a chair. Out of the corner of her eye she saw the video camera and wished she could just turn it off. After the first few days her constant awareness of the lens had subsided, but now she felt self-conscious again, knowing that David would view the tape later and see everything, including his brother's behavior with her.

On impulse Kate left her chair and walked out of the camera's range. The room was much like the activity room upstairs, minus the video game machine and the ping-pong table. Instead, there were tables and chairs and cabinets full of art supplies and writing paper. The group discussions were held in the part of the room used for viewing movies and television in the evenings. The low sectional furniture was placed in an arc around a large rear-projection screen against one wall. Beside the screen was an ash cabinet containing nothing but videotapes of both old and new films. The patients lacked nothing on the ranch. Nothing but wholeness.

Kate sighed and returned to the table. Margaret had written half a page on baseball rules and abruptly shifted into a description of a white building with rust stains that resembled blood. Kate wasn't surprised. Another persona had emerged and taken over before Randy could finish.

Sally would begin a beautiful drawing of a flower and the next day Beth or Kevin or one of her other dozen personas would arrive to stare in confoundment at the drawing and eventually wad it up to start anew.

Putting the pictures and the personas together, introducing Sally to Beth and Margaret to Randy and allowing the tone-deaf Vicki to hear herself singing like a bird as Laura was the ultimate in gratification. Kate felt no resentment toward the women because of their background of wealth. They had been abused regardless of money and power. Or perhaps because of it. They had suffered the worst form of human injustice and survived the only possible way they knew . . . by becoming someone else. Kate had nothing but pity and hope for these women. Hope that they would emerge from treatment with a love and respect for the person as a whole, with all its facets. Hope that they would come to accept their full worth as human beings and never have to suffer another minute of the mind-numbing depression that made their lives unbearable now.

Kate's lips tightened as she thought of the people responsible for bringing these three seemingly healthy, outwardly normal young women to this place. People who were allowed to walk free while hiding their true selves from society.

Her thoughts paused as she noticed Margaret looking at her with an intent expression.

"What? What is it?" Kate asked.

"What happened to your face? You never answered."

Randy again? Kate wondered. "I was out in the sun too long on Thursday." She put a hand to her face and felt the rough, flaky skin. The area where the blisters had been was a bright pink and still tender. "I look funny, don't I?"

"It looks awful," came the reply. "You shouldn't go out into the sun without a hat. Ever."

Kate sighed. "You're right, Randy."

"My name's not Randy," Margaret said immediately. "I'm Tom. Why are you always calling me Randy?"

"I'm sorry," Kate told him. "I wasn't thinking, Tom."

"I could tell you something if I wanted to," the impish Margaret/Tom went on. "Something about Cindy."

Kate's chin lifted. Tom was the most talkative of Margaret's personas, but he was also the most bratty.

"I'd like to hear it, Tom."

"What'll you give me?"

"What do you want?"

"A Garfield eraser."

"I can try, but I won't promise you," Kate said. She hadn't the faintest idea where she would find a Garfield eraser.

Margaret/Tom screwed up her face in indecision until the answer was deemed acceptable. "Okay. She sneaks out of her room at night. Not every night, but sometimes. Once I followed her."

"And . . ." Kate prompted.

"And I saw her go outside. She went in the poolhouse and took off all her clothes. Then a man came in and—"

"Okay, Tom," Kate said, suddenly aware of the interest being displayed by the other two women.

"Who was the man?" Sally asked.

"Tom, I don't—"

"I couldn't tell," Tom said with a shrug. "It was dark and I couldn't see his face too good."

Kate stood and pushed back her chair. "Who wants to paint now?"

The three women merely looked at her. She was saved when a frowning Mel entered the room.

Kate turned from the patients and mouthed, "What happened?"

"Tell you in a minute," Mel whispered. Then, "Come on, gang. Give Katie your poems and we'll start our discussion without the good doctors. Just go on and sit down and I'll be with you in a minute."

Reluctantly, the three women did as Mel bid them. When they were far enough away, Mel took Kate by the arm and put her mouth close to her ear. "It was a battle when Raleigh suggested putting her under to find out what happened. Guerin didn't want him to hypnotize her for some reason. Old Silver Tongue finally talked him into it, but Tammy wouldn't come out. Would *not*. It was weird, Kate. Like something was keeping Tammy from talking. Finally Natalie came back and started crying a flood. They couldn't calm her down, so Guerin's giving her a sedative."

As Mel finished, Dr. Raleigh entered the room. He looked at the waiting women and gestured impatiently to Mel. Kate gathered up the patients' papers and sat down nearby as the discussion began. All three patients were unusually animated during the session. Kate listened and attributed their verbosity to the excitement aroused by the peeping Tom's tale. Thankfully, he repeated none of his story to Dr. Raleigh. Kate guessed it was the bribe of the Garfield eraser that kept him indebted to no one but her. Mel ended the session with a quiet story and a request for each of the women to take out their journals and write in them for a few minutes. The journals were then put away and the women were free to go. Dr. Guerin and Dr. Raleigh would pore over the journals, poems, and drawings to use them as a guide in later discussions and private sessions.

Kate couldn't imagine the two men arguing. They worked so well together. She wanted to ask Mel more about what had happened with Natalie, and to tell her what the tattletale Tom had said, but Mel waved her on and said they would talk later. With a shrug Kate left the room and found herself face to face with a smiling Jay.

"How about riding into town with me?" he said. "It'll do you good to get away from the ranch."

Kate hesitated, until she remembered the need to look for Tom's Garfield eraser. "Are you sure you won't be embarrassed to be seen with me?"

"Never," said Jay. He led her out of the house and around to the garage where his Jeep and two identical black Mercedes were housed. Kate stopped when she saw a huge Labrador sitting in the seat of the Jeep.

"Are you taking the dog?"

"I usually do," Jay told her. "He'll ride in the back."

Kate's smile was weak. "I . . . changed my mind, Jay. I'll go some other time, okay?"

"Why?" he demanded. Then he looked at the dog. "Is it because of him? He won't hurt you."

"I'm sure he won't," Kate said. "Just the same—"

"We don't have to take him," Jay said quickly. "Come on, Charge. Out. You can't come today."

The black dog lumbered out of the Jeep and ignored Jay's outstretched hand to snuffle at Kate. She froze.

"Get him away," she breathed.

Jay frowned at her and gave a short, sharp whistle. The moment the dog turned away, Kate bolted in the other direction. Jay called after her, but she didn't stop until she rounded the garage and ran directly into a hard chest.

"Slow down." David held her away from him. "What's wrong? What happened?"

"Nothing." Kate was breathless. "I think I just broke my nose."

David looked past her. "Has Jay left yet?"

"No, he's in the garage." Kate felt her throbbing nose. "Are you going into town with him? If you are I need—"

"More chocolate?"

"A Garfield eraser, if you can find one."

David looked strangely at her. "If I can find one."

# 16

"WHAT'S WITH HER?" Jay asked as he started the engine. "The dog sniffed her and she freaked."

David glanced at the large black animal in the back. He wouldn't be happy about being sniffed himself.

"She doesn't like animals," he said.

"I noticed. The day I took her around the ranch she flinched at every four-legged creature we saw. Why?"

David couldn't see the harm in telling. He had asked the same question. "Bryan told me she was mauled by a dog as a child. It traumatized her."

"I see." Jay stared at the road ahead a moment, then he said, "That was a dog. What does she have against other animals?"

"I don't know." David wondered himself, since she obviously had nothing against parrots. But the human mind was a funny thing. If it could turn shadows into shapes and put monsters in closets, it could easily turn one episode with a dog into a lifelong phobia of animals. Kate had a right to a phobia, he guessed, just like everyone else. Everyone was afraid of something.

He was afraid of fat women with M&M eyes. Last night he had dreamed of Augusta. Not the Augusta in the bed on the third floor, but a thin and lovely Augusta with shining russet hair and a secretive smile. When he had begun to feel sexually aroused, he shook himself awake and lay there in his bed, feeling disgusted. He also had the distinct feeling of being watched by someone. Unable to sleep again, he had wandered downstairs and searched through the kitchen stores until he found some candy bars. Mel had been right about the Mormon stockload. The place was a fat person's paradise. A Dolly Madison mecca. It was unbelievable.

"Jay," he said abruptly. "Can you tell me what your mother wants from me?"

Jay didn't look at him. "I don't know. Why don't you ask her?"

"I have. She's convinced something is going on at the ranch and she wants me to find out what. What do you think?"

"I think she's infatuated with you and wants your attention. But don't flatter yourself. You're not the first man she's lured out here. Sometimes I think she does it just to annoy my father."

"Does it work?"

"No. He doesn't care. His interest is in his patients and nothing else."

David thought for a moment. "Who else has she brought out here?"

Jay shrugged. "Mystics, an occultist, a few of her old doctor buddies. Then there was this male nurse. My father fired him and hired Rosalie."

"Why?"

"He was trying to talk my mother into changing her will."

"Your grandfather must have been very wealthy," David said in a bland voice. "Was he into production, exporting, or both?"

Jay finally looked at him. "What are you talking about?"

"Oil."

"Ted hated the oil business," Jay told him. "My grandfather's interests were in hotels and warehouses."

"Warehouses?" David repeated in surprise. "Where?"

"Los Angeles, Boston, Cleveland, and Nashville," Jay answered.

"Port cities and distribution centers," David said. "Sounds profitable."

"Better than retail and office space. He also owned part of a winery in Napa, a racetrack in Louisiana, and a private research facility in West Virginia."

"Researching what?"

"Synthetic blood."

David wasn't surprised. The Guerin family was big on blood. "Your grandfather must have been quite a man. Who takes care of the business now?"

"My mother and her ten accountants."

This was another surprise. David couldn't see Augusta participating in anything connected to the business world. He couldn't see her participating in anything but a game of Yahtzee and a carton of Ho-Ho's.

"I meant to tell your brother that the lock on my gun cabinet had been tampered with," Jay said.

"What?"

"They grilled me about the pistol this morning. When I took it upstairs I found the wood splintered and the lock damaged. The patient used something metal to get the cabinet open. I still don't know how she got inside the room itself."

"Don't you have a security system?" David asked.

"Only for the pieces inside the glass cases. I added the cabinets later and never got around to updating the system. If she had broken the glass, an alarm would have sounded."

"Does anyone else know that?"

"Everyone but the patients."

"Are the guns behind the glass kept loaded?"

"Of course not," Jay said. Then his mouth tilted downward. "And that's why she broke into the cabinet, I suppose. But how would she have known?"

Someone told her, David thought. Someone who knew the

guns with the ammunition were kept in the cabinets. Someone who knew the cabinets weren't protected by the alarm.

He glanced up to see the town just ahead. He didn't look forward to seeing Wally and his three shelves of convenience items again, but he wanted to use a phone away from the house. Admit it or not, Mel's story about the Guerins had fired his curiosity. David wanted to know what the papers had said about Ted Arnette's death, and if there was any mention of Augusta's being a psychiatrist. He didn't know what he was looking for, or why he wanted to know, but he had been unable to think of anything else that morning.

If his friend at the *Star* was still employed, David could have every printed piece available sent to him within the week. Just for his own information, he told himself.

"I've got some packages to pick up at the post office," Jay said. "Where can I drop you?"

"At Wally's," David told him. "How long do I have?"

"As long as you like. I'll wait for you."

"Thanks." David got out of the Jeep in front of Wally's place and wondered why Jay was being so friendly. The look in his eyes that day in Kate's room had been anything but that of a cordial host.

"Hello again," David said to the round man behind the store counter.

Wally nearly dropped his wad of Red Man. When he finally got his chew reinstated, he looked at everything in the store but David.

"Is there a pay phone in here?" David asked.

Wally pointed. His cheeks took turns bulging as he switched the tobacco around to speak. "Five minutes is the limit."

David stopped. "Why?"

"Just the way it is," said Wally.

"All right." David looked at his watch and turned his back on Wally as he picked up the receiver. Next to the phone was a rack of magazines. He eyed the faces on the covers as he dropped in his money. Exactly four minutes later he hung up. His friend at the paper was happy to help. David turned and gave Wally a friendly smile. "Do you have any erasers in stock?"

"Erasers?"

"Pencil erasers."

"They'd be by the pencils."

David looked. "Where are the pencils?"

"By the writing tablets. Those two over there." Wally pointed again. He appeared nervous.

Wally's phobia was clearly a fear of mental patients on the loose.

David examined the stationry stock and found nothing but standard pink erasers. He turned back to Wally again. "Do you have any Garfield erasers?"

"Garfield?"

"The comic-strip cat. Garfield."

Wally's mouth opened. Was he going to scream for help? David wondered.

"Only got bookmarks," Wally said finally. "My little granddaughter likes him."

"Where are the bookmarks?"

"By the greeting cards. There."

David went where he was pointed and saw exactly five greeting cards. There were two bookmarks. He decided to buy both of them in hopes they would prove an acceptable substitute for the eraser.

"You like Garfield?" Wally asked as he rang up the purchase.

"Sure." David threw a couple of candy bars on the counter as well. "He's a favorite back at the ward."

He couldn't resist.

Wally's smile was thin as he took David's money and gave him his change. "They don't let you make phone calls there at the ranch?"

"Just local ones," David said. Then he smiled. "Look, I'm not really a patient. It was a joke."

"Right," Wally said with a forced laugh. "A joke."

"Have you seen Deputy Waltman around?" David asked.

"Deputy Waltman?"

Was it him, David wondered, or did Wally echo everything everyone said to him?

"Yes . . . Deputy Waltman."

"No, I sure haven't."

"All right. Thanks, Wally."

Jay was waiting in the Jeep outside. Beside the dog in the back were three large parcels. As David rounded the Jeep, he caught a glimpse of a West Virginia return address. The research facility?

Before he could ask, Jay pointed to the tasseled Garfield bookmarks in his hand. "A secret obsession?"

"Kate asked for them," David said as he climbed into his seat. Jay waited until he was buckled in, then the Jeep shot forward.

"Do you mind if I ask you a personal question, Raleigh?"

"I won't know until you ask."

"Okay. Is there anything between you and Kate?"

"I mind," David said.

Jay nodded. "Then I guess I have my answer. I didn't want to horn in on anyone."

David looked at him.

"But then again," Jay continued, "Kate is the one I should ask. Right?"

"Suit yourself," David told him.

"Did you make your phone call?" Jay inquired.

David looked at him again.

"I know you didn't go in there to buy bookmarks and candy bars. We've got candy at home."

"Tons of it," David agreed.

It was Jay's turn to look. David looked away from him and was silent for the rest of the trip back to the ranch. In the garage he asked Jay if he needed any help with the parcels in the back. Jay shook his head. "I can handle them, thanks."

"Mind if I ask what they are?"

"Yes," said Jay.

*Touché*, David thought. But he didn't really need to ask. The markings on one carton indicated that the contents were temperature controlled. Combined with what Jay had told him earlier about the research facility, it wasn't hard to figure out. Jay had just picked up a shipment of blood.

# 17

## Thursday, May 19, 8:00 p.m.

Mel sat on the rocks and waited. The temperature had dropped slightly, but the rocks were still warm from a day of sun. Chelsea grazed on the sparse grass below the small ledge, occasionally looking up when Mel spoke her name. Beside Mel lay a dead prairie rattler, its head crushed by the heel of her boot. The snake had been coiled up on the rocks when she arrived, and not seeing its small form, Mel had walked right over it and had the mind-boggling experience of seeing a real live snake strike at her boot. Without further ado she had done a vigorous, adrenalized stomp dance on top of the rock. The poor little snake never had a chance.

She almost regretted killing it. They could have shared the rock ledge. It was a prime spot for viewing wildlife, she had discovered. Yesterday she had seen three scampering brown rabbits, a quivering little prairie dog, and not twenty minutes ago another fat, furry badger had come meandering by the ledge. Mel was still holding her breath, hoping the badger would return, but a strange cry and a loud snort from Chelsea had hastened its plodding steps. Mel thought the badger was headed to a nearby trickle of water for his last sip of the day, but he seemed to have disappeared into the slope.

She thought about the sound that had startled Chelsea. A bobcat? she wondered. According to David they could sometimes sound like a screaming woman. Did bobcats eat people?

"I'm in a world of hurt if they do," she murmured aloud.

Chelsea's head lifted. Her ears pricked, but not in Mel's direction. She looked and saw a rider approaching from the direction of the ranch. As the horse neared she recognized Denny, the blond stable hand. She waved to him from atop the ledge and saw him wave back. Within minutes he was leaving his horse beside Chelsea and preparing to climb the ledge.

"What's wrong?" Mel asked.

"I was worried," he said as he climbed. "I thought you might have gotten lost. It'll be dark soon."

Mel stood to pull him up onto the flat rock with her. "I've been coming here for the last couple of days, so I pretty much know my way around now. But thanks for thinking of me."

Denny gave a small start as he nearly sat down on the dead prairie rattler. "Thought it was a live one. Did you do that?"

Mel nodded. "Guilty. These cowboy boots saved me."

Denny tossed the snake off the ledge and sat down beside her.

"How long have you been looking for me?" Mel asked.

"Not long. I just followed the direction you took when you left. Mr. Raleigh was asking about you and I realized you hadn't come back yet. I told him I'd find you."

"Which Mr. Raleigh?"

"The doctor."

"Oh." Mel shrugged it off. Then she looked at Denny. "Are there any caves around here?"

He frowned. "Not that I know of. Why?"

"Just curious," Mel said. "How long have you worked here?"

"Almost two years. Still trying to save money to go to college. I'll probably be thirty by the time I get there. I'm twenty now." He leaned back on his palms then. "You know, come to think of it, I did hear of a cave found near Cassoday, so I guess there could be one around here."

"But you've never seen one?" Mel asked.

"No. But I've never looked. Did someone tell you there was a cave around here?"

"Not in so many words." Mel shivered as a sudden breeze cooled her flesh. "Denny, I'm not being nosy or anything, but how well do you know Jay? Do you ever talk to him?"

Denny took off the work shirt he wore over his T-shirt and put it around her bare shoulders.

"He's only talked to me a couple of times, like when one of the horses is sick and needs a vet. Most of the time he deals with Tim and Grant. Grant's my brother."

"He got you this job?"

Denny nodded. "I needed a place to live after Mom died. Grant told Jay I was good with horses."

"So it's just you and Grant?" Mel asked.

"Yeah. He went to college for a while and dropped out. I'm going for a degree. I don't want to be stuck out here with these nuts."

"They aren't nuts, Denny," Mel said. "They have an illness, but they aren't nuts."

"I wasn't talking about the patients," Denny replied.

Mel looked at him. "Mrs. Guerin? Have you met her?"

"No, and I don't intend to. I hear enough stories from everyone else. Someone said she drinks blood."

Mel laughed. "I wouldn't be a bit surprised. Is that kitchen gossip?"

"No," Denny told her. "Someone saw Rosalie toss a bunch of glass beakers into the garbage. There was blood in them."

"Who is this someone?"

Denny shook his head, and Mel laughed again.

"I'm not going to blab, Denny. I wouldn't get my favorite stable hand into trouble."

He smiled at her. "I may have a thing for you, but I'm not crazy. I wouldn't survive without my job."

Mel stared at him. "I would never do anything to hurt you, Denny. Honestly. And I'm flattered that you like me, but you don't know anything about me."

"Yes, I do," he said. "I know and I don't care. I heard Grant and Tim talking about you. Mrs. Guerin said something to Jay, and Jay told Grant."

That explained Jay's avoidance of her lately, Mel thought. She couldn't believe he hadn't known before. She had assumed Dr. Guerin would tell him, since Bryan had seen fit to warn the good doctor before their arrival, in case of any religious and or moral prejudices against people like her.

Perhaps Augusta thought she was getting back at her for their tumultuous chat. As for Jay, she didn't know what his problem was. Maybe he still resented her intrusion on his Sunday morning bleeding service.

"Mel? Are you upset that I know?"

"What?" She looked at him. "Me? No, of course not. Denny, did you know Jay was a bleeder?"

"A what?"

"A hemophiliac. His blood doesn't clot the way ours does when we're cut. He just keeps on bleeding."

Denny frowned. "I heard the old man was, but I didn't know about Jay."

"Have you ever seen him walk around with a bandanna tied to his wrist?"

"Not that I can remember. You think he's the one using the blood?"

"Could be. Hemophiliacs need transfusions. I'm sure he does it somewhere upstairs rather than in a hospital."

"That's right," Denny said. "I heard there's a room on the third floor with some medical equipment in it."

Mel rubbed her eyes. She knew she should shut up and not ask any more questions, but a little voice in the back of her head was telling her that blood for transfusions came in bags, not beakers, and she couldn't get the vision out of her head of Augusta drinking a beaker of blood.

"Where?" she asked. "Where is the room?"

"I don't know. Close to Mrs. Guerin's room, I think. Even Juana's not allowed to go in there."

Aha, Mel thought. Juana. The inconspicuous little maid was the someone doing all the gossiping. How else would Denny know Juana wasn't allowed in the room unless she had told someone who had told him?

You should have been a detective, Mel told herself. You're so smart I can't stand it. She smiled at Denny and then shivered. "Ready to head back now?"

He looked disappointed. "If you like. The doctor didn't say it was urgent or anything."

"Aren't you getting chilly?"

"When I'm with you? No."

Mel chuckled. "You are such a flirt. What am I going to do with you?"

"I have a suggestion," Denny said.

"I'm sure you do, but I know better than to rob that particular cradle."

He laughed and touched her arm. "You're funny, you know that?"

"I've been told."

"Let's go down to the lake," Denny suggested. "The water will still be warm and we can go swimming."

"It'll be dark."

"I'll be with you."

"I'm sorry," Mel said. "I can't go to the lake. I don't like it there. And I'd hate myself if anything happened between us. I really would, Denny."

"Only for a little while," he told her. "But you'd get over it. Right now you're thinking that you should probably try to avoid me for the next few days. Then you'll try being cold to keep me away. When that doesn't work you'll start treating me like a kid, hoping to make me mad. Finally you'll give up and accept the fact that you're as attracted to me as I am to you, regardless of age or anything else."

Mel was staring at him again. "Is this in a manual some-where?"

"It's called horse sense. Horses are a lot like people, believe it or not."

"In your vast experience, I'm sure," Mel said. "What if I told you we'll be leaving at the end of the month?"

Denny's smile wilted. "You will?"

"As far as I know. Guerin's in the process of finding his own assistants. He knows how our program functions now. He's fly-ing into Kansas City to do some interviewing tomorrow. If you're lucky, he'll find some sweet little thing just your type."

Denny looked away from her. "I thought you were here to write a book."

"David is writing the book. All he needs are the doctor's notes, a few files, and the videotapes. He can write the book any-where."

"Why the big rush to leave?"

"No rush. Dr. Guerin has familiarized himself with our meth-ods, so he doesn't need us anymore."

"Well, what about the patients?" Denny persisted. "Won't they be upset with you for leaving when they've just gotten to know you?"

"Probably," Mel admitted. "But we have our own patients to think about. Dr. Raleigh is growing anxious to return to his program. He left everything in the hands of his associates."

Not to mention his unease over leaving Frieda alone for so long, Mel silently added, and she marveled all over again at what David had told her about his affair with Frieda. Mel would have given anything to see the Golden Boy's face when he found out.

"You haven't even been here a month," Denny said.

"No," Mel agreed. "Did you think we'd be here all summer?"

"I wanted you to be here that long. Are you sure Mrs. Guerin isn't scaring you away?"

"She could do it," Mel said. "The whole family is scary if you ask me. David doesn't seem to think anything is weird, but I guess he's used to weirdness." She clasped her arms then. "Denny, I'm cold. Let's go back now."

He gave a reluctant nod and climbed down to get the horses. As he helped Mel into the saddle, his hand lingered on her thigh. "I'll be sorry to see you go, Mel."

"Me too, in a way," she told him. "But I . . ." She paused as she heard the strange, eerie sound she had heard earlier. It seemed to echo against the rock ledge.

"What *is* that?"

"A bobcat," said Denny. He turned away from her and swung up into his saddle.

They rode to the ranch in silence, with Denny casting an occasional look at her. In the stables Mel gave him back his shirt and said a quick goodbye as he moved to take care of the horses. He merely nodded to her.

Mel felt almost guilty as she left the stables. She trudged up to the house and wondered if she should in fact avoid him in the future. If she did, she wouldn't be able to ride out to the ledge and look at the little animals, or talk Chelsea into avoiding the paths of any Mexican steers. She sighed to herself as she opened the front door.

"Where the hell have you been?" demanded Bryan. He strode across the room and grabbed her by the arm.

"Take it easy," Mel told him, and she struggled to pull herself free. "I was out for a ride and forgot the time."

Bryan released her and stepped back to run a hand through his hair. "I didn't know what to think. When Natalie turned up missing I thought she might have done something to you this time."

"Natalie? She's missing?"

"Since this afternoon."

"She was at the session," Mel told him. "And then she put on her suit to go swimming."

"No one has seen her since. Sally said she never showed up at the pool. We were going to hypnotize her again this afternoon."

"Did she know that?" Mel asked.

"I don't think so. She knew we wanted to talk to her again, but she didn't know why."

"So she really had no reason to run away," Mel said. "I thought Guerin had been sedating her since Monday."

"He didn't today. We wanted her clean for the hypnosis. Now that you're back, I'm going out to help them look."

"Want me to come?" Mel asked.

"No, I think—" Bryan paused and turned as the door opened. David, Jay, and Dr. Guerin stepped into the foyer. Their faces were grim.

"Well?" asked Bryan.

"It's too dark to see anything now," Guerin said. "We can try again in the morning. I'll reschedule my trip for next week."

Mel watched him and shivered at the thought of Natalie out there in the dark, wearing nothing but a skimpy red bikini. Then she remembered the sounds at the ledge.

A bobcat, Denny had said.

A screaming woman.

Tomorrow, Mel decided, she would find out.

# 18

## THURSDAY, MAY 19, 10:00 P.M.

KATE WALKED INTO David's room and found him sitting on the edge of his bed. His expression became annoyed when he looked up and found her staring at his naked chest.

"Don't you ever knock?"

"You wouldn't let me in if I knocked. And you feel free to walk into my room anytime you please." She walked to the bed and sat down beside him. He was holding what appeared to be copies of newspaper articles. "What are you doing?"

"Reading about Augusta and her father. What are you doing?"

"Looking for company. Nothing on Natalie?"

"No." He glanced up again. "Your face looks a lot better. Still tender?"

"A little. Where did you get these copies?"

"I called a friend. I was curious."

"Why?"

"Because of some things Mel told me. Has she said anything to you?"

"About what?"

"Never mind," David said.

Kate lifted her chin. "Don't do that to me. I'm a part of this too, you know. Tell me what's going on."

"What's Bryan doing?"

"I don't know. Why?"

David stood up. "Just wondering. I'm going to take a shower. You can read these if you like."

"Sweetheart," Frank called from his covered cage.

"Hello, Frank," Kate said to the parrot. She left the bed and went to lift the cover. "Not asleep yet?"

David muttered something under his breath and stepped into the bathroom. After a brief chat with the parrot, Kate replaced the cover on his cage and went to plop down on the bed. She put the articles in chronological order and began to read. She was still reading when David came out of the bathroom with a damp towel around his waist. He frowned when he saw her.

"I didn't say you could read the articles here."

Kate ignored him.

He walked to the closet and pulled out a pair of pants before disappearing into the bathroom again. Kate smiled to herself as the door closed.

"Modest, aren't we?" she said when he came out a second time.

He scowled at her. "Are you about finished?"

"Almost." Kate slid over to the opposite side of the bed and put her feet up to lie down. "It's bizarre about Mrs. Guerin being a psychiatrist. After everything I've heard, she doesn't sound like the most stable person in the world."

"She's not," said David. "Trust me."

"I do. What exactly is paraphilia?"

"It's the psychiatric term for sexual perversion."

He sat down beside her and began to gather the pages she had finished reading.

Kate lifted her brows. "She treated perverts?"

"Treated and studied, according to the articles." David leaned over to find a particular article for her. "From all indications, she was on her way to making a hell of a contribution. It's hard to believe she suddenly decided to quit. Here, read this one next."

Kate took the page and put it behind the one she was reading. "I don't understand why she didn't go to work with her husband. The two fields are related in a roundabout way."

"Who knows?" said David. He swung his feet up and propped a pillow behind his head. "Where's the obituary on Arnette?"

"Here." Kate patted the small stack beside her.

"Let me have it. I haven't read it yet."

She sifted through the pages and handed it over to him. They read in silence for a while, until Kate made a face of frustration and put down the article he had handed her to read.

"David, what is a coprophiliac?"

He turned his head to look at her. "A feces freak."

Her eyes rounded and she turned to him in disgust. "You mean there are people who actually . . . ?"

David nodded.

"Ugh," said Kate. "What about a klismaphiliac?"

"Enemas."

"Someone who loves . . . enemas?"

"Yes."

"Mrs. Guerin actually worked with these people? No wonder she's become a recluse. David, how do you know all these terms?"

His mouth curved. "Are you worried?"

"Should I be?"

"No." David settled back against the pillow. "You know I read somewhere that the man who gave his name to a popular brand of breakfast cereal was thought to be a klismaphiliac. The strange part is that he supposedly created the cereal to combat lust. Antisex all the way."

"That is strange," Kate said with a yawn. "Didn't he believe in procreation?"

"Go to bed if you're sleepy," David told her.

"I'm not," she lied. "I still want you to tell me what Mel told you. And then I'll tell you what one of the patients had to say about Natalie."

"Tell me now," he said.

Kate started to argue, but his expression changed her mind. His look turned pensive when she finished.

"Tom didn't see the man's face?"

"No. What is it, David? You know something."

"Mel said she caught Guerin with Natalie on his lap one night in his office."

Kate automatically shook her head. "No, I don't think so. Not Dr. Guerin. He's far too dedicated."

"What makes you so sure?"

"I don't know." But Kate was certain it wasn't Guerin in the poolhouse with Natalie. It could have been anyone. Even David. Mel had told Kate he liked to swim at night. And hadn't Natalie picked him out that first day?

"What?" David said to her.

She blinked and realized she'd been staring at him. "Nothing. I was just thinking. Would you like to play some cards?"

David groaned. "Go to bed, Kate."

"I don't want to. I've been having bad dreams the last few nights."

"Sorry, but I'm ready to go to sleep." He paused then. "What about?"

"My dreams?" Kate said. "They're not really about anything. I hear someone calling my name over and over and I can never find them. Then I wake up. The scary part is that sometimes I can still hear the voice after I'm awake."

"Where is it coming from?" David asked.

"My head." Kate looked at him, then she gathered up her courage and moved the articles aside to slide over beside him. He sucked in his breath as she put her head against his chest and laid one arm across his stomach.

"Kate . . . don't," he said. "I'm asking you."

She lifted herself to look at him. "Why?"

"Because I don't want this. I don't want anything."

Kate put her head down again. "Is it because of me? You don't find me attractive?"

"You know better than that."

"Then why?"

"I told you. I don't need this right now."

She pressed her face against his skin and said, "What if I told you that I do? What if I said I have the feeling that something is wrong, really terribly wrong in this house, and that you're the only one who seems right to me."

David's sigh sounded like an ocean wave in her ear. "Is that your intuition talking?"

"Yes. Sometimes I feel like . . . like someone is watching me, especially after one of those dreams." She lifted her head once more to look at him. "Does that sound crazy?"

"No," he said, watching her. His expression was thoughtful.

"Have you ever had the same feeling?" she asked.

David didn't answer. Kate looked at him, waiting, and suddenly she smiled. "You got it."

"What?"

"The spot you miss shaving every day. You got it."

He frowned. "What are you talking about?"

"Here." She lifted a finger to point, but on impulse she leaned forward and pressed her lips against the spot instead.

David's breathing stopped. He grew still.

Kate moved her lips slowly across his face to his mouth, where she dropped a light kiss and leaned back. They gazed at each other a moment, then his hand moved up to gently squeeze her shoulder and cup the back of her neck. He drew her to him and kissed her gently before forcing her away from him. She held her breath as she looked at him.

"You're not ready for me," he said in a whisper, "and I know I'm not ready for you."

"Why?" she asked.

He opened his mouth to tell her, but Kate was there to catch the words with her lips. His hands immediately came up to her shoulders, but they lingered as she splayed her fingers across his chest and kissed him deeper still. When she settled herself along the length of him, he abruptly broke the contact and sat up to push her away.

"I'm not what you're looking for," he told her in a harsh voice. "You may not see me again after we leave here. Have you thought of that?"

"No," Kate admitted. "But you wouldn't do that to me. I know you wouldn't."

David stared at her. "What makes you think I wouldn't?"

"Because you're not the kind of man your brother says you are," she answered. "And you do like me. You don't touch me with your hands, but you're always touching me with your eyes. You watch me on the tapes and you stop the picture when it's just me. I know you do because I saw you do it today." Kate paused and cleared her throat.

He was still staring at her.

"Anyway, that's why I don't think you would do that to me."

David lifted his hands and rubbed at the lower half of his face. After a moment he reached out and pulled her onto his chest again. Kate wrapped her arms around him and inhaled deeply of his fresh, clean scent.

"I don't know what to think or feel," David said. "All I know is that I don't want to hurt you."

"That means you care about me."

"No, it means I have a lousy track record in personal relationships."

"You do care about me. You bring me candy bars."

"I did it for Mel, too."

Kate raised her head. "Do you wish I was a little more like her?"

"What difference would that make?"

"You might not be so afraid of hurting me."

David filled his chest with air. "Let's not talk about this anymore."

"Are you going to let me stay here?" she asked.

"If you promise not to move . . . at all."

Kate nodded and pressed her lips against his chest.

"Don't do that either," he said.

Kate was jarred from sleep when David placed her arms around his neck and lifted her from the bed. She opened her eyes and looked at him. "What are you doing?"

"Putting you in your own bed," he answered. "I have to get up early to help look for Natalie."

"Couldn't you sleep?"

"No."

"Okay," she mumbled. There was a draft on her skin as they crossed the hall, but she was already closing her eyes again. She opened them briefly when her head touched her pillow. David took her arms from around his neck and leaned down to kiss her. "Goodnight, Kate."

"Goodnight." She put a hand to her mouth to trap the warmth of his lips. Several seconds passed before she heard him cross the room and close the door.

# 19

## FRIDAY, MAY 20, 1:00 A.M.

ROSALIE STOOD NEAR the bed with a towel, ready to catch any drips before they reached the carpet. The plastic under Augusta's head didn't always work; sometimes the sheets were stained and had to be discarded. When it looked like the blood was going to pool and stick in Augusta's hair, she backed up with the towel and stepped over the pillows on the floor to sit down in the chair at the foot of the bed.

The ritual had bothered her the first few times, even made her sick. Now she was used to it. She was used to the blood sipping and dripping and the vacant expression in her employer's small, glassy eyes. Rosalie had tried talking to her once and had soon discovered that the glassiness signified some sort of trance state. If she checked vital signs now, Rosalie knew she would find indications of a stage just one step short of clinical death. Augusta's heart would be beating at a rate so low as to be almost indiscernible by now. Her pupils would be fully dilated and completely unresponsive to light.

Rosalie didn't know how she did it. Or why. She supposed this was something close to what the old men in India did when they lowered their heart rate and controlled their breathing. Why did they do it?

She didn't know. Sometimes she wondered if she knew anything. This job had sounded like a dream to her in the beginning. The patient wasn't dying. Rosalie wouldn't be forced to watch any more vomiting or wasting away. No more bedpans or sponge baths, no more globs of phlegm or soiled sheets to clean up. Just blood.

And not even real blood.

She was paid well. Extremely well. More, in fact, than Rosalie had ever been paid in her life. And for what? To fetch meals and people, to spy on those people, to listen to occasional ranting, and to give Augusta her daily massage. The rest of the time she simply guarded the door.

Rosalie knew Augusta got up out of bed on a regular basis. From outside the door Rosalie often heard sounds in the room. Augusta bathed herself at least once a week—usually after the blood ritual—but her other forays away from the bed included more than trips to the toilet. Rosalie was sure of it. In the last few days she had heard a door to a connecting room on the right open and close. When Rosalie tended Augusta there was always an occasional table placed before that door. Rosalie had never been in the room to the right. Augusta had threatened her with dismissal the day Rosalie asked about it.

Rosalie wouldn't have been a bit surprised if Augusta kept a refrigerator full of blood and bonbons in there. The beakers of blood used in the fat woman's ritual were always slightly cool to the touch.

And what did she do when Rosalie went to bed at night? Rosalie's room was to the left of Augusta's and she often awakened in the early hours of the morning to hear her employer's voice through their connecting door. She could never make out any of the words, but it sounded as if Augusta were talking to someone besides herself. Who it was, Rosalie had no idea. As far as she knew, no one visited Augusta at night. It was Augusta's own rule.

Rosalie wished she could go to bed now. She was tired. But Augusta didn't like her to leave until the trance was over and the bloody plastic had been taken away.

Her employer had been testier than usual because of that David Raleigh fellow. At least once a day Rosalie was sent down to find him, but he continued to ignore Augusta's command to visit her. Privately, Rosalie thought it was funny. But she didn't dare let her mirth show. She didn't dare let anything show where Augusta was concerned. The woman was unusually sensitive. Maybe even a bit psychic.

Even more privately, Rosalie was beginning to be afraid of what would happen if David Raleigh didn't come to see Augusta soon. Each time Rosalie returned with his refusal, Augusta's rages grew longer. She was used to getting what she wanted. Her husband and son pampered her enough, the son more than the husband. And her money had been sufficient enticement for the other men she had lured into her third-floor lair. They had come and listened to her strange, esoteric ramblings with smiles and nods, hoping that Augusta's infatuation would become money in their pockets. For some it had, the mystics in particular. But the last one had left the house over ten months ago and Augusta's attention had turned to the journalist.

She was fascinated by his magazine and newspaper stories and by what she proclaimed to be his interest in the arcane. Rosalie couldn't see it. David Raleigh was different, true, but he wasn't like the other men Augusta had dragged up to the third floor. Rosalie had a feeling Augusta intended to break David Raleigh in some way, to punish him for not living up to her expectations and giving her the attention she felt she deserved.

In other words, Rosalie thought, David Raleigh was going to pay for not believing Augusta's practiced line of help-me-I'm-a-prisoner bull. She used that on all of them initially, and it always worked. Until now.

David Raleigh hadn't believed her, and even if he had, Rosalie didn't think he cared one way or another. He couldn't be bought, prodded, or threatened into showing obeisance, and that was exactly what was driving Augusta crazy. What she wanted from him Rosalie couldn't possibly fathom, but that sullen bit about seeking revenge and fame had made Rosalie uneasy. More than anyone else in the house—including family members—Rosalie knew that Augusta Guerin was insane. And insane people, particularly the brilliant ones, were people to be afraid of.

A sob made Rosalie look up. She rose from her chair and carried the towel to the side of the bed. Augusta was back and blinking away tears.

"Mrs. Guerin?" Rosalie asked quietly.

"I found him," Augusta whispered. "I found him this time. I really did."

Rosalie wanted to ask who, but she decided to simply wait and listen. She couldn't trust herself to speak normally while the woman was wiping clots of blood and sticky mucus from her face.

"Now I know what I was doing wrong. Just one little change made the difference. I found him, Rosalie. And he was so happy to see me. Everything is going to be all right now. I finally found him."

Rosalie couldn't stand it any more. She offered the towel to Augusta and asked, "Who did you find?"

Augusta looked at her and it was all Rosalie could do to keep from backing up. There was nothing warm or even remotely human in Augusta Guerin's eyes.

"My father, Rosalie," Augusta said. "I found my father. Everything is going to be all right. I have his blessing to do what needs to be done."

"That's wonderful," Rosalie said in a cracked voice. "What needs to be done?"

Augusta smiled and Rosalie saw that even her teeth were covered with blood. "Lots of things, Rosalie," she said. "Lots of things need doing."

# 20

## FRIDAY, MAY 20, 7:00 A.M.

KATE MET DAVID on the stairs as he descended and covered his face with kisses before bounding up and away from him again. David watched her departure and shook his head before continuing down the stairs. He had the feeling he was making a big mistake. Everything in him said not to do it, not to get involved with her and risk destroying that unbelievably pure and guileless nature. She would be disgusted if she knew his own true nature. She would learn to hate everything about him.

He should have continued to avoid her and keep things just below the level of civility. He had been the paranoid one, telling her not to like him. Obviously, it had generated the opposite effect, just like Bryan's telling David to stay away from her.

Kate didn't know him. She didn't know what he was . . . and what he wasn't.

He should stop it now, he thought. Now, before it progressed any further and someone got hurt.

Mel and Bryan were standing by the door as he left the stairs. Bryan was holding a map and Mel was pointing to something on it.

"Morning," David said.

"Sleep in?" Bryan asked. Then he turned back to Mel. "You can look west of the lake. If you find her and she's injured, use your radio to let us know. Kate will be manning the base, ready to call for an ambulance if we need one. David, you can take the area north of the lake. Here's a list of the names for you to call out."

David frowned as he took the piece of paper.

"In case someone besides Natalie is present," Mel explained. "Cindy, Tammy, or whoever."

"We'll do a check by radio every half hour just to make sure no one has run into trouble," Bryan said.

David looked around. "Jay and his dad go out already?"

"They left before dawn. Here's your radio, David. Are you ready?"

He nodded and followed them out the door. Bryan was in rare form this morning. The weekend games of splatball in the woods had paid off for his take-charge older brother.

David didn't go in for pretend war games. He had covered a war or two and he had seen enough splatters in his time, the kind where the wounded didn't say "Shit" and get up to go drink a beer.

In the stable he noticed a strange look pass between Mel and the hand named Denny, but he didn't have time to ask her about it. She rode out of the stable before David was in his saddle. Bryan, unaccustomed to riding, had secured a small four-wheel, all-terrain Yamaha. He putted around the side of the stable as David rode out.

"Radio check in half an hour."

David saluted him. "At your command, Captain."

Bryan glared and gunned the Yamaha. David looked at his watch and reined his horse toward the lake.

Mel missed the fifth radio check. David wiped the sweat from his forehead and listened as Bryan repeatedly asked for contact.

Finally he picked up his own radio and said, "She would answer if she could hear you, Bryan. Who's closest to her?"

There was a crackle, then Bryan said, "You are. Why don't you see if you can find her?"

Before David could answer, another voice came over the radio. "This is Kate. Mel's horse just came back to the ranch without her. The stable hand wants to know if he can go out and look for her. He thinks he knows where she might be."

"Tell him to go ahead," said Jay Guerin's voice.

"Okay. Forget it, David," Bryan said.

David looked around himself and decided to ride in the direction of Mel's appointed search area anyway.

He kicked his horse into a canter and heard the stable hand Denny's shouting long before he caught sight of him. The lanky blond was standing atop a rock ledge and yelling Mel's name. The picture he made and the hoarse note in his voice told David all he needed to know about the look that had passed between Mel and Denny. The ranch hand had it bad.

David rode up to the ledge and dismounted. Denny merely glanced at him. David rubbed his sore parts and looked around himself. "What made you think she would be here?"

Denny dropped to a sitting position. "Because she likes this spot and we were here yesterday. I thought she might have come back here when Chelsea ran off."

"Is Chelsea in the habit of running off?"

"No, but what else could have happened?"

Plenty, David thought. "Have you seen her radio anywhere?"

"That's the first thing I looked for."

"What about fresh tracks? Have you checked to see if she's been here at all today?"

Denny looked at him. "Of course."

"Well?"

"Like I said, we were here yesterday." Denny kicked at a rock shard and sent it flying off the ledge.

David stepped back and scanned the area again. It was an

unusual spot, unusual because there were actually a few trees and other forms of plant life, mostly weeds, around.

"Is there a stream around here?"

Denny pointed. "About a hundred yards. Right where the land dips. It's just a little one."

Little wasn't the word, David decided as he walked the distance and found the small branch. It wasn't any wider than his arm was long. He followed the course of the stream until it became nothing more than a large patch of muddy earth and standing water. The flow went underground there, he guessed. He searched the mud for prints and saw nothing. Fifty yards to his left was a small slope with thick clumps of dotted brush. He walked to the top and saw a large herd of cattle grazing on the green expanse below. He swatted a fly from his nose and walked back to the rock ledge in time to hear another radio check in progress.

He took the radio strap from around the horn of his saddle and responded just as Bryan asked for contact a second time. "No sign of Mel. I'm going to keep looking in her section."

"Fine," said Bryan's voice. "We'll be out to help you after we check out Natalie."

"You found her?" He looked at Denny and the hand gave a shrug.

"Kate did," Bryan said. "Weren't you listening?"

"I wasn't near the radio," David explained. "Where was she?"

"We don't know. She just wandered into Guerin's office. Kate said she was pale, but she doesn't appear to be hurt. We'll check in with you as soon as we can. Keep your radio with you. Over."

David ignored him and strung the radio around the saddle horn again.

"Which direction do you want?" Denny asked.

"The one you don't."

The hand climbed down from the ledge and approached his horse. When he was in the saddle, he looked at David.

"Mel acts tough, but she's really not."

"I know," said David.

* * *

It was dark when he finally made his way back to the ranch. David left his horse in the hands of Grant and walked painfully up to the house. His backside was aching and his hair was matted with a day's worth of sweat. Kate was waiting at the door. Her brows became pinched and her face grew a shade paler when she saw that he was alone.

"Oh, Mel," she murmured.

David pulled her to him and found himself leaning on her. "Are the others still out looking?"

Kate shook her head.

"Where are they?"

She pulled away from him. "In the dining hall. They came back around dusk. Are you all right?"

"I will be if I can make it into that elevator," he said. "I don't think I can handle the stairs."

"Are you stiff?"

"Getting that way. If I'm going to be any good tomorrow I need to get in a warm tub now."

Kate put an arm around him and walked with him to the elevator. In his room she took off his shoes and went into the bathroom to turn on the water.

David watched her and his mouth curled at the irony. They had been in this situation before.

"I'll go and get you something to eat," she said as he unbuttoned his shirt.

"Make it something cold," he said. "You can leave it on the desk."

She nodded and left the room. David finished undressing and had been in the tub only minutes when she opened the bathroom door and stepped inside. He opened his mouth and she held up a can of beer.

"I thought you might want one," she said.

He did. "Thanks."

Kate showed him a tube of Ben-Gay. "I can put some of this on you when you get out. Juana gave it to me."

Not burn cream this time. Ben-Gay.

"The beer's open." Kate handed him the can and sat down on the lid of the toilet. "I think I might come along tomorrow. Dr. Raleigh said there are several four-wheelers available."

"I wouldn't advise it," said David.

"Why not? I wouldn't get lost. I'd stay close to you and—"

"Not with me. It's hot, dirty, and you wouldn't be comfortable around my horse."

Kate blinked. "Who told you?"

"It doesn't matter," he said.

"Fine." Her irritated gaze traveled over the length of his submerged body and back to his face again. "You need to wash your hair," she finally pronounced.

"I know that. You can leave now."

She slammed the door on her way out. David tilted the beer and downed half of it in one breath. When he was finished, he put it beside the tub. "Kate?"

"What?" she said from the bedroom.

He knew she would be there. "Fetch me another beer?"

There was no answer, but he heard the door to the hall open and close. When the water cooled he drained the tub and washed his hair in the shower. By the time he was finished, Kate hadn't returned. He decided he had made her mad with the fetch business. He got out of the tub, toweled himself dry, and opened the door to find her asleep on his bed, the tube of Ben-Gay still in her hand. A wet can of beer sat on the desk beside a plate of food.

David went back for a towel to wrap around his waist before moving to shake her awake. "Kate. Come on."

She opened her eyes with a start. "Oh. Sorry." She pulled her skirt down over her hips and swung her legs over the side of the bed. "Are you ready?"

No anger left. Nothing but concern. David could only stare at her. He thought of his earlier decision to halt things with her and decided the timing might be bad. Maybe tomorrow, if they found Mel.

"It's late, Kate. Why don't you go to bed."

"I was just dozing." She stood and kicked off her sandals. "I'm not very good at massage, but the Ben-Gay should help you."

David weighed the proposal only a moment before stretching out facedown on the mattress. Kate hiked up her skirt and climbed over him to straddle his thighs. "Am I hurting you?"

"No. Don't put that on too thick."

"I won't," she said.

He was glad he was tired. Any other time, the feel of her bare legs against his thighs and her small hands on his flesh would have been irresistible. He closed his eyes and thought about Julia to keep arousal completely at bay. There was a slight chill as Kate removed his towel.

"I think you're going to bruise," she said as she began to spread the ointment over his buttocks.

David made a noise into the mattress.

"What?" Kate's hands paused. "Is that painful?"

"Yes," he said clearly.

"Sorry." She softened her touch. "The reason I thought I might come tomorrow is because I felt so useless just sitting around the house today. I want to help. Mel is my friend and I'm worried about her."

David lifted his head and twisted around. "You're not coming with me, Kate."

She looked at her hands and wiped them on the towel. "All right. I'm done now. There's a ham sandwich and some turkey breast on the desk."

He caught her before she could move away. He pulled her down to the mattress and made her look at him. "You'd be more hindrance than help. I don't want to have to worry about you, too."

"I'm going to bed," she said. "Let go."

David couldn't. "Don't look at me like that."

Her gaze shifted. "I don't need to ask your permission. I

thought it would be nice to be close to you while I helped look for Mel."

"If something has happened to Mel, I don't want you to be there when we find her."

"Fine. You've made that clear. I'm tired and I'm ready to go to bed now."

David made a noise of frustration and held on. He was going mental over her. She made him feel like he was caught in some adolescent time warp, where the game hadn't been learned yet and it was okay to argue because arguing was a release for the tension that arose as a result of physical attraction.

He held her chin and lowered his mouth to hers. She hesitated several seconds before opening her lips to him. Her fingers came up to touch his cheek.

I could, he thought as he tasted the inside of her mouth.

And she could. She could make him want to stop and kiss on stairways at seven A.M., and make wonderful body-sore love with a smelly coating of Ben-Gay. He could lose himself in her.

Suddenly she pulled away from him. "You need to get some rest, David."

He looked at her, a question in his eyes.

"It wouldn't feel right," she murmured. "Not now. Not when Mel—"

"May be lying dead somewhere," David said in a flat voice. "Right."

Wordlessly, Kate left the bed and crossed the room. At the door she paused. "I'm sorry I disappointed you. But I'd know if Mel was dead. She's not."

"How?" he asked. "How do you know she's not?"

"I just do."

"Good for you," David said.

# 21

## FRIDAY, MAY 20, 11:45 P.M.

MEL BELIEVED SHE was dead for the first ten seconds after she regained consciousness. She thought she was dead and buried, because her present location was as dark as the inside of a casket and her eyes felt dilated to the max.

It was the pain that told her she was alive. Not to mention the fact that all five of her senses still seemed to be working. She found her head with one hand and a quick examination uncovered a sticky gash above her right ear. When she tried to sit up she felt so dizzy she nearly passed out again. She took a deep breath and promptly lost the meager contents of her stomach to the ground—which she quickly realized wasn't ground at all, but something that was pliable and had an unbelievably foul, dead-animal-in-a-garbage-can smell.

"Please, oh please don't let me be sitting on something dead," she prayed aloud.

But she was sitting on something dead and she knew it. Her fingers felt hide, hair, or something non-groundlike beneath her. It had probably saved her life when she fell through the cave entrance, but she wasn't the least bit grateful. Where there were dead things, there were maggots.

And what had she hit her head on? A rock wall? She wished she could see. She wished even more that she could survive without breathing, because the nausea was going to kill her.

Mel didn't want to know what she had landed on, and she was afraid to move because she could hear the sound of running water and there was a distinct draft coming from somewhere very near. She could be on some sort of ledge or precipice that dropped away in the next few feet.

*A bottomless cave.*

Now there was a cheery thought. Just what she needed to be thinking about. But go ahead, she told herself. You might as well get the fear and panic over with so you can start thinking of a way to get out of here.

She screamed.

It opened the gash in her head and hurt like hell. And it echoed, giving credence to her bottomless-cave theory. She shut up.

How did I get into this? she asked herself. And was it day or night? It had to be night. If it were day, she thought, she would be able to see light coming in from the cave entrance somewhere above her. And if it was in fact night, then it meant she had been unconscious for a long, long time. Now that was scary.

She felt the gash again and noted that it was swollen. A concussion wasn't out of the question. And she would probably need stitches—not to mention brain surgery, for ever getting off Chelsea to begin with.

Chelsea had wanted a drink from the stream, so Mel had gotten out of the saddle to stretch and do some knee bends. Then she had strolled up the slope to look at those ugly, godforsaken cows grazing on the plain below. It was on the way down that she had spotted her friend the badger. It skulked into a clump of brush and disappeared. Mel went after him for a closer look, and the moment she parted the thick brush she had spied the opening, a wide, yawning hole directly in front of her. Then the badger, the clever little fiend, had attacked her from behind, causing her to stumble and fall back . . . then down. Down into the cave in the side of the slope. The slope that was covered with brush that no one would think to part unless they were looking for some vicious, boot-chewing badger.

Mel began to feel real fear as the realization set in. No one would find her here. No one would know where to look. No one but Jay, the lying jerk. And would he look? Would he even consider the possibility of her having found his secret cave? Mel didn't think so. And even if he did consider the possibility, she wasn't so sure he would make tracks to get her out.

A terrible thought.

"Stop it," she said aloud. "You're not going to wait around to be found, anyway. You're going to get yourself out of here, remember?"

Yeah. Okay. Now . . . how?

Radio, she thought suddenly. Her fingers went immediately to the hip pocket of her jeans and found nothing but denim.

"Figures," she muttered. But the radio had been there when she fell in, so it had to have fallen in with her. She automatically reached out . . . Then she stopped.

Do I really want to do this? she asked herself. Maggots and all?

Do you really want to get out? came the instinctive reply.

"Oh, yes." She didn't have to close her eyes, but she did anyway. Her stomach gave an alarming heave as she encountered a short, hairy leg. It was thin and knobbed in the middle. A cow. Not full grown, judging from the size. Maybe a heifer or a steer.

She pressed on, making her fingers skip lightly, until she found the head. Gritting her teeth, she tried to feel under the head to see if there was ground beneath. She found another leg, this one much smaller and with a slightly different texture. It was fur. And there were pads rather than hooves at the end. A dog? she wondered.

Had these animals wandered in here and fallen to their deaths? Or had they fallen in and eventually *starved* to death.

Another cheery thought.

Mel stretched to her left as far as she could and felt around the corpses with no luck. Surprisingly, she hadn't felt anything maggoty yet, which worried her in a way. If there were no maggots, then these corpses hadn't been here very long. Long enough for rigor mortis to have come and gone, but not long enough to . . . rot. Why that should worry her at the moment, she couldn't say. But it did.

After a pause she began an exploration to her right, feeling the flank and then the back of the calf she rested on. She jerked her hand away when she found another bovine head.

No, she thought. This was just too much. Two calves and a dead dog. She trailed her hand back over the flank and felt one finger slip into something sticky.

"Yuck," she whispered as she recoiled. Then she frowned. It hadn't been squirmy sticky, just *sticky* sticky. Holding her breath, she made herself go back over the flank again until she relocated the spot. She felt around the edges and finally realized what she had found. It was a hole. A round, neat hole. Like a bullet hole.

Mel sat back. She didn't want to think about what that meant. She didn't. All she wanted was to get out of there.

Abruptly, she leaned forward and began to feel around in front of herself. She immediately felt more hair. Only this hair was different in texture than that of the calves and the dog. And there was much more of this hair. In fact, it felt like human hair.

A high keening noise began at the back of Mel's throat. She wasn't aware of it. When her hands found the head, she screamed. And when her fingers encountered the dents in the skull she fell back and returned to blessed unconsciousness.


When Mel awakened again she was immediately aware of where she was and just what she had found. The smell clued her in right away. She opened her eyes and prayed that she would see light. She did. About ten feet above her. It was weak, but it was light. Then she looked for her radio. She looked at everything in the cave before she looked at Melanie Martin. Then she screamed again.

In the dimness she could see the crusted, blackened screwdriver wounds . . . and she could see a dozen or more puckered holes in the naked back of the corpse. Without wanting to, Mel quickly realized that the calf beneath her also had more than one wound. And the dog wasn't a dog, it was a coyote, also shot to death. Its muzzle had been blasted completely away.

"Jay," Mel said weakly, already battling nausea again. "Sometimes you like to shoot targets, don't you, you sick sonofabitch."

She closed her eyes, swallowed, and wondered if Dr. Guerin knew. Melanie had no relatives, he had said. He must have known, she decided, because he had asked Jay to put her on the jet rather than do it himself that day. He must have known that Jay never intended to send her to a hospital in Kansas City. He must have.

All of them, thought Mel. Everyone in the whole damned family was sick.

She slowly forced herself up from the dead calf to look past Melanie's corpse. There was a drop-off, but it amounted to only a few feet. Water took over from there. Mel looked at the swirling surface and realized her radio was probably in that water. Then she realized she was thirsty. Her screaming hadn't helped the situation any; her throat was raw.

No more, she told herself. Save your breath and your strength to get out. Which brought her to the really big question now that there was light to squint by. The walls of the cave looked impossible to scale; there were no visible handholds. The ledge she was on measured only about five feet wide and maybe twelve feet long before it disappeared into the wall on both sides. Across the drop-off was another, similar ledge. Mel guessed that at one time the ledges had been one and the floor of the cave had been a lot closer to the entrance. The running water had likely caused the rift in the middle, because the ledges themselves were mostly earth, not rock.

The cave probably flooded during the rainy season. And the water in here most likely found its way to some pond where cows slurped and ate their way to butcher heaven.

Spring-fed ponds, right, Dr. Raleigh?

Mel cursed him as she looked for a way out. When it hit her, she nearly threw up again.

But she had to. She had to do it or still be sitting there the next time Jay came to dump another corpse.

The muscles in her back and shoulders screamed as she pulled at the second calf in an attempt to place it atop the first. The second calf was on its way to becoming maggoty. Both were stiffer than she had thought and heavier than she would ever have dreamed.

She pulled and grunted, grunted and pulled, almost losing her balance several times. Some deep dark part of herself was worried about the calf's head coming off in her hands. Shuddering at the vision, she renewed her attack with a strength born of panic. If it did come off, she would lose it. That's all there was to it. She would be gone, on her way to Augustaville.

The head didn't come off, but she soon realized the calves would not stack on top of each other if they were both facing the same direction. She spent countless more minutes getting the calf on top twisted around, so that its black limbs stuck out in the opposite direction of the dead calf below it. Then she wiped her hands on her jeans and started to climb.

Mel cried as her fingers clawed in vain at those last twelve inches. It wasn't enough. And the little coyote wouldn't help by itself.

She would need Melanie as well.

*Lord, please,* she begged. I don't want to do this. Don't want to, don't want to, please don't make me touch her. . . .

The keening noise began after she placed the coyote on top of the calves. She turned to Melanie and dropped to her knees. "Forgive me. I don't want to do this, but if I stay here another hour I'll go insane. You understand, don't you? Please understand, Melanie. I have to do this. But I'll get him. I will. I swear I'll get the man who did this to you, so please just forgive what I'm about to do."

She had to stop twice so she could bend over and heave. Nothing came out, but her eyes bulged and her face hurt with the attempt. She was making that noise again, and it grew louder as she moved Melanie into position and tugged her bloated, gassy corpse onto the top of the stack.

When it was done, Mel lay down on the ledge and sobbed until she couldn't sob any more. Then she stood up and made her face stiff, her resolve firm.

There was a sickening crunch as she finally stepped onto Melanie's white, bullet-riddled back.

Mel felt the blood leave her head for a frightening instant. She was either going to heave again or faint. She strained her face toward the entrance and made herself breathe deeply of the clean air. After the fetid stench of the cave, it smelled like heaven. Mel closed her eyes, then she quickly opened them again as an image of Jay, waiting just outside with a gun, filled her mind.

No, she told herself. It's paranoia, Mel. You've got every reason to be paranoid about him, but he won't be there. He's either bleeding onto the ground or filling some other dumb animal with bullets from his precious guns.

The veins in her arms stood out and the nails on her fingers broke to the quick as she pulled herself up and over and finally out of the entrance. When she was clear she put her throbbing head on her arms and panted for breath. There was no Jay.

When she could stand without falling she got up and pushed her way out of the brush. Her gaze went automatically to the rock ledge in the distance, and what she saw there made her eyes well up in relief.

"Denny!" she called. "Denny, over here!"

He twisted around; then he bolted from the ledge and leaped onto his horse. Mel tried hard to remain standing, to wait until he reached her, but the pain in her head was bringing a darker shade of daylight with each throb. She went to her knees to try to fight the dizziness, but it was no use. As her vision faded she felt herself go tumbling down the slope.

# 22

## SATURDAY, MAY 21, 10:00 A.M.

KATE STOOD PATIENTLY by the door as the doctor and Rosalie treated Mel. Kate hadn't realized Rosalie was a trained nurse, but the doctor had asked for her the moment he arrived. Now Rosalie was handing him things from a tray and swabbing at the ugly gash in Mel's head as the doctor prepared to stitch the wound. It was the same doctor who had been called in for Melanie Martin the day David and Mel found her in the boathouse. The doctor didn't appear to like the Guerin family, but Kate supposed the money offered for his services was too good to turn down.

The stitching itself made Kate feel nauseous. She turned her gaze to the window and wondered where Mel had been. According to Denny she had appeared on the side of a slope and called his name. Before he could reach her, she collapsed. She had been unconscious ever since.

Denny was still waiting for word downstairs. Before leaving for Emporia on ranch business, Jay had told Denny to get back to work, but Dr. Guerin had kindly countermanded the order and allowed the young stable hand to stay.

Kate was the only one allowed in Mel's bedroom. The doctor

and Rosalie had been with Mel only moments when Rosalie came out to find Kate. Together they had removed Mel's soiled clothing and sponged her down. The smell of the clothes had been putrid. Kate guessed the doctor had been unable to work on Mel until her clothes were gone. Kate and Rosalie had glanced at each other as they stripped the garments away, but neither said a word. Comment was unnecessary. Both recognized the odor of putrefaction.

Kate glanced back to the doctor and saw him snip off a suture. Rosalie was waiting with disinfectant and a bandage. Her broad face was expressionless.

The doctor put his instruments down and stood back. After a moment he took a small light from his pocket and examined Mel's pupils a second time. Kate moved forward.

"Concussion?" she asked.

"I'd say so, yes."

"Is that why she's still unconscious?"

"I don't know. I'd like to take her back to Marwell for some x-rays and keep her under observation for a while. Put a gown or something on her, would you? I wish these people would learn to call an ambulance before calling me. Save me a lot of time and trouble. I do have a practice, you know. And these men are trained doctors themselves. Rosalie, go phone for the ambulance."

Rosalie left the room and Kate moved to Mel's dresser. She'd wanted to call for an ambulance, but Jay had stopped her before she reached the phone. He told her the doctor was already on his way and it was best not to move Mel until the man could examine her.

Kate hadn't argued.

She found a nightgown in the top drawer and went to look in the bathroom for a robe. When she came out, the doctor was looking out the window and shaking his head.

"Whatever became of the other young woman? The one who damaged herself with a screwdriver? Did Guerin's fancy neurosurgical friends get back to him?"

Kate blinked. "I don't know. No one has spoken of Miss Martin since the day it happened."

The doctor shrugged and turned back to the bed. "I'll lift her, you slip the gown over her head. No, forget it. Just put the robe on her for now. You can bring some clothes to the hospital later."

Mel shifted and slowly opened her eyes as they moved her. When she saw Kate, her chest heaved with what looked like relief. "I'm really out. Water, Kate."

Kate hurried into the bathroom and came back with a full glass of water. The doctor supported Mel's back as she sipped. "Don't gulp," he warned. "You'll throw up."

Mel looked at him with unfocused eyes. "Doctor?"

"That's right. You're coming into Marwell with me to have an x-ray or two. Is that all right?"

"Fine," Mel mumbled. "Have to get away from these sick, sick people . . ." Her eyes drifted closed again.

Kate looked worriedly at the doctor. "She's going to be all right, isn't she?"

The doctor lifted a brow. "Sounds like it. But I'll let you know."

"Maybe I should come with you," Kate said.

"I'd rather you didn't. I want her to get as much rest as possible, and you'll just be in the way."

Kate's mouth tightened. She was tired of people telling her that. "Will you call as soon as you know anything?"

"The very minute."

"Call me or Dr. Raleigh," Kate said suddenly. "Don't leave a message with anyone else."

The doctor frowned at her and Kate realized how strange the request must seem. She didn't care. She didn't trust the Guerin family. The entire stay at the Guerin ranch had seen one mishap after another, and Kate was beginning to wish she had never come to the place.

When the ambulance arrived she followed the stretcher downstairs and listened while the doctor told everyone his intentions.

Bryan's face was pale with a concern that Kate thought Mel would enjoy hearing about later. Guerin merely nodded and looked at his watch while the doctor spoke. Denny looked worried, and David was nowhere to be seen. Kate found him upstairs in his room, working at the word processor. She crept in and stood behind him a moment, reading the screen.

The paragraph he was writing wasn't about multiples, it was about Augusta Guerin.

"Sweetheart," said Frank.

David swiveled in his chair and Kate smiled. "Hi," she said. "The doctor is taking Mel to the hospital for x-rays and observation."

"Good," said David. "Did she ever come around?"

"For a few seconds." Kate approached David's chair and moved his arms so she could sit on his lap. "She sounded like her old self, but the doctor wants to be sure she's all right."

The chair groaned as David shifted his legs. "I'm trying to work, Kate."

"I can see that. You're writing about Mrs. Guerin."

"Snoop." He pushed at her. "Come on. You're heavy and I'm still sore."

Kate stood and moved behind him to look at the screen once more. "She'll probably sue you."

"Only if it's published. I thought I'd show it to her and let her see how pathetic she is."

Kate stepped around the chair again to look at him. She wanted to see if the cruelty in his words was in his face. "Would you really do that?" she asked.

"If you met her you wouldn't be so concerned," David said in a dry voice. "But no, Little Miss Conscience of us all, I wouldn't do something like that. I'm writing it for me. Because her situation and her story interests me, and the interest eats away at me until I can get it down on paper."

"Does this happen every time?" Kate asked.

David looked at her. "Does what happen?"

"Do you become surly and mean every time you write something?"

"I'm not my brother, Kate. I can't turn on the charm when it's convenient to do so."

"I wouldn't want you to. Jerk."

Kate pinched him on the last word and he swatted at her. She pinched him again, and Frank squawked as David left his chair and went after her. Kate shrieked and jumped up on the bed to get to the other side. David caught her by the heel and she felt her sandal come away as she tumbled face-first onto the mattress. She punched and batted at him as he twisted her around and pinned her beneath him.

Then she heard him laugh. Not his usual restrained chuckle, but real laughter. She was stunned into complete motionlessness at the transformation in him. His face lost ten years, and he was twice as handsome as his brother. Kate's chest filled with sudden emotion as she stared at him. She put her arms around his neck and hugged him hard.

"That won't get you off," he said against her ear.

"David, I love you," Kate said.

He grew suddenly still. She could feel his breathing slow until it seemed to stop completely. Kate cringed inside and waited for him to pull away. He didn't. He remained completely still.

After a moment she leaned back. She wanted to see his eyes. They were closed.

"I guess I shouldn't have said that," she whispered. "I mean, people are usually having sex when they say it for the first time. They don't just blurt it out—"

His lids flew open, and with one look at her face he started laughing again.

"What's so funny?" she asked.

"You," he said. "You were serious."

Kate frowned at him. "Of course I'm serious. Did I say something wrong?"

He stopped laughing and looked at her. "I'm sorry. You

didn't say anything wrong. It's just that sometimes you seem so . . ."

"What?"

"Forget it." He kissed her on the nose. "Unless you want to have *sex* right now, I suggest you get out of here and let me go back to work."

Kate's eyes narrowed. "You're making fun of me. You're amused by what I said."

"No," he repeated soberly. "I'm anything but amused, Kate."

She looked at him a long moment, trying to decide what he was if he wasn't amused by her declaration of love. She couldn't tell. She was surprised to find that she didn't want to leave. She had the feeling that if she didn't become intimate with him now, right at this moment, that something precious, never to be re-captured, would escape her.

With trembling, uncertain fingers she took his hand and placed it over her left breast. She touched his cheek. "I don't want to go."

He studied her face, then opened his mouth. Before he could speak, the bedroom door was flung open.

"David, have you seen—" Bryan stopped and stared at the two of them on the bed. He backed slowly out of the room. "Kate, we need you downstairs," he said in a stern voice. "Now."

Kate looked at David and whispered, "He sounds mad."

Wordlessly, David rolled away from her to sit on the edge of the mattress. Kate sat up beside him and straightened her skirt and blouse. The set of his jaw bothered her.

"David . . ."

"You'd better go," he said.

"I'm going. Will you eat dinner with me tonight? I hate to eat alone in that dining hall."

He wouldn't look at her. "If I'm not working."

"*Kate,*" Bryan said from the hallway.

"Coming," she called. She kissed David on the cheek and stood up to slip on her sandal. "I'll check back with you later, all right?"

He nodded.

Kate hesitated a moment longer. His expression worried her. "David?"

He reached up to swat her bottom. "Go on, before he starts turning blue."

She smiled and hurried from the room. Bryan's face was lined with anger as he took her by the arm and pulled her down the hall. "What the hell were you doing with him?"

Kate tried to yank her arm away. "What did it look like? Not that it's any of your business."

Bryan stopped and swung her in front of him. "You have no idea what you're getting into with him, Kate. I know he's smooth when he wants to be, but he goes through women like typewriter ribbons. When the impression begins to fade he just throws them away. I don't think you're ready for his method of operation."

"Let me be the judge of that," Kate responded. "You're not my guardian, Dr. Raleigh. And David himself warned me about his past. I'm willing to take the risk. Now will you please let go? You're hurting me."

Bryan released her arm. "I'm trying to save you from being hurt. Remember the last—"

"Don't say it," Kate snapped. She turned on her heel and walked away from him. Bryan hurried after her.

"I want you to remember, because the same thing could happen with David. He's the same kind of man. Kate, you have to wait until you discover genuine feelings for someone. Someone who can respond in kind. I'm telling you that David can't."

Kate kept walking. "Was there any particular reason you came looking for me?"

Bryan sighed and followed her into the elevator. "Yes, there is. We decided to talk to Natalie again to find out where she was hiding. Before we could even ask, she said she wanted to talk to you."

"Me?" Kate said in surprise. "Why me?"

"I don't know. She became flustered when we asked her why

she wanted to see you. Dr. Guerin is growing very worried about her. He thinks she's regressing rather than improving. Four different personas have appeared in the last half hour or so, each of them extremely agitated about something they refuse to talk about."

"Which personas?" Kate asked as she preceded him out of the elevator.

"Everyone but Tammy. Tammy is still hiding from us for some reason. Maybe you can find out why."

"I can try," said Kate.

Dr. Guerin stood as they entered his office. Natalie was seated behind his desk, a vacant expression in her eyes. Bryan ushered Kate to the chair in front of the desk and moved to stand beside Guerin. "Who?" he mouthed.

"It's Cindy," Guerin told him. "Cindy, Kate is here. Did you say you wanted to speak to her?"

"Yes, but not in front of you."

Bryan shook his head when Guerin turned to him. "How about if we go to the other side of the room? Will that be all right?"

A shrug. "I guess."

When the two men had retired to the sofa along the back wall, Kate leaned forward. "Cindy?"

She looked up. "Hello, Kate. I wanted to talk to you about . . . the cold was in me for a long time, you know. It hurt."

"What?" Kate said. "What hurt?"

"Cold. Coldness can hurt you when it's inside."

"I don't understand, Cindy."

Her mouth drooped. "I don't either. I just hate feeling that cold inside. Has anyone ever . . ." Her voice trailed off and she sighed. "I can't say any more. This was a bad idea. I want to go."

"All right," said Kate. "Do you mind if I ask you a question first? You didn't answer the last time I asked."

"What's the question?"

"Just a little one. Where were you before you came in here and found me yesterday? Where did you go?"

"I was—" Abruptly, Natalie's face changed. Before Kate could move, the woman brought an open switchblade from under the desk and planted it deep in the top of her own hand. "Not supposed to tell!" a new voice wailed.

Kate recognized the knife as the one Mel kept under her pillow. She lunged across the desk and grabbed for the hand wielding the blade. Natalie promptly pulled the knife out of her hand and placed the point at Kate's throat.

Bryan and Guerin halted just behind her chair.

"Tammy?" said Guerin in a hoarse voice. "Is that you? Don't hurt her, Tammy. No one is going to ask you any more questions. I promise you."

Kate closed her eyes and swallowed as she felt a tiny trickle of warm blood course down her throat.

Natalie's youngest persona began to sob. "My *hand* hurts. Can you make it stop?"

"Put the knife down and we'll fix it, Tammy. We'll bandage it up and give you a treat just like at the doctor's office."

"Not you. I don't want you to make it stop, I want the nice lady to make it stop. I'll be good, I swear."

"I . . . I can't make it stop with you holding me," Kate whispered.

Tammy whimpered in frustration. "I'm not talking to . . ." She paused and cocked her head, as if listening to something. Her face began to redden in anger. "I *do* have to. I do. I'm going to get a big surprise if I do this one last thing for—"

Guerin and Bryan looked at each other in confusion.

"She's talking to someone else," Guerin said finally.

The sobbing slowly ceased. Natalie's color gradually whitened, and suddenly a look of horror filled her eyes. She dropped the switchblade and clamped her seeping hand over her mouth. "Oh, God," she mumbled. "What have I done?"

It was Kate's first glimpse of the real Natalie.

And her last.

As Guerin reached for her, Natalie snatched up the knife again and plunged it into her own throat. A bright arc of warm blood jetted across the desk and sprayed Kate's face as she opened her mouth to scream.

In the main room, David's head swiveled. His beer fell to the floor and spewed foam as he pushed away from the bar and ran down the hall. He burst through the office door in time to see Guerin pull Mel's pearl-handled switchblade from Natalie's gushing throat. Natalie's limbs were jerking. Her face was white.

Kate's face was red with spattered blood.

Her screams became soundless as Bryan attempted to steer her away from the desk. She resisted. Her stunned gaze was fixed on the dying Natalie.

"Kate," David said sharply.

Her lids blinked.

Bryan's mouth went into a grim line as she bolted away from him. The blood on her face smeared David's shirt as he caught her against him. He put his arm around her and turned to drag her out of the office. As they reached the doorway, a final whistling of air came from Natalie's throat. David paused. Accompanying that dying breath was the low, barely discernible sound of soft laughter.

# 23

## SATURDAY, MAY 21, 2:00 P.M.

DAVID DECIDED IT was time to pay a visit to Augusta. He glanced at Kate and knew she would sleep for at least another two hours. It had taken him that long to calm her babbling and clean up her face. For the first hour she had stood over the toilet in an attempt to heave, gargle, and spit the taste of Natalie's blood from her mouth. It had been painful for David to watch her.

Now he could think of nothing but the cut he had found on her throat . . . and the sound of that laughter.

As gently as he could, he pulled himself free of Kate's arms and left the bed. She shifted once but didn't awaken. David closed the door of her room behind him as he went out. Instinctively, he moved toward the stairs rather than the elevator. No sense in forewarning them of his intentions. He liked the idea of a surprise visit much better.

He himself received a surprise when he reached the dim third floor and saw no Rosalie guarding Augusta's door. He padded down the hall as quietly as possible and paused beside Rosalie's empty chair. Maybe she was in the bathroom. He assumed Rosalie functioned like everyone else and found it necessary to empty the bladder or the bowels on occasion. Just to be sure, he waited.

When ten minutes had passed with no sign of the bodyguard and no sounds from within the room, he reached out and gently twisted the doorknob.

When his eyes adjusted to the dimness inside the room, he saw that Augusta was wearing a mask of some sort. He moved closer and realized it was the kind Julia had used after a night of boozing. Fill it with cool water and it was supposed to reduce the swelling. Too bad Augusta didn't have a body mask of the same kind; she could stand to have some swelling reduced.

Shit. Don't start that again, David told himself.

He watched her until he was sure the even rise and fall of her breast meant a nap was in progress. Just as he was about to make a quick exploration, he heard the low hum of the elevator in the hall outside. After a moment of indecision, he opted for covert action. For lack of anywhere else to hide, he slid noiselessly under the huge bed. Within seconds the door opened and he saw a pair of white-clad feet step inside the room. Rosalie had returned.

"Mrs. Guerin," she said loudly. "I've brought your afternoon snack."

There was a snort from somewhere above him. David felt the mattress shift. Augusta was sitting up.

"What is it?" Augusta asked sleepily.

"Cherry pie, just like you asked for."

"Good. What did you see, Rosalie? What's going on down there?"

"Not much. Sandy said the ambulance left a few hours ago. Dr. Raleigh is having a talk with the patients, and Dr. Guerin is sitting at the bar. He's drinking quite heavily."

Augusta clucked her tongue. "He must be devastated over the loss of Natalie. He never drinks, you know. He knows I don't approve."

There was no response from Rosalie.

David heard the flick of a switch, followed by the sound of his brother's voice, low and soothing: ". . . how important it is for all of you to concentrate on your own therapy. Most of you are making remarkable progress and I want you to know how pleased I am to . . ." The voice faded.

"I wonder how much longer he'll hang on, Rosalie. He certainly is a tenacious sort. And ambitious. He may have to finish that paper without dear Russell's help. And speaking of tenacious, did you happen to see the other Mr. Raleigh anywhere?"

"No, Mrs. Guerin. I checked the second floor but he wasn't there. I don't know where he could be."

Augusta's voice became stiff. "Why do I get the feeling you didn't look very hard, Rosalie?"

"I don't know, Mrs. Guerin."

"Get out," snarled Augusta.

Rosalie left, and for the first time, David wondered how long he was going to be there. As the clink of utensils reached him he moved closer to the foot of the bed. Then he heard more switches being flicked.

"Hello, Kate," Augusta mumbled, her mouth obviously full. "Sleeping, are we? Well, at least he isn't with you."

David frowned and peered through the eyelets in the bed ruffle. He pulled himself along until he could lift the ruffle and see the opposite wall. His intake of breath seemed deafening to his own ears as he saw Kate on the large screen above the stereo system. She was sleeping just as he had left her.

"Kate . . ." Augusta sang softly. "Oh, Kate . . ."

On the screen, Kate began to move. A tiny frown pinched the skin between her brows.

Augusta chuckled. "God, you're such a pitiful little thing. Did all that blood frighten you? I'll bet it did. I heard you scream and scream. Just the way I screamed the day I found my—"

Kate sat up suddenly and opened her eyes. "David?"

He watched and wished he was there with her. Her eyes were round and frightened. She called for him again, then she hugged herself and sank back down to the mattress.

"I want to go home," she whispered. "I just want to go home."

Augusta flicked a switch. "Why don't you, you anemic little bitch?"

Since Kate didn't appear to hear this, David assumed Augusta had turned off the mike part of her set-up. He looked at Kate again and wanted to get up and strangle the woman on the bed above him. He wanted to throttle her until she told him just what she had been doing and why. He wanted to rip out those spying little M&M eyes and shove them down her throat.

Then Kate disappeared from the screen and he saw his own room. David studied the screen intently to try and determine the location of the camera.

In that moment he knew he wasn't going to do what he should. He wasn't going to throttle Augusta or go to Bryan and tell him they should leave. He couldn't. He couldn't because his blood was racing and his mind was humming and he was already wondering how he was going to expose Augusta Guerin without incurring the lawsuit Kate had mentioned.

He wanted this. He wanted to put Augusta's life in print and play the ultimate prying-eyes game by letting the entire country have a peek into *her* bedroom.

"Rosalie!" Augusta shouted suddenly, and David barely had time to duck back under the bed before the door opened and Rosalie appeared.

"Take the plate away and fetch me some eggs from the kitchen. Raw eggs. I didn't get all the blood out of my hair. Does it look dull?"

Blood, David thought. Jay's package?

"It looks fine, Mrs. Guerin," said Rosalie.

"How can you tell?" Augusta snapped. "Never mind. Just go."

Rosalie was back within minutes this time. After she delivered the eggs she was ordered from the room. As the door closed, David felt the mattress heave. Augusta was getting out of bed. He saw two white pudgy feet making their way across the room. Then he heard another door shut and the sound of running water. She was in the bathroom.

David eased himself from under the bed and froze when the door to the hall opened. Rosalie put a finger to her mouth and gestured for him to hurry. David did.

In the hall he wanted to ask her a dozen questions, but she shook her head.

"Just tell me about the blood," he whispered.

"I can't," Rosalie replied, also in a whisper. "Please go. All of you should go. She's getting worse every day. I think she might . . ."

"What?" David prompted.

"I don't know," Rosalie told him. Then she jumped as sounds from within the room reached her. She gave David a shove and reluctantly he went, his entire opinion of Rosalie greatly changed. If he could get her alone he knew she would talk to him. For now, though, he had some peepshow equipment to take care of.

He went first to Kate's room. She was asleep again. He sat down on the bed as gently as he could and eased the pillow from beneath her head. She stirred, but her eyes remained closed. He removed the pillowcase and unzipped the outer lining to thrust his hand inside the thickly packed goose down. After seconds of probing he located what he was looking for. He withdrew his hand and looked at a small black transmitter the size of a pack of cigarettes. On the back was the name of the manufacturer: *Arnette Electronics*.

Funny that Jay hadn't mentioned that particular source of revenue the day he and David had talked.

David examined the thing and found that it had both sending and receiving capabilities. It was more sophisticated than any transmitter bug he had ever seen, though he admitted to himself that he wasn't up on the latest in nouveau-techno surveillance equipment. He shoved it into his hip pocket and quietly left the bed to approach the mirror above the dresser. He hoped Augusta wasn't watching at the moment.

With a low grunt he shoved the dresser away from the wall. Kate mumbled something and he waited until she grew still again before taking the mirror from the wall. Behind it was a square niche, inside of which rested a small camera with a convex lens.

Two-way mirror. Camera. Bugs. Augusta Guerin was a serious voyeur.

David went back to the dresser and opened the top drawer to find a piece of dark clothing to cover the lens. He sifted through panties and bras and smiled to himself when he found a lacy black nightgown.

He almost hated to use it.

After wrapping the filmy fabric around the lens, he replaced the mirror. Kate sat up just as he finished pushing the dresser against the wall.

"What are you doing?"

David turned. "Going through your lingerie. I'm the type who likes to sniff."

Kate stared at him and he could see that she didn't know whether to believe him. Then she gave him a shy smile.

"What does it smell like?"

"You," he said, thinking of the lacy black gown. He moved to the bed and sat down beside her. "Sometimes I like to wear it, too."

Kate's smile widened. "You're lying."

"I am." He lifted a hand to touch her hair. "You okay?"

"Now I am. I woke up once and thought I heard someone calling my name again. Where did you go?"

"To check on Frank. I haven't paid much attention to him lately. He misses me."

"Oh." Kate looked away from him. "David, I want to leave here. I think we should all leave before anything else happens. Something isn't right."

"More intuition?" he said casually, and he was surprised to see her cheeks fill with angry color. Her eyes darkened as her gaze locked with his.

"Don't," she said. "Don't you dare treat this lightly. You may thrive on fear and death and blood, but the rest of us feel nothing but pain when we watch another human being die before our eyes. You wouldn't be so cavalier if it had been someone you cared about. Or maybe you would, I don't know. Maybe you would have gotten a rush out of seeing her slit my—"

David clamped a hand over her mouth. "You know that's not true, so don't even say it. Not another word."

Kate's hands came up to shove him back, and in the blink of an eyelash she was sitting on his chest. Her eyes were almost black with fury.

"Don't *tell* me what to say, David. And don't ever touch me like that again. I won't be treated like some whimpering female simpleton who needs to toe your line to get along. You've been taking advantage of my good nature and my feelings for you and it's going to stop."

David was speechless. All he could do was stare at her pink cheeks and heaving breasts and wonder what else she had in store for him. She glared back, and slowly her eyes regained their softness. Her breathing returned to normal.

"Are you going to tell me you're sorry?" she asked.

"No." He slid both hands under her skirt to rest his palms on her thighs. "Did you ever notice how fast you talk when you're excited?"

Kate made a noise of frustration and rolled away from him. He turned on his side and propped his head on his hand. "All right. I'm sorry. You made me mad."

Her back was to him. "You made me mad, too."

"I noticed. I can't wait to see what happens when you're ecstatic."

Kate favored him with a smirk. "I doubt you'll be around. I might not see you after we leave here, remember?"

David smiled and slid off the bed. "We'll see. Meet me downstairs in an hour and we'll get something to eat . . . if you're up to it, that is."

"I'll be there," she said distantly.

David went to her and turned her around. Her eyes refused to meet his.

"What?" he said.

"Nothing. I don't like to argue."

"I don't either." He bent his head and lifted her chin to kiss the cut on her throat. While his lips were there, a sudden thought popped into his head. "Kate, did you say Natalie was pale when she showed up in Guerin's office? After she had been missing?"

Kate frowned. "Yes. Why?"

"How pale was she? Scared-pale or sick-pale?"

"Sick. Almost white. Why, David?"

He was already on his way out of the room. "I'll see you downstairs in an hour."

He needed a beer in his hand and a notebook in front of him to think. He sat at the bar and scribbled down his thoughts as he drank.

Guerin had been sedating her, so that made Natalie the perfect choice. A needle mark would have gone unnoticed.

The patients had free run of the house. It wouldn't have been too difficult to lure Natalie upstairs.

Augusta could do it, David thought.

And that was it. Natalie hadn't been missing at all, she had been upstairs having her veins robbed by a corpulent vampire. But why? Was Augusta tired of fake blood?

David leaned back on his stool and wondered what the hell was going on. Fake blood, real blood . . . what was she doing, drinking it or washing her hair with it?

Or maybe she was back to re-creating her father's death and using the real thing this time.

Bull's-eye, he thought.

Next question: Why wouldn't Natalie tell anyone where she had been?

That one stumped him. He closed his eyes and tried to remember what Kate had babbled to him earlier. Something about Tammy being the one using the knife. Tammy had also been the one who allegedly talked Cindy into pulling a pistol on Kate. But why would the hole-poking Tammy take a knife and deliberately hurt . . .

He slowly opened his eyes. Of course. Someone *told* Tammy to do it. Someone told her to keep the other personas from talking. Probably the same someone who told her where to find the guns with ammunition in Jay's room.

David sucked in his breath. "Augusta, you are one cunning fat lady. How did you do it?"

Considering what he had found in Kate's bedroom, there was only one possible way that David knew of, only one way to make people stab themselves with knives or deliberately walk into fires. Post-hypnotic suggestion. Augusta was all too familiar with hypnosis. She had over a dozen books on the subject in the library upstairs.

And what better subject than a multiple? Pick a persona, preferably the weakest or the most violent, and plant a few seeds. Multiples were no strangers to suicide or self-inflicted wounds. They were easy prey.

David picked up his notebook and left the bar.

Natalie's room was easy to find; there were three large suitcases just outside the door. David checked the hall and then slipped inside.

There was no niche behind the mirror and nothing in the pillow. It didn't surprise him. Augusta was doubtlessly clever enough to clean up after herself. He sat down on the bed and looked around the room as he pondered the most important question. He was sure he knew the what and the how, but he was uncertain as to the why.

The fact that Augusta was crazy wasn't enough. David wanted to know what had motivated her to bug rooms, install cameras, and terrorize people through dreams and hypnosis. Everyone had a motive for their actions. Even crazy people.

When he heard a noise in the hall he checked his watch and left the room. Kate was waiting for him at the bar. She smiled when she saw him and David felt something turn over in his chest at the sight of her. He wasn't making much progress in shutting her out. He didn't know if it was because she wouldn't let him, or because he really didn't want to.

"Ready to eat?" she said.

He nodded and felt himself smile as she clasped his free hand and gave it a little swing.

Suddenly he wondered if debugging her pillow and covering up the camera was enough to ensure that she would be left alone. He had decided to leave his own room as it was. Augusta might become suspicious if more than one set of equipment had been tampered with.

"Hey," said a voice behind them, and they turned to see Bryan enter the main room from the hall David had just left. He looked at their entwined hands and frowned. "The doctor just called. Mel came around and she wants to see us. She's causing quite a fuss."

Kate immediately stepped forward, but Bryan lifted his hand. "Not you. Just me and David."

"Fine." Kate bristled at his tone. Boldly, she turned and kissed David on the mouth. "I'll see you later. Tell Mel that I'm thinking about her."

Bryan was still frowning as he and David walked out the door.

# 24

## SATURDAY, MAY 21, 6:00 P.M.

MEL BARED HER teeth at the nurse with the little white cup in her hand. "You come near me with that dope and I'll bite you. I swear it."

The nurse blinked. "Doctor said to—"

"I don't care what Doctor said. I've slept all day and I'm not going to sleep any more. Got that?"

"Yes," said the nurse.

"Good. You might take it yourself. You look pretty wired. Are my friends here yet?"

"No."

"Yes," Bryan said from the door.

The nurse hurried away, obviously glad to be relieved by the visitors. Mel held out her arms as the two men entered the room. "Come here, Golden Boy. I thought I'd never be glad to see you."

She saw the look of surprise on David's face as Bryan leaned down to give her a hug. Mel winked at David behind his brother's broad back.

"Are you all right?" Bryan asked as he pulled away from her.

"I'm fine, now. I guess I was in shock or something. Sit down, you two. We need to have a discussion about the Dude Ranch of Death."

"Mel—" Bryan began.

"Let me speak," she said firmly. "First of all, I know about Natalie. These nurses are better than a telephone. Sounds like the whole town is keeping a body count. But just to get the facts straight, did she really slit her own throat?"

"No," Bryan told her as he pulled a chair close to the bed. "She stabbed herself in the throat with your knife."

Mel cringed. "Oh, no. How did she get it?"

"No one knows."

"Did she hurt anyone else?"

"She frightened Kate, but she's fine now."

Mel looked at David for confirmation. He nodded from his chair under the window.

"Are you going to tell us what happened to you?" Bryan asked. "Where were you?"

Mel told them. As she spoke, Bryan leaned farther back in his chair, his face growing paler with each sentence. David leaned forward. His eyes held a strange light.

Finally, Bryan said, "I can't believe it. I can't believe Russell would be a part of this."

Mel stared hard at him. "Has he ever called the hospital to check on Melanie Martin's progress?"

Bryan lifted a shoulder. "I don't know. He's never spoken of it. And I never thought to ask."

"None of us did," said Mel. "Which just goes to show you how nearsighted we are. Out of sight, out of mind."

"But how can you be sure this was Jay's doing?" Bryan asked her.

"Who else loves guns?" Mel replied, and as an afterthought she related Kate's experience with Jay in his collection room. David's expression immediately clouded. Bryan showed his anger openly. "Why didn't she tell us?"

"Why should she?" Mel said. "He didn't do anything to her."

Her eyes rounded then. "Where's my head? Is Kate alone at the ranch with him now?"

"No," Bryan said quickly. "Jay left town right after you were found this morning. He's gone to Emporia on ranch business."

"When will he be back?" Mel asked.

"I'm not sure. I wasn't paying attention."

Mel sat up. "Let's move now then. We can take the police to the cave while he's gone. When he comes back they can have a warrant ready."

Bryan didn't move. He was frowning.

"Don't," Mel said. "Don't do this to me, Raleigh. You're not going to sit on this one for some stupid paper. People are getting killed."

"Just one," he said. "And I still can't believe Russell had anything to do with it."

"Even if he didn't we still have to do something," Mel snapped at him. "I could have died down there myself."

Bryan lifted his head and reached out to squeeze her hand. "You're right. We have to report what you found. David and I will go. I want you to stay here."

Mel automatically shook her head. "No way. No one but me knows how to find that cave."

"I know the slope you're talking about," said David. "I walked right over it."

"If you walked right over it, why didn't you find me?" Mel asked him.

David smiled. "Good point."

"Okay." Bryan stood and sighed. "Get your clothes on and we'll go. I'll speak to the doctor."

When he was gone, Mel looked at David. "I don't have any clothes. Did you bring any?"

"No," he said.

Mel eyed him. "There's more, isn't there? Something else has happened that I don't know about."

David left his chair and helped her out of bed. "I'll fill you in later."

"Something your brother doesn't know?"

"That's right. And tonight I want you to sleep with Kate in her room."

Mel started to ask why, but at that moment Bryan returned with the doctor in tow.

"I don't think this is wise," he said to her.

"Maybe not," Mel answered. She put on her robe and turned to face the Raleighs. "Come on, boys. Let's ride for the law."

The head lawman in Marwell was the chief of police. He listened politely to Mel's story, all the while eyeing her robe with a slightly raised brow. When she finished he checked his watch and stood up behind his desk to say that the Guerin ranch was out of his jurisdiction. He would have to call the county sheriff and let him handle the problem. And as there were only a few hours of daylight left, very little could be done that evening. When Mel began to protest, Bryan put a firm hand under her arm and lifted her from her chair.

"We can expect to hear from the sheriff in the morning then?" he asked.

"If not sooner," the chief of police responded.

"Thank you," said Bryan. "We won't trouble you any further."

Mel sulked as Bryan put her in the front seat of Dr. Guerin's black Mercedes. David sat in the back and thrummed his fingers against his knee. Mel twisted around to look at him. "Did you get the feeling that guy thought I was a little weird?"

"*I* think you're a little weird," said Bryan as he sat down in the driver's seat and started the engine.

She scowled at him. "I mean I don't think he believed me. He acted like he thought I was slightly screwy. In a big city there would have been cops crawling all over the place within an hour, day or night."

"We're not in the big city," David said. "And you're a stranger in these parts."

Mel smiled at his drawl. "I'm serious. I really don't think he believed me."

"We'll know by tomorrow," Bryan said. "If the sheriff doesn't call, then he didn't believe you."

Mel faced the windshield. "Do you want to go out there tonight? I can show you."

"No," said Bryan. "I want you to go straight to bed. I'm going to have a talk with Russell."

"About what?" Mel gave a disbelieving laugh. "You think he's going to own up under a little pressure from the righteous Dr. Raleigh?"

"Don't start with me, Kierkes. I have to know for myself."

"Okay, okay." Mel could respect that. She fell silent and let her head roll back against the seat. She was surprised to find that she was tired again.


When she opened her eyes, she found herself in a bed in a darkened room. "Hello?" she called. When no answer came she left the bed and padded across the carpet to open the door a crack. She almost closed it again when she saw Kate and David. They were standing just inside the doorway of his room, locked in an embrace that made Mel sigh. She wished someone would kiss her like that. Just once.

She backed away from the door and returned to the bed. Within minutes Kate slipped into the room and began to undress. Mel propped herself up on an elbow. "You've got to be kidding me."

In the dimness, she heard a sharp intake of breath. Kate came to sit on the bed. "You scared me. I forgot you were in here."

"Why didn't you stay with David?"

"He wouldn't let me," Kate told her. "Let me get my gown on and we'll talk."

Mel waited patiently while Kate fumbled into a cotton nightgown. She bumped her shin on the frame before finding the bed. "How are you feeling, Mel? Are you all right?"

"I think so. My skull wasn't cracked, but I keep getting tired. I'm not now, though. Talk to me, Kate. There's only one thing that follows kissing like that."

"Apparently not."

"Why wouldn't he let you stay?"

"I'm not sure. He said he had too much to do. I'm beginning to think he's more shy and modest than I am."

Mel grinned in the darkness. "Somehow I doubt that." She thought there had to be another reason for David to send her away.

"Am I doing something wrong?" Kate asked.

"Didn't look like it to me. But don't worry about it, okay? Maybe he's just waiting for the right time."

"I am worried about it, Mel. Sometimes he's so strange. I can almost see a tug-of-war going on inside him when he's with me. I don't understand it."

Mel sighed. "It's probably because of Julia."

"His wife? Do you know about her?"

"A bit."

Kate sat up. "Mel, will you tell me? Please. I want to know what happened."

Mel was touched by the note of desperation in her voice. "If I do, will you promise not to say anything?"

"I promise," Kate said solemnly.

"It's heavy-duty stuff," Mel warned, and then she started talking.

When she was done, Kate lay silent beside her. After a long moment, she said, "He didn't love her. He's never loved anyone, has he?"

"I don't know," Mel said. "David is a different breed."

"Yes," Kate said. "I'll let you go to sleep now, Mel. Sweet dreams."

"I hope so," Mel murmured. "If I'm lucky I won't remember any dreams at all." She rolled over onto her back and stared at the ceiling. The silence stretched into minutes and the room seemed to grow even darker. For a brief, frightening moment,

Mel found herself imagining she was back in the cave and that this—lying here beside Kate in a warm bed—was just a dream. If she extended a hand she knew she would feel dead, brittle hair and cool, unyielding flesh. She could almost smell the stench in her nostrils. . . .

"Kate," she said abruptly. "Would it bother you if I turned on the bathroom light?" Her voice broke on the last syllable.

Without a word, Kate left the bed and crossed the room to flick on the light. When she returned, she put an arm around Mel and hugged her. "David told me about the cave."

"Everything?" Mel whispered.

"He said there were dead things in there. But you're safe now."

Am I? Mel wondered. Are any of us?

Kate hugged her again. "You're shaking. You'd feel better if you cried, Mel. It's just me. No one else is going to see."

Mel was glad to.

# 25

## SUNDAY, MAY 22, 12:45 A.M.

DAVID COULDN'T SLEEP. Whether it was because of the camera or his lust for Kate, he didn't know. He decided it was a little of both. Hours later and he still squirmed uncomfortably on his mattress each time he thought of her. He had to roll over on his side to keep Augusta from tuning in on his state of wakefulness.

He wished he hadn't had the bright idea of asking Mel to sleep in Kate's room.

After flopping around for several more minutes, he swung his legs over the side of the bed and reached for his pants. As he slipped a T-shirt over his head, Frank stirred behind the cage cover and called out to him. David went to lift the cover. "Just going down for a shot of whiskey. Go back to sleep."

Frank made a few grumbles that threatened to become squawks, so David stayed with him until he was quiet again. It didn't take long. Kate had given him an extra ration of beer that day, not knowing that David had already given him his supply. He imagined Frank had suckered her in with his special plaintive look. When the hangover arrived, the little con artist would be sorry.

David left his bedroom door open as he entered the hall. On

his way to the stairs he noticed that Bryan's door was open as well. He found his brother at the bar in the main room, drinking straight from a bottle of scotch.

Bryan merely glanced at David as he walked around the bar for a bottle of Jack Daniels. David picked up a glass and came back to sit on the stool beside Bryan.

"I take it the talk with Guerin didn't go very well?"

Bryan grunted. "He passed out before I got to the good part. I decided he had the right idea."

"So he doesn't know about the cave yet. Or what was in it."

"No, he doesn't know. Right now he doesn't know anything."

David detected a slur in the answer. He poured himself a drink and raised the glass to his lips. The burn felt good on the way down. When he lowered his glass he felt Bryan looking at him.

"You're a hard sonofabitch, David."

David sighed into his glass. He didn't want another confrontation.

"I resent that in you, but at the same time I admire it," Bryan went on. "Does that make sense?"

"Bryan," David began, "let's not—"

"Well, it doesn't make sense to me. *You* don't make sense to me. You've never once asked me for anything, ever. Even when we were younger you never wanted my help. If I tried to show you how to do something, you'd just look at me and go out to play alone. You were always like that. You wouldn't let me do anything for you."

David wasn't prepared for this. He didn't know what to say. He opted for refilling his glass.

"I hated that about you," Bryan said with a sigh. "I hated it that you were so stubborn about doing things for yourself. That's why I started picking on you. After a while it became habit. I guess it still is." He looked at David with watery eyes. "I know you didn't kill that neurotic bitch."

"What?" said David.

"Julia. I know you didn't kill her."

"I'm glad you believe me," David told him. "But I would appreciate it if you dropped the subject, Bryan. Permanently."

Bryan took a long drink from his bottle and wiped his mouth. "Believing you had nothing to do with it. I knew you didn't kill her because Julia told me what she was going to do. She told me while I was in bed with her." He glanced at David to see his reaction. David's face was impassive.

"You knew, didn't you? You knew I slept with her."

"She told me."

Bryan's laugh was harsh. "Of course she did. We were both trying to punish you for being you. The trouble was, you didn't care. I laughed at her when she started ranting about the cyanide and how she was going to make you sorry you had ever met her. I didn't believe she would do it. I thought it was her pain talking. No woman would have that much spite in her. But Julia did. And no matter how badly I wanted to see you crack, I couldn't play it out. I gave that little bastard fifty grand for a false autopsy report. Fifty grand and a one-way ticket to L.A."

David swirled the contents of his glass as he let the confession sink in. After a while he said, "Fifty grand. Frieda must've had fits."

"I told her I lost it in the stock market. But she wouldn't have cared. She always hated Julia. So did I, for that matter. I still don't know why you married her."

David shrugged. "To have someone. I just picked the wrong someone."

"You're doing it again," Bryan said, and the look in his eyes made something in David's gut tighten.

"What do you mean?"

"I mean you're picking the wrong woman again. Kate is my patient, David."

David's glass slipped through his fingers to the bar. His vision went suddenly dark.

*Don't do this to me,* he thought. *Don't do this, Bryan.*

The thought surprised him almost as much as his brother's statement.

"I guess I handled it badly," Bryan said. "I thought you would stay away from her if I warned you off. I should have known better."

"You're lying," said David.

Bryan took another drink and shook his head. "In all fairness, I haven't treated her professionally for the last four years. But technically, she is my patient."

He wasn't lying. David took a deep breath and filled his lungs. "Tell me."

"I can't."

"Bryan . . ."

Bryan studied him a long moment. Then he sighed. "All right. Briefly. I met her almost ten years ago when some Mennonites brought her to me. She had been with them since she was eleven. Before that, she was in the care of an older sister and her husband. On a farm. The sister's husband wasn't your average pedophile. Instead of sexually abusing her himself, he liked to—"

"Animals," David murmured. "He used animals."

"Yes," said Bryan. "It took nearly two years for Kate to tell me that. It ended the night her sister sneaked her out of the house and threw her in the truck. The next day, Kate woke up with the Mennonites. They gave her to the state, and she ran away from three foster homes until the Mennonites finally agreed to keep her. She felt safe with them."

David ran a hand over his cheek. That explained a lot of things. Why she was always dressed in simple skirts and blouses. Her lack of artifice, and her uncomplicated nature.

"Didn't the Mennonites have animals?" he asked Bryan.

"Only a milk cow and some chickens. The family she lived with farmed the land. They knew something was wrong with her, but they thought they could handle it with prayer and hard work. It was only when her bouts of depression became life-threatening that they brought her to me. In the middle of the night I opened my door and saw all these people dressed in black. The man said, 'She's ill. She hasn't eaten in over a week.'

"They found my name in the phone book, they said. I looked at her and told them they should take her to a hospital. The man told me it wasn't that kind of illness. He said, 'She doesn't belong with us.' Then they left."

David put his head in his hands to think. "Is she a multiple?"

"Yes, but a minor leaguer compared to some of Guerin's patients. She had only two other personas. The one causing all the trouble was bent on suicide. To keep her safe, I talked a friend from the hospital into boarding her. She got Kate a job in the hospital cafeteria and enrolled her in school. Later, when she went on to get her license as an occupational therapist, I asked her to come to work for me."

"She was well by then?" asked David.

"For the most part. I wanted to see how she reacted to other multiples. She's turned out to be one of the best people I have in the program."

"What do you mean, *for the most part?*"

Bryan looked up and discovered he had talked himself halfway to sobriety. He reached for his bottle again and took a long drink before answering.

"Four years ago she met a nice young intern. He took her out for dinner and a movie a few times. One night he took her home to his apartment. For the next three days Kate didn't say a word to anyone. She sat at home like a stone. When my friend asked the intern what happened, he claimed Kate had 'weirded out' on him during sex."

"Did you talk to her?"

"I tried. She called him an animal and refused to go within fifty feet of him."

David closed his eyes and shook his head when he thought how close he had come to making love with her.

"She hasn't been with anyone since?"

"Not to my knowledge," said Bryan. "She's dated off and on for the last four years, but there's been nothing serious."

"Would she tell you if there was anything serious?"

Bryan lifted his bottle again. After he drank, he said, "I don't know. She's steadily growing away from me, and it's my own fault, I suppose. In the last year or two I've been looking at her less as a doctor and more as a man. She can sense the difference."

"Do you love her?" David asked.

"Not in the way you think, no. But I do have feelings for her." Bryan turned his head to look at David. "What about you? Has the indomitable David finally fallen?"

David looked away from him. "I don't know."

"You don't know. Well, that'll never be good enough, little brother. That's why I tried so hard to keep you away from her. She needs someone stable. Someone who'll be patient with her and take his—"

"You want me to walk away from her," David interrupted. "She's already told me she loves me. What do I do about that?"

Bryan looked up. "Kate did? She actually said she loves you?"

David frowned at his brother's surprise. "Is that unusual in some way?"

"For Kate it is." Bryan's voice became earnest. "David, you can't let this go on. In any emotional and physical relationship Kate enters she's going to require tenderness and care and patience and understanding. She's going to need someone she can depend on."

David looked at him. "You're saying that I'm incapable of fulfilling those needs."

"Aren't you?" Bryan said frankly.

David was silent. He didn't know if he was or not. He had never tried. He thought of how she had returned his kiss earlier, how she had strained against him. He wondered if her professed love for him would make the difference between thinking of him as a man or as an animal.

Bryan put a hand on his arm. "I'm not taking any joy in this, David. It's obvious that you do care for her, but it's not in you to care enough. A year from now you may not care at all. I want to protect Kate from that if I can. You understand, don't you?"

When David said nothing, Bryan sighed. "Maybe you should

leave. I promised her I would never say anything about her being my patient. Even Mel doesn't know. Kate is uncanny when it comes to sensing things. She'll see right through you to me."

"I'll think about it," David said abruptly. He got up from the bar and took his bottle with him. "See you in the morning."

"Hey," said Bryan. "I'm sorry."

David forced himself to reach out and lay a hand on his brother's shoulder. "Don't worry about it."

Bryan seemed grateful for the contact. "I'll see you tomorrow."

"Tomorrow."

David disappeared around the alcove and started up the stairs. As he climbed he knew he had lied to his brother. There was nothing to think about. He wasn't going anywhere.

# 26

## Sunday, May 22, 2:00 a.m.

AUGUSTA POPPED HERSHEY'S Kisses into her mouth and watched the screen on the far wall. David had drained the bottle in less than thirty minutes. He sat now with his back to the camera, a strangely desolate cant to his shoulders. His brother had staggered to bed only seconds ago. The conversation in the bar had been a tiring one, she guessed.

So interesting about sweet Kate. It explained why there was so little personal information available on her. Unlike Melvina Kierkes, or the brothers Raleigh, Kate's past had been carefully hidden. It was unlikely that Berquist was her real name. Augusta wished she knew the name of the molesting brother-in-law. What juicy dream fodder that would make. On impulse she hit the video switch for Kate's room. Too dark to see any . . . wait. Augusta glanced at the moonlight streaming in through her own window. It should have been in Kate's room, as well. Did she have the drapes completely closed?

Augusta tried the audio switch and received nothing but a hiss over the console.

"Damn," she muttered to herself. She would have to ask Jay to investigate. He wasn't half as good with his hands as Augusta's father had been, but if it was something trivial he could handle it. The animal dream would have to wait. Strange to think that both the video and the audio had malfunctioned at the same time.

What of Melvina, fresh from the hospital? she wondered. She chuckled to herself and hit another switch. The screen showed her an empty bed with filmy rays of moonlight decorating the covers. She flicked a succession of switches and found no sign of the petite brunette.

Sleeping in Kate's room? she wondered.

No doubt. The mouthy harlot was trying to escape the dreams of Duane and his hatchet. And maybe a few new nightmares as well. Augusta wondered how Kate enjoyed sleeping with the lesbian, if she lay quivering on the edge of the bed, hoping she wouldn't feel a hand in the middle of the night.

Augusta laughed to herself. Then her smile slowly died as she let herself think about the white-haired Kate. Augusta had been aware of her from the moment of her arrival, aware of her on a level that frayed the nerves and made her inexplicably uncomfortable. It was good to have this extra information about her past, this extra ammunition, so to speak, against her. Just why, Augusta couldn't say. But she was glad to have it.

With a lengthy sigh, Augusta went back to David. He was staring directly into the mirror now, and Augusta started and felt herself shiver at the loathing in his red-rimmed eyes.

Did he hate himself so much? she wondered. What kind of man looked at his own reflection with such intensity?

Tonight would have been perfect, she realized. Every man in the house was drunk. David himself was nearly in a stupor. It would have been easy.

"Damn you, Jay," she murmured.

At the foot of her bed, he stirred. His clothes were crusted with dirt and he reeked of liquor. He was worthless to her in his present condition.

Augusta unwrapped another Hershey's Kiss and settled back against the pillows to think. She had a new pillow tonight. Rosalie had fetched it for her first thing that morning. The pillowcase still smelled of poor Natalie's shampoo.

# 27

Kate shivered as the first drops of rain pelted her skin. Merciless gusts of wind drove a herd of thick black clouds before the sun, leaving the morning light bruised and weak. She glanced at Mel and saw that her flesh was prickling. Her dark eyes were fastened on the cave entrance, where just seconds ago a deputy had disappeared from sight. The rope he had used to lower himself was still twitching with his movements. Kate let her gaze follow the rope to the bumper of the patrol car it was attached to, and then to the man who sat behind the wheel.

The deputy in the car was watching her. He touched the curved brim of his hat and smiled when he saw her looking. Kate looked away from him and wondered where David could be. Dr. Raleigh had prevented her from knocking on his door that morning, claiming that David needed to sleep. The two of them had been up late, he told her. Before Kate could ask why, three cars from the sheriff's department had arrived, lights flashing.

Dr. Guerin bent over and threw up on the foyer floor when Mel explained why she had brought the police to his home. He still looked queasy, Kate observed, and Dr. Raleigh appeared to be pale and hung over as well. The hand he had on Mel's arm was firm, but his other hand was trembling slightly.

Kate wondered if David had been drinking with them. She had seen him drink a lot of beer, but she had never seen him become drunk. She eyed the anticipation on the faces around her and knew he would be angry that no one had roused him.

Kate was already angry with *him*. He had lied to her about the contents of the cave.

Well, he hadn't actually lied to her. But he had said nothing about Melanie Martin. And neither had Mel. Kate wouldn't have known at all if she hadn't overheard Mel's explanation to Dr. Guerin. Kate resented them for constantly behaving as though she needed protection. She thought she had a right to know what was going on. And now she understood why Mel's sobs had been so wrenching the night before.

As if sensing her thoughts, Mel turned to look at her. "Kate, it's cold. Why don't you go sit in the car?"

Kate glanced at the Mercedes parked behind the patrol cars at the bottom of the slope. "I don't want to."

A deputy turned to look at her. Kate ignored him and moved closer to Mel and Bryan. A drop of rain landed on the tip of her nose. Another landed on her eyelid. She rubbed it away and shivered.

Mel's intake of breath drew her attention back to the cave entrance. Kate saw two hands and then a head emerge. The deputies outside the hole began to pull on the rope. The rain fell harder.

"Well?" Mel stepped forward as the deputy got to his feet and wiped his hands on his pants.

"There's four corpses down there, all right. Three coyotes and one badger."

Mel's head began to shake. "No, no. Two calves, one coyote, and one dead woman."

The deputy glared at her. "I was just down there, ma'am. There's no dead woman."

Dr. Guerin nearly collapsed with relief. Mel darted forward, but Bryan caught her and pulled her back. Mel's eyes were round as she whirled on him. "He's been here, don't you see? He's been here and moved her."

The deputy shook his head. "There's nothing. No body, no blood, no anything. It's not against the law to shoot coyotes. He probably tossed them in there so the smell would keep the cows away from the cave. Being professionals, I'm sure you people have heard of hallucinations. It's easy to do that down there in the dark, especially when there's a head injury involved." He looked pointedly at the bandage above Mel's right ear.

Mel struggled to break away from Bryan. "I didn't imagine anything, you stupid rube sonofabitch. She was down there. She was down there and she was *dead*. Don't you dare talk to me about hallucinations and head injuries."

The deputy took a menacing step forward and Bryan jerked Mel against him. His voice was low and full of warning. "Mel, don't say another word."

Tears of anger and frustration welled up in Mel's eyes. "Bryan, they don't believe me. She was there. The calves, too. How do they think I got out? I didn't have any rope."

Bryan looked at the deputy. The man shrugged. Guerin gave up the struggle to remain standing and toppled to the ground. Deputies rushed forward to pick him up. Bryan directed them to the car and dragged Mel after them.

Kate turned as she felt a presence behind her. It was the deputy from the car. "Hello, ma'am," he said. "I'm Deputy Waltman. Can I give you a lift back to the ranch?"

"I rode up here with them," she said, and pointed to the Mercedes.

Waltman looked. "I don't think there'll be much room left. They're putting Dr. Guerin in the back. Come on, now. You're getting wet."

Bryan opened the driver's door of the Mercedes and shouted to her. "Kate, can you ride with him?"

She nodded and waved him on. Mel was sitting in the passenger seat of the Mercedes. Her face was taut with anger.

"This way . . . Kate, is it?"

"Yes," she said as she followed him. "How did you know my name?"

"He just said it," Waltman explained with a smile.

"Oh."

At the car she waited while he tried to untie the rope on his bumper. The rope was wet and Waltman cursed under his breath at being unable to loosen the knot. Finally he took a pocketknife from the pants of his uniform and sawed the rope away.

"Jay won't mind, I'm sure," he muttered.

Kate got in the front seat when Waltman finally thought to open the door for her. She nodded away his apology and drew her fingers through her wet hair as he climbed in the driver's side and started the engine.

"It's pretty," said Waltman. "Your hair, I mean."

"Thank you." Kate turned to look at him. "I've seen you before, haven't I?"

"Probably. I was here the day they found the woman in the lake." Waltman reversed the car and turned it away from the slope. "I'm glad to see none of the kooks are on the loose today. Every time that Raleigh fellow comes to town old Wally nearly wets his pants. Wally thinks he ought to be locked up."

Kate stared at him. "What Raleigh fellow?"

"Mr. Famous," the deputy replied. "The writer who killed his wife. I heard he got off on diminished capacity and was remanded to the care of his brother, the doctor. I can't believe what passes for justice these days. The man looks sane to me."

"That's because he is," said Kate in a flat voice. "I don't know who you've been listening to, but someone has been filling your head with nonsense. David Raleigh's wife committed suicide."

Waltman snorted. "I'm sure that's what he told you. Hell, he made *me* think he was on the level. But he let it slip to Wally that he was a patient here. I felt like a fool when I found out."

"Wally told you?" Kate asked him.

"What difference does it make?" Waltman concentrated on his

driving as he guided the car over a deep rut. "If I were you, I'd stay away from him. These suicides seem to follow him around, if you know what I mean."

"If you're talking about Natalie Parks, I was in the room when she stabbed herself. David was nowhere in sight."

Waltman lifted a brow in interest. "You were there? Can I trouble you with something?"

"What?"

"To your knowledge, was Miss Parks having sexual relations with anyone at the ranch?"

Kate looked at him in surprise. "Why do you ask?"

Waltman glanced over. "There was some interesting data in the coroner's report. We don't usually commission an autopsy on obvious suicides, but in view of all the recent problems here, the sheriff wanted one done. Miss Parks had some peculiar bruises in her vagina and her . . . uh, alimentary canal. I thought you might have an idea as to how she got them."

Kate felt sick. Cold, Natalie had said. Coldness hurts inside. Had she been talking about something inserted inside her?

"No ideas," she said to the deputy, though she had plenty. "You could ask one of the doctors later. They might be able to help you."

Waltman sighed as he pulled up outside the big house. The rain pounded on the roof of his patrol car.

"Officially, I'm not a detective," he told her. "But I have a feeling, Kate, that you should be careful around here. And I'd keep an eye on Mr. Raleigh."

Kate put a hand on the door and looked at him. "I suggest you run one of your makes on him if you don't believe me. And after you find the truth, I'd look at the person doing all the talking and wonder what the noise is covering up. And one more thing, Deputy Waltman. If Mel Kierkes says she saw a body in that cave, then you can bet those muddy boots of yours there was a body. Thank you for the ride."

Waltman stared at her as she shoved open the door and left the car. When she reached the shelter of the front entry she turned back and saw the deputy frowning as he put the car in gear.

Kate searched the main floor until she found Mel and the two doctors in Guerin's office. The righteous anger and indignation in Kate deflated when she saw their faces. Mel was seated behind the desk, her head in her hands. Dr. Guerin was on the couch against the back wall. He still looked pale and weak.

"What's going on?" Kate asked.

Mel lifted her head. "We just called Kansas City. They said Melanie Martin died a few hours after she arrived at the hospital. According to the morgue, her body was claimed by a member of her law firm the next day and flown to Minneapolis for burial."

Bryan moved behind the desk and put his hands on Mel's shoulders. "Kate, take Mel upstairs and get her into something dry."

"I don't want to go upstairs," Mel argued. "I want to leave."

Bryan ignored her and continued speaking to Kate. "Try to get her to lie down. And take a look at her stitches. I think the wound might have opened and I don't want it to become infected."

"Maggots," Mel muttered.

Kate looked at Bryan in alarm.

"That's the sedative talking," he said, and he bodily lifted Mel from the chair. Kate rushed to take Mel's arm as her legs began to wobble.

"I didn't imagine anything, Katie. You know I didn't. We need to get out of here."

Kate helped her across the room. At the door, Kate stopped and looked back. "Mel's right, Dr. Raleigh. We should leave."

Bryan sighed and glanced at the couch, where Guerin had fallen asleep. "I know what you're saying, Kate. I've already spoken to him about it. We'll have to wait until the storm clears. Right now, I need to see about the patients. Take care of her, would you?"

Kate nodded and pulled Mel into the hall. They went to Kate's room, where she helped Mel undress and get into a robe. While Kate was changing Mel's bandage she thought of Waltman's preposterous statements. She couldn't wait to tell David.

"Infection," Mel mumbled as she lay on the bed.

"Doesn't look like it," Kate told her. "Just a little bleeding. One of the stitches worked loose."

"Great. Just put a few nuts and bolts in and call me Kierkenstein."

"Try to rest, Mel."

"I don't have any choice," came the reply. "That jerk put something in my coffee. I'm not some raving hysteric who needs to be dosed up and closed away in the attic. I may sue that bastard for this. I may . . . as soon as I get up I'm going to . . . Oh, Kate, I hate this feeling. I hate feeling out of control. I have to . . ."

Kate finished the bandaging and sat still until Mel's eyes remained closed. After tucking in her sedated patient, Kate took a warm shower and dried her hair with a blow dryer. A light sweater went over her blouse, and for once she decided to wear a pair of slacks instead of a skirt.

She looked at the closet and wondered if she should begin packing her things. Then she decided it could wait. She wanted to talk to David.

Outside his door, Kate paused to listen. There was no sound from inside. She gently knocked.

"David, are you awake yet?"

There was no answer. Kate knocked again and shifted her feet as she waited. Finally she twisted the knob and opened the door. "David?"

His bed was rumpled, but it hadn't been slept in. His closet doors were open, the closet was empty. Frank's cage was gone. On the desk, propped between the rows of keys on the word processor, was a note. Kate strode forward to snatch it up. There were only two short lines:

Kate: Bryan told me everything. I decided it was best to leave. I'm sorry. David.

A noise of pain escaped Kate's throat. She looked wildly around the room again and caught sight of her reflection in the mirror above the dresser. The raw pain in the face of the woman in the glass made her wince. An old enemy waited there. A child full of hopelessness and despair.

"No," Kate said between her teeth. "*No.*"

She whirled away from her reflection and left the room to find Bryan.

# 28

## Sunday, May 22, 12:00 p.m.

MEL AWAKENED TO the feel of a hand stroking her arm. She kept her eyes closed for a moment, enjoying the sensation, until it occurred to her to wonder just whose hand was doing the stroking.

"Hi," said Denny as she opened her eyes.

Mel sat up. "What are you doing here?"

Denny smiled and removed his hand. "I just wanted to see how you were. How are you?"

"How did you get in?" Mel asked.

"In the door and up the stairs. No one stopped me." Denny looked over his shoulder. "The door's locked. I wanted some time alone with you."

"Where's Kate?"

"Downstairs. She's arguing with Dr. Raleigh about something."

"Kate? Arguing? Are you sure?"

Denny nodded. "I didn't hear much. I think Dr. Raleigh's brother left and didn't tell anyone. They found Mrs. Guerin's car at the bus station in Marwell a little while ago."

"David? Why would he leave?" It was a rhetorical question.

Denny wouldn't have an answer. Mel leaned back against the headboard and felt his hand cover hers.

"You didn't answer me. How are you?"

"When did they discover the car missing?" Mel asked.

Denny sighed. "When everyone came back from the cave. Dr. Raleigh left Dr. Guerin's car in front of the house, so Grant put it in the garage. He didn't think anything of the other Mercedes being gone until your friend Kate went storming around the house trying to find out how Mr. Raleigh left."

Mel looked at him, thinking. None of this made sense to her. The David she knew would not have gone without knowing what was in that cave. And why bail out when things were going so well with Kate?

"Is Jay back yet?" she asked Denny.

"I don't think so." Denny leaned forward then, and before Mel could say another word, he pulled her face to him to kiss her. Mel felt a shock go through her at the warmth of his lips. Her hands came up to push him away, but they stopped just short of touching him. When her entire body felt as if it were melting, he pulled away.

"Denny . . ."

"I had to do that," he told her.

"You did."

"Yes. I've been wanting to for a long time."

"Denny, let's talk. I think—"

"I know you didn't make up that story about the cave, Mel. All the guys were laughing about it, but last winter I found a dog shot full of lead out by the lake. It was sickening. I didn't say anything about it today, but maybe I should have. Not to Waltman, though, because he's good friends with Jay."

Mel pulled her robe tighter around her. She was having trouble concentrating. She kept looking at his mouth and thinking how wonderful it would be if he kissed her again. She forced her eyes away and said, "Are they going to press charges against David for taking the car?"

"No. Dr. Guerin refused." Denny's eyes were fastened on her lips.

"How . . . would David have gotten the keys?"

"No one knows."

Conversation ceased, and they came slowly together again. This time Mel's arms found their way around his neck, and his hands came up to hold her close to him. Their kisses grew impassioned, and soon Mel was consumed with heat and urgency and the need to feel his young, strong flesh beneath her hands.

Half an hour later she was consumed by guilt and remorse.

She lay quietly with him, hardly daring to breathe while he stroked her neck and twined her hair around his fingers.

What have I done? she asked herself over and over. My God, what have I done? He's only a child. I'm sixteen years older than he is. I was dating when he was conceived. I was married when he was in preschool.

"Mel," Denny said quietly. "Don't do what you're doing."

"What am I doing?"

"Berating yourself. Don't. You needed it and I wanted it."

"I needed it?"

"To reaffirm your existence after your brush with death."

"You read that somewhere."

"I did."

"Denny . . . I think you should go now. The other hands are probably looking for you."

He rose up on one elbow. "You let me stay here longer than I thought you would."

Mel looked at him and frowned. "What?"

"I figured you'd boot me out a lot sooner. What are you going to do when I come to the city and knock on your door?"

"Put on the deadbolt. I'm serious, Denny, this was a big mistake. Please go now."

Without a word he left the bed and reached for his clothes. Mel forced herself to look away from his lean, tanned body as he dressed. He would mature into an incredible man, she found herself thinking. Gorgeous. And by the age of thirty-five her name would be lost in a thick book of years lived and women loved. She pictured him smiling and shaking his head when he thought of her . . .

"Mel."

She blinked. He was at the door.

"Come and say goodbye to me before you leave. Will you do that?"

"Yes," she said. "I promise."

He opened his mouth once more, then he simply nodded and left the room. The expression of resignation on his face stayed with her long after he was gone. Finally she left the bed and went into Kate's bathroom to take a shower and wash the smell of him from her skin. When she came out she dressed in her still-damp clothes and walked to the window. The rain had ceased only momentarily. The clouds were still rumbling with thunder and emitting streaks of lightning. A large colorful bird landed in the dripping cottonwoods across the lawn. The bird fluttered its wings as if shuddering from the cold.

Mel squinted at it and shuddered herself. I know how you feel, she thought.

She stepped away from the window and crossed the room to open the door. Her breath left her in a rush as she saw Jay Guerin standing on the other side, his eyes as dark and full of thunder as the clouds outside.

"What are you—" Mel didn't finish. Jay lunged for her and she jumped instinctively back. She slammed the door on his nose and frantically twisted the lock. Her fingers crossed in the next second as she prayed that he had no key. What was he doing? she asked herself in a panic.

"I hear you've been spreading some nasty rumors about me," he said from the hall.

Mel couldn't speak. Her throat was frozen with fear. His voice was normal, charming almost. But she knew better. Her pulse pounded as she leaned against the door and waited. After a moment she put her ear to the wood to listen. She couldn't hear anything. No breathing. No retreating footsteps.

How long had he been back? she wondered. Had he seen Denny leave and then made a plan to come in and silence her? Perhaps even blame it on the stable hand?

The doorknob slowly began to twist. Mel backed away, and her heart did a series of cartwheels in her chest. Jay had gone for a key. He had left and come back with a key.

Suddenly there was a loud knock.

"Mel? It's Kate. Are you in there?"

Mel unlocked the door and threw it open. "Katie, he's back! Did you see him?"

Kate's face was pale and strained. "Who?"

"Jay Guerin. I opened the door and there he was. Boy, did he look pissed. He reached for me but I jumped back and locked the . . ." She stopped at the worried expression that darkened Kate's eyes. "Why are you looking at me like that?"

"Mel," Kate began quietly, "Jay Guerin just called from Emporia to say he was on his way home. I spoke to him myself."

Mel heard someone laugh, but she didn't realize it was herself until she saw Kate's frown deepen.

"It won't work, Katie. You people are all trying to make me think I'm crazy, but it won't work. I don't like people messing with my mind. Pull out my toenails, steal my money, and shave my head with a rusty razor, but *don't* mess with my mind. The sonofabitch called you from somewhere inside this house."

She pushed past the startled Kate. "Get out of my way. I'm going downstairs to find my blade. And then I'm going to pack my bags and fly that jet myself if we're not out of here by nightfall. I wish I'd known David was leaving. I would've gone with him."

She ignored the flash of pain in Kate's eyes and moved down the hall to the elevator. Her blade, her bags, and a parting of the clouds was all Mel wanted at that moment.

And maybe a straight shot of bourbon.

# 29

## Sunday, May 22, 4:00 p.m.

It was easy to let the scenery hypnotize you, Rosalie thought as she leaned her head against the window. Easier yet to look forward, rather than back. She had a lot to look forward to if she thought about it. She had always hated the cold Kansas winters. They seemed to get longer every year. New Mexico had winters, too, but they couldn't be as bad. Especially south, down around Alamogordo. The missile range was close by, so she'd go first in the event of nuclear accident or disaster. That was good. And the Mescalero Indian reservation was near, as well. Being one-fourth Apache herself, Rosalie had always been interested in learning about the Indian way of life.

Now she had the time.

She thought she might even try out some of those herbal remedies she'd been reading so much about, like using wild ginger for colds, and elm bark tea for sore throats. If she could find some seeds of bladder nut, she was sure it would relieve her chronic constipation. And what about using milkweed for warts and oak bark for burns? Her grandmother had used all of them, she was sure. It all sounded lovely and peaceful. Harmless.

Rosalie closed her eyes and felt the engine of the bus vibrating in her bones. Not too many people traveling west on this dark, rainy day. Rosalie had been to the bathroom in the back of the bus three times already and never once had to wait. Three times to open her purse and look inside, just to make certain the money was still there.

Big money. Bundles of it, with the bank paper still around the bills. Two years' salary.

And a huge bonus.

The smell of it amazed Rosalie. She sat on the tiny toilet in the back of the bus and simply inhaled the aroma. When she opened her eyes and looked at the money it was easy to forget about David Raleigh. Easy to forget the ropes that bit into the skin of his bare chest and held him in that wheelchair. Not so easy to forget the look in his red eyes when he opened them up and saw Augusta Guerin standing over him.

But that would pass. Rosalie was sure of it. Mrs. Guerin wasn't going to hurt him any. Not really. She was just going to keep him in the wheelchair . . . for a while.

Rosalie squeezed her eyes shut.

And Augusta's son wouldn't hurt anyone, either. Not sweet, crazy Jay with the inflatable penis.

No. They were both harmless.

They were . . .

No sense denying it to herself. Rosalie knew good and well what Augusta was planning to do. She had figured it out the moment she saw what was in the other room. But she didn't care. She *couldn't*. Not with all that money staring at her and filling her nostrils with its wonderful smell.

Rosalie sighed and opened her eyes. The old man in the seat across the aisle looked over and smiled at her. Rosalie smiled back and rose from her seat to trundle down the aisle toward the tiny bathroom. It was time to look at the money again.

# 30

## SUNDAY, MAY 22, 6:00 P.M.

DAVID'S NOSE HURT. Augusta had broken it the last time she hit him. Three hundred pounds behind a punch could do that. His arm was sore, too, where she had jabbed the needle into his vein and taken three vials of his blood. She was going to take more, he knew. But not before she found out what she wanted to know.

He could hear her in the adjoining room, smacking her lips and scraping away at a dish of peach cobbler brought up by Juana. David didn't know where Rosalie was. He had seen her that morning for just an instant. She was probably gone. He had overheard something about Augusta's car turning up at the bus station in Marwell.

His staged departure, no doubt.

Augusta had assuredly made it worth Rosalie's while to play out the ruse and disappear. David wished he could do the same. His limbs ached from being in the same position for so many hours. The rope had cut deep into his arms and chest, leaving the skin raw and bleeding in places. A deep breath was out of the question. Not that he could take one anyway, given the shape his nose was in.

Augusta had hit him for looking at her. She didn't like the light in his eyes, she had said, or the way he didn't blink. He should blink when he looked at her. He should blink and perhaps even tremble.

The clinking sounds next door quickened. Augusta was finishing up. David leaned his head back and let his eyes travel around the room. The lab equipment was dusty, but everything looked relatively new. Augusta obviously wasn't interested in keeping her little hematology lab clean. And he imagined none of the housekeeping staff had ever seen the place. The look on Rosalie's face had been enough to tell him that.

Funny. David had been convinced the nurse-gofer-guard had more character. But he guessed anyone could be bought.

At least Frank had gotten away. The bird was probably halfway to Mexico by now. That, or Jay had gone out and shot him down. Jay's first idiotic reaction to Frank's name-calling had been to open the cage door and try to grab the angry, frightened parrot.

David looked at the broken window above the dusty bookcase and wondered if Frank had been hurt when he flew through the glass. Frank wouldn't like the cold rain. He would fly until he found someplace dry. If he was alive.

David's head swiveled toward the connecting door when he heard Augusta begin to snarl at someone.

"Where have you been all day?"

"Around. I've just formally arrived back from my trip."

Jay, thought David.

"Did anyone see you before your arrival?"

"That little lesbian bitch. She's still causing trouble for me. I almost had her, but then Kate—"

"What?" Augusta cried. "What is wrong with you? Why did you let her see you?"

There was no answer from Jay.

"I'm tired of this, Jay. I want you to leave these women alone. You're drawing too much attention. First you had to go and take Melanie Martin from that morgue for your target practice, and then you shoved that pistol inside Natalie Parks. I'm sick of cleaning up your messes."

"Then why don't you help me?" Jay shot back. "You promised to help me, Mother. Do you think I enjoy these impulses? Do you think I can control them? When are you going to start helping me?"

"Soon," said Augusta in a calmer voice. "I still have some work to do."

"On what? Raleigh? What are you going to do with him?"

"You're pushing me, Jay."

Jay's voice cracked. "I'm sorry if I'm *push*ing you, Mother, but I am losing ground every day and I need your help. I don't want to be like this. I want to have a life and maybe even a relationship someday. If what you heard about Kate is true, then maybe I can have one with her. But first you have to help me."

"I will," Augusta snapped at him. "I've said I would and I will. But you have to trust me, Jay."

David's forehead creased into a deep frown. Now he knew what the others had found in the cave that morning: nothing. Jay hadn't been away at all—he had gone to the cave and done something with Melanie Martin's body. A body he had picked up from the morgue in Kansas City.

Why? David asked himself. What kind of illness did Jay have? What made him put bullets into animals and pistols inside women?

The way they talked about Kate worried him. If he could have, David would have gotten up from the wheelchair and kicked himself for forgetting about the intercom while talking to Bryan downstairs at the bar.

Even more worrisome was the fact that they were talking at all with him in hearing range. It confirmed something he had been tossing around in his head most of the day.

He wasn't leaving the room alive.

"Before you go," Augusta was saying, "I want you to promise me you'll leave Melvina alone. She can't do anything to you now. She has no proof."

Melvina? thought David.

"I know that," Jay said to his mother. "It doesn't stop me from wanting to strangle her. Anyway, she's attached herself to Dr. Raleigh. Grant says he'll fly them out first thing in the morning. He won't go before then. He doesn't like flying in storms, and Dad won't make him go if he doesn't want to."

David heard Augusta chuckle. "Just how is your father? I haven't heard much out of him today."

"That's because he's ill with a hangover. I think Dr. Raleigh is afraid to leave him."

"I think he's more afraid to leave the patients with no one in command," said Augusta. "Don't you?"

"I don't know. And I don't care. I don't want Kate to go, but I realize I can't have a relationship with her until I learn to control myself. When can you start helping me, Mother?"

There was a long pause. Finally, Augusta said, "We'll start tonight."

"Do you mean it?" Jay's voice was grateful.

"Of course I do. Run along now and let everyone know you're back. I've ignored my work long enough."

You mean me, David thought. He closed his eyes and attempted to prepare himself for whatever.

In a sense, he felt sorry for Jay Guerin. The man knew he needed help. He was begging for it. But he was asking the wrong person.

David opened his eyes when Augusta pushed open the adjoining door. Once again, he was amazed that she could even stand. Give an elephant tits and toes and you've got Augusta, he thought. He could imagine the strain on her heart. One little hard-working muscle to push around all that blubber. And most of the blubber was visible; Augusta seemed to love wearing gowns ten sizes too small.

She couldn't possibly think she looked sexy, David told himself. There was nothing sexy about folds of fat or a belly that visibly swung with the slightest movement. The cheeks of her buttocks were another story entirely. Two tomes' worth.

Augusta waddled directly to David and backhanded him across the face. "I'm going to do that for every day you ignored my request to come and visit," she told him.

David blinked away the stinging wetness in his eyes. His nose was throbbing and threatening to bleed again.

"I know you heard everything," she continued. "Do you have any questions?"

"How many will you answer?" David responded.

"As many as I feel like answering. Are you getting hungry yet, or do you still feel sick?"

He wasn't hungry. Watching Augusta would rob anyone's appetite.

"Suit yourself." She moved away from him to a large refrigerator-freezer beside a cluttered cabinet. She pulled open the refrigerator side and her hand came out with a carton of chocolate milk. She opened the top of the carton and began to drink.

David watched her and decided to begin with confirmation of his theories. "I know you've been using hypnosis on some of the patients. You use transmitters in the pillows."

Augusta stopped chugging and looked at him. "My, you are a bright one, aren't you?"

"If I was, I wouldn't be here," he said.

Her eyes went dull. "Who else knows about the electronic equipment?"

David allowed himself to smile. Let her worry about that. He said, "You picked women with personas who were prone to violence and erratic behavior. Correct?"

Augusta shrugged. "Multiples are vulnerable and at times extremely volatile creatures, David. The problem with hypnosis, however, is that you cannot force a person to do something against his or her own nature. Rather than hurt someone else under post-hypnotic suggestion, these poor unfortunate women chose to hurt themselves."

She was smiling. The bitch.

David's stomach did a slow roll as he thought of the day he found Melanie Martin stabbing herself in the head with a screwdriver. When she had screamed "Get out," she hadn't been talking to David, she had been talking to someone inside her own head.

"Who?" he asked Augusta. "Who did you want these women to hurt?"

Augusta belched loudly and took another long drink of chocolate milk. Finally, she said, "Russell, of course, and, later, Kate. But I really miscalculated with Natalie. I should have started with Cindy rather than Tammy. Cindy was by far the more dominant persona. Tammy was instructed to get a gun from Jay's collection and shoot Kate. The kink in the plan occurred when Jay met Cindy in the poolhouse and . . . assaulted her, shall we say, with one of his pistols. Cindy flaked out and Tammy suddenly had a gun. But by the time she reached Kate's room, Cindy came back and refused to relinquish control to Tammy. Too bad. I'm certain Tammy would have pulled the trigger."

The blood vessels in David's head were pounding after this calmly delivered confession.

"Why would you want to hurt Kate, Augusta?"

Augusta wiped chocolate from her curling mouth. "Jay is so misguided sometimes. He really doesn't know what's best for him."

"What about Melanie Martin?" David asked. "And the woman in the lake? Why them?"

Augusta smiled and came to smooth his hair with one doughy, ringed hand. David's stomach hitched.

"You forgot the woman I led into the fire," she said. "She was an experiment, really. After my success with her I'm afraid I got a bit carried away with my newfound powers. I attempted to hypnotize two separate personas in the woman found in the lake. There must have been a great deal of confusion when Cilla the runaway got to the top of the tree only to encounter another very hostile persona trying to take over and jump. I wish I could have seen it.

"As for Melanie Martin, well, like Natalie she was a bit too close to Russell for my liking. He becomes very attached to his patients, you know. Too attached, in my opinion. He becomes a doting father figure, playing with them, giving in to their silly little whims. He has never thought of Jay the way he should. The way a real father would."

"Why?" asked David. "What exactly is wrong with Jay, besides being a bleeder and having a sick fetish for pistols?"

Augusta grabbed a handful of David's hair and pulled viciously hard. "Don't you dare speak of my son in those terms. You can't afford to."

"On the contrary," David said between his teeth. "I don't think I have anything to lose."

Augusta released him and laughed. "That's what I love about you. Ever the realist, aren't you?" She walked to the refrigerator and put the chocolate milk inside. When she turned again she had a half-pound Hershey's bar in one hand and a plastic bag of whole blood in the other.

David wondered if the blood was also part of her daily diet.

In the next moment he stopped wondering.

She slit the bag open and came to pour the crimson contents over David's head. He blinked as it ran into his eyes. He gagged as it streamed over his lips. It smelled like spoiled meat.

"Not much fun being a 'bleeder,' as you so callously put it," said Augusta. "In addition to coming into the world as a hemophiliac, Jay was born with a condition known as micropenis. His testicles were fully developed, but he had no penis to speak of. You can imagine the devastation suffered by Russell and myself."

"Wait a minute," David said, remembering Mel's story about the erection in the gun room with Kate. Augusta laughed merrily when he told her about it.

"It's a specially designed apparatus that inflates and deflates by hand control. Jay was probably showing off for Kate. He can have sex with it if he likes, but he prefers to use his pistols for that."

David stared at her. He shook his head to flick a drop of blood from his eye. He thought he understood now. He thought he understood everything.

"That's why, isn't it?" he said to Augusta. "That's the reason you stopped treating paraphiliacs. You moved out here to the ranch and discovered that your own son was sexually perverted. That's why your father, Ted, wanted you out here so badly. He wanted you to come and help Jay."

Augusta began to shake her head.

"But you didn't, did you?" David continued. "You turned away from the field altogether and went on some paranormal goose chase. When your father died you were suddenly faced with dealing with Jay on your own. You decided to hide up here instead and eat your way to some Nestle's nirvana. Your husband doesn't know about Jay's gun fetish, does he? He doesn't know anything."

"You're the ignorant one," Augusta said in a voice just above a whisper. Her eyes were dead. "*You* don't know anything, David. Russell turned away from Jay the moment he was born. He was too busy to care for a son born with Jay's condition. And so was I. I had to get back to my work. I didn't have time for the bruises and the elastic bandages. I didn't have time for the ice packs and the bleeding joints and the hundreds of transfusions he was going to need. Daddy knew how to do it. Daddy knew how to pad the furniture, cushion his joints, and keep Jay alive through the most dangerous years. He had the money for all the doctors, teachers, and nurses. And he knew how to give the transfusions himself. Daddy loved me, and he was sorry for passing on the gene and making me a carrier.

"He tried to warn us, but Russell wouldn't listen. There was a chance we wouldn't have a hemophiliac son, and Russell wanted to take it." Augusta paused to smirk. "God laughed at us for daring and compounded the curse by sabotaging Jay's manhood as well as his blood."

It was David's turn to shake his head. "So you handed him over to your father and walked away."

"Only until he was past puberty." Augusta ran the big chocolate bar over her lips like a lipstick. "When they're finished growing there's less danger. There was a time when over half of those afflicted with hemophilia died before they reached the age of five. I honestly don't know how my father survived. He was lucky his own father had money."

She nipped at the chocolate bar and smiled suddenly. "They used to call it the disease of kings. Did you know that?"

"Yes," said David. He had learned about hemophilia while reading Julia's book on Rasputin.

"I believe Queen Victoria was behind it all," Augusta said, warming to the subject. "She had no history of the hemophilia in her own family, but for some reason a gene changed. Spontaneous mutation, they call it. Her son, Prince Leopold, was a hemophiliac, and both her daughters were carriers. The daughters of those daughters were carriers as well. They married into the royal houses of Russia and Spain and had hemophiliac sons. Does Alexis, son of Alexandra and Nicholas, czar of Russia, ring a bell? I believe Rasputin was reputed to have helped the boy."

Augusta ignored David's sudden stare and went on. "Life has always been ghastly for hemophiliacs. Many become addicts, you know. The drugs they take to ease those bleeding joints and organs can be dangerous. My father was fond of using hypnosis on himself, and later Jay, rather than drugs. Daddy learned it from a doctor who used it on him as a child, when some people were still calling it mesmerism. Even Jay knows how to do it. I was the last to learn."

"And the first to abuse it," said David. "Tell me just one thing. Rather than clean up his so-called messes, why haven't you tried to help Jay?"

The chocolate bar hit David square in the nose and made him bite the tip of his tongue in pain. Augusta snatched a piece of rubber tubing from the counter and came to tie off his arm. "You'll be happy to know your blood has passed the usual gamut of syphilis, hepatitis, and HIV tests. Do you know what plasmaphresis is, David?"

He couldn't speak for the blood running thickly down his throat.

"Well," said Augusta as she retrieved a sterile bag from somewhere behind him. "I would have thought you did, but what it amounts to is this: I take your whole blood, put it in the centrifuge, and separate the red cells from the plasma. Then I give you back the red cells and keep the plasma. Your red cell and hemoglobin levels will remain the same, and your plasma protein levels will return to normal within two or three days. How does that sound?"

"Why?" David managed.

"For Jay, of course. I want him to have your plasma. Oh, I know he can buy the AHF protein he needs in a concentrated form, but I want him to have yours."

David closed his eyes as she reached for the needle. He hated this part. "What . . . is AHF?"

She smiled at his flinch. "Ooops. I missed the vein. I'll have to try again. AHF is Anti-Hemophilic Factor, what Jay's plasma is missing. It's one of a dozen or more plasma proteins necessary for proper coagulation. You should have paid more attention in biology class, David."

"I took chemistry," he said.

Augusta jabbed him hard with the needle. "Hah-hah. You are so funny. You really make me laugh, David. That's why I'm going to keep you around for a while. You can open your eyes now."

He didn't want to. "For how long? How long are you going to keep me around?"

Augusta ignored the question. "Did you know the Romans used to drink blood? Egyptians took baths in it, but the Romans thought the power would be lost unless it was taken internally. What power do you suppose they meant, David? Could it possibly be the life force itself? I think so. All the scientists in the world can't change the aura of superstition surrounding blood. Do you know why?"

David knew. Because if you lost it, you died, and the aura of superstition surrounding death would be around long after all the mysteries of blood chemistry had been solved.

"Blood contains everything about you," Augusta told him. "It can tell all your secrets, and it can pass those secrets on to the next generation, undetected. I never knew my father was a hemophiliac until the day Russell and I were married. He kept everything hidden from me. And he offered to take Jay when he was born, David. We didn't ask him to take him. We really didn't. He offered to take Jay and raise him, because he knew what my career meant to me, and he knew how much of a burden Jay was going to be. My father loved me so much. After my mother died I was all he had in the world, until I gave him Jay."

Augusta sighed and David finally opened his eyes. Her vacuous gaze was fixed on the blood bag that was filling. David glanced at the dark red fluid and looked slowly away again.

She's going to take my blood, he thought. Not just this bag, but all of it. She's going to take it and give it to Jay to try and make him different. To help him.

"Daddy would have done this, I know," Augusta murmured. "He was very interested in the blood of strong, healthy individuals. He funded a research institute in West Virginia. They're trying to create synthetic blood. Why? Because we're a greedy country, David. We sell blood. We sell life. My father wanted to change that. He wanted to have enough blood for everyone who needed it. He was such a wonderful man."

Maybe so, David silently told her, but you didn't turn out so hot, Augusta. And if he was so wonderful, how did Jay get to be such a warped gun-loving monster? Theodore Arnette had to have pushed his collection on Jay as a healthy masculine outlet, one that ultimately backfired, possibly as a result of the sheltered life Jay had been forced to lead.

What had Mel said about Jay while she was in the hospital? Something about men using guns as an extension of their penises. With Jay, the pistol *was* his penis.

"Daddy said I should try every means at my disposal to help,"

Augusta said suddenly. "And he looked so happy when I told him I would."

"Who . . . Jay?" David asked.

"No. My father. I finally found him. I had to use the real blood. That's what was missing. I'd been trying to make the trip with the synthetic blood, but I never had any success until I used the blood I took from Natalie. To be on the safe side, I drank it *and* bathed in it, just like the Romans and Egyptians."

David closed his eyes again. A trip. The fat vampire had gone on a trip and found her dead father. Wonderful.

"Augusta, you need help," he said. "So does Jay. Please—"

A thick hand was clamped over his mouth, and in the next second the hand was replaced by adhesive tape.

"You've seen too much of your parrot's Oprah, David. You surprise me, really. I thought you kept an open mind. I've admired you for so long, and now all you've done is disappoint me. I looked forward to long afternoons spent talking to you and getting to know you. I just knew you'd want to write about me and my life once you knew me."

Got that right, David thought.

"I have to go," Augusta said as she looked at her watch. "Don't worry, though. I'll be back after dinner. I'm having steak tonight."

David leaned his head back as she left. He could scarcely breathe. With any luck, he thought, she would choke on a chunk of meat and die on her silk-covered bed.

# 31

## SUNDAY, MAY 22, 8:30 P.M.

AFTER MAKING HER fourth nervous circuit of the house and grounds, Kate finally wound up at the bar in the main room with Mel and Bryan. Bryan's gaze immediately sought hers, but Kate refused to look at him. Mel looked at nothing but the bottom of her glass. As promised, Mel's bags were sitting by the front door. A wood-handled knife of some kind protruded from her jeans pocket.

Kate seated herself and declined when Bryan offered her a drink. She didn't want anything from him.

"You're being childish, Kate," said Bryan.

"Why shouldn't I be?" she responded. "That's the way I'm treated." She looked at Mel. "What happened to your knife? Did the police take it?"

Mel patted her pocket. "They took it. But Denny gave me one that he made. It's sort of a miniature switchblade, with a little button and everything."

"Good with his hands, isn't he?" Bryan commented.

"He certainly is," said Mel, and as her cheeks began to flush she picked up her glass and tossed back another shot of whiskey. She looked at Kate and Bryan. "I guess the rumors are true. I heard you two were feuding, but I couldn't believe it. Take my mind off my mind and give me a little hint here. What's the problem?"

"It's none of your business," snapped Kate.

Mel blinked in surprise. "Whoa."

Bryan sat up. "Mel, why don't you call down to the stable and see if Denny's had any luck with Grant?"

"Here," said a voice from the foyer, and the three at the bar turned to see a dripping Denny approach. He took off his hat and said, "Grant won't change his mind. He won't fly in a storm."

"So we're stuck here until morning for sure," Mel said sullenly.

"Looks like it." Denny wiped his wet forehead. "I'm sorry, Mel. I'd take you into town, but there's nowhere to stay in Marwell."

Kate saw Mel's hand fall to the knife in her pocket. "That's all right, Denny. Thanks for talking to Grant for us."

Denny seemed to be waiting for something. Finally, he caught Mel's arm and took her aside. Kate saw Mel immediately begin to shake her head, then the shaking slowed and stopped as Denny spoke to her. Soon Mel's brows lifted. She said, "You do?" loud enough for everyone to hear, and Denny nodded.

Mel exhaled and turned to face Kate and Bryan. "You two are on your own. Denny has a twelve-gauge shotgun in his room. I'll see you in the morning."

Kate and Bryan looked at each other as Denny put his arm around Mel's shoulders and led her away.

"She's such an extremist," Bryan said as the front door closed. "I hope she knows what she's doing with him."

"If she doesn't, will you run Denny off?" Kate asked.

"That's enough," Bryan said in a level voice. "I've told you my reasons for doing what I did. You can see I was right, can't you?"

"No. I can't."

"David is gone, isn't he?" Bryan said in exasperation. "If he cared for you he would have stayed, Kate. He would have stayed and worked it out somehow."

"He does care for me," Kate said firmly. "I know he does. And I'm going to find him."

"How? And what are you going to do once you find him? David doesn't like to be cornered, particularly by women."

Kate looked away. "I haven't decided what I'm going to do yet. I just know I have to find him."

Bryan stared at her. "Why him? Will you tell me that much? Why David?"

The question was simple, but Kate sensed that her answer was important to Bryan. Important in relation to how he regarded his brother.

"It's difficult to define," she told him. "In the beginning, I found his aloofness intriguing."

"That's not aloofness," Bryan said bitterly. "It's contempt for the human race."

"Whatever it is," said Kate, "it drew me to him. The more I came to know him, the more I realized how caring he could be without appearing to care. Then one day I caught him watching me on tape. He's in love with me already and won't admit it to himself."

Bryan was staring at her. "What makes you so sure?"

"I don't know. But I am."

"And you love him?"

Kate's eyes were dark and very blue as she looked at Bryan. "I do."

"What about sex, Kate?"

"What about it?"

"Do you think you can handle it?"

"With David I can."

"Are you sure of that, too?"

"I want him," she said simply.

Bryan shook his head. "It'll never work, Kate. David will expose you to a side of life you never knew existed. He'll drag you through human slime until you're just as hard and cynical as he is, and if you don't want to go with him, he'll leave you behind. He's addicted to the exploration of human madness."

Kate said nothing, only looked at the glasses above the bar.

Bryan sighed and reached over to refill his glass. "I never knew you were so stubborn. Where is this aggression coming from, Kate?"

"From my feelings for David," she answered. "I'm not going to lose him."

"Fine. But what if you're wrong about his feelings for you? Have you thought about that? What if he doesn't, or can't, love you?"

"I'm not wrong," Kate said.

Bryan took a long drink. "Ten years and I feel like I don't even know you. Why didn't I see this coming?"

"I'm not your patient anymore," Kate told him. "I've been out in the world for some time now."

"And obviously learning your lessons well. You used to have a certain amount of affection for me. What happened to that?"

"It's still there," Kate admitted. "But now it's different."

"Different how?"

Kate lifted a shoulder. "I still respect and admire you, but I have a problem with the constant touching and the way you're always trying to protect me. And I don't like the way you treat David. You remind me of a big schoolyard bully who likes to pinch girls and beat up boys who don't agree with him. A lecherous, egotistic bully."

Bryan looked at her in consternation. Then he suddenly began to chuckle. "You know, Frieda says the same thing."

"Do you miss her?" asked Kate.

"A little. When you've been married as long as we have you begin to look forward to the time apart just so you'll be happy to see each other again." Bryan gave her a sidelong glance. "That's the way it works outside of fairy tales."

"Meaning?" Kate inquired.

"Meaning don't get your hopes up where my brother is concerned. Remember how long it took me to find him. If he doesn't want to be found, he won't. And if you do happen to find him, don't be disappointed if he turns to stone on you. David has never believed in happily-ever-after, or people fated to be together. He might even laugh in your face."

Kate got off her stool and merely looked at him.

"Right," said Bryan. He looked at his watch. "Are you going up?"

"I need to pack my things. How was Dr. Guerin when you saw him?"

"Still weak, but I think he'll be all right. Jay was with him. Some of the patients have been calling home. They don't know what's going on and they're uneasy. A few of them are talking about leaving."

"They should," Kate told him. "Dr. Guerin can't help them anymore."

Bryan looked at her. "What makes you say that?"

Kate didn't know. She wasn't sure. All she knew was that something in Guerin's eyes had died, as if he had given up a battle and surrendered himself to the enemy.

"I'm not sure he can," she said.

"Maybe you're right." Bryan got up from his stool. "I'll come up with you. I have some packing to do myself."

Once in the elevator, he laughed. "You know, I just realized something. I'm a better doctor than Russell Guerin ever was. He got the fame because he had the money to fund his own research. And it wasn't even his money. Here I am, begging to co-author a paper with him, when most of the valuable work being done is mine. The irony stinks, doesn't it?"

Kate eyed his broad grin, and on impulse she gave him a hug. "I think you're the best doctor in the world."

"You're biased," Bryan said. Then he stepped back. "About David . . . I hope you find him, Kate. I really do."

Kate smiled at him as the elevator came to a halt.

"Goodnight, Bryan."

He smiled. "Goodnight, Kate."

She went directly to her room and packed her things in a flurry of activity. Then she went to David's room and sat down on the bed. After a while she clutched his pillow to her and swung her legs up to lie down. She would find him. She knew that like she knew her own name. He still felt close. His smell was on the pillow and the room was still imbued with his presence. Not to mention that of Frank.

Kate dozed and awakened to the sounds of someone knocking on her door across the hall.

"Kate?" a voice called. "It's me, Jay. I want to talk to you before you go."

She held her breath and lay silent. She heard a door open and knew he had gone into her room. The knowledge made her angry. Who did he think he was?

There was the sound of something heavy being moved, a pause, and then the same sound again. After a moment she heard him shut the door and enter the hall.

Before she could act, he opened the door to David's room and flicked on the light. His dark brows met above his nose when he spied her on the bed.

"What are you doing in here?" he asked.

"Dozing," she answered. "What are you doing with that?" She pointed to the lacy black nightgown in his hand.

"This?" He smiled. "I wanted to have something to remember you by." He approached the bed. "Are you angry?"

Kate didn't know what she was. She didn't think it was fear she felt, but it was uncomfortably close. She sat up on the bed. "Where did you find it? I thought I'd lost it in the wash."

Jay ignored her and came to sit on the bed. "I want to talk to you again, Kate. I know we haven't been able to spend much time together, but it must be obvious that I'm very attracted to you. I have some things to work out, but once I do would it be all right if I came to see you in Kansas City?"

Kate couldn't answer; she didn't know what to say. If he had done the things Mel suspected him of, it was best not to upset him.

He viewed her hesitation with immediate mistrust. "Have you been listening to Mel Kierkes? Do you believe her?"

Instinct made Kate feign ignorance. "I'm not sure I know what you're talking about. What do you mean?"

Jay seemed to relax. "Nothing, I guess. I just heard she caused a lot of problems while I was gone. I understand she did have a serious head injury."

"Yes," said Kate. "Mel really hasn't been herself lately."

"I know how that goes." Jay leaned back on his hands. "The isolation here can really get to you sometimes."

Kate looked at his arms and saw a cut on one wrist. He saw her looking and said, "In case you haven't already guessed, I am a hemophiliac like my grandfather. But it won't interfere with a relationship. At least it doesn't have to. Everything else I'll explain to you later. For now I just need to know if I can come and see you."

The hint of desperation in his tone unnerved Kate. She tried to smile and make her voice convincing. "I think that would be nice. I could show you around."

Jay smiled. "Great. That's great."

It took her by surprise when he suddenly leaned forward and kissed her. She forced herself to pull away slowly.

"I'm not very good with men, Jay."

He smiled again. "That's okay. Don't worry about it." He looked around himself then. "You never told me why you were in here."

Kate looked at the door. "Mel wanted to sleep in my room tonight. She says she has bad dreams in her bedroom."

"Little wonder," Jay said with a snort, and he suddenly seemed angry again. He left the mattress and moved to the door. "I'll see you at breakfast in the morning."

Kate nodded. When he was gone she breathed out a pent-up

breath and used the sheet to dab at the sudden line of perspiration that had collected at her hairline.

With a long shudder she gathered the pillow to her and tried to close her eyes. Only one thought comforted her: By the time Jay came to the city she would be with David.

# 32

## Sunday, May 22, 9:00 p.m.

Mel paced and Denny watched her. Denny's room was only nine by twelve or so, so she didn't have much walking space. Each time she passed the bed, Denny's wagging foot would brush her thigh. She could hear other sounds in the ranch house: stomping, clomping boots, and the sounds of male voices. No one but Denny knew Mel was there.

She looked at his room and wondered why the walls were free of the usual young male decoration. No pin-ups, no posters, nothing but a calendar and a clock. There were no strewn clothes, socks, or underwear. The bed was made to army perfection, and the dresser top was neat and orderly.

"What are you?" she asked. "Some kind of prairie geek? You're not normal."

Denny laughed and continued to wag his foot.

"Seriously," said Mel. "What do you do besides take care of horses?"

"Ride them," Denny answered. "Open the top drawer of that dresser."

Mel did. Inside were dozens of ribbons and plaques for everything from calf roping to barrel riding.

"Why aren't these on the wall?" she asked.

Denny shrugged. "It's enough to know I have them. I don't need to display them."

"Dare I ask what you're going to major in at school?" Mel asked. "It wouldn't be equine medicine, would it?"

He laughed again.

Mel made a face at him and closed the drawer. She went to the closet and made another face when she opened it and saw more evidence of compulsive neatness. "Denny, you must know this isn't normal. Guys your age—guys any age, for that matter—are not this fastidious."

Denny left the bed and came to stand behind her. He reached past her and stuck an arm between the shirts on hangers to drag a rope from a hook in the back of the closet. "I guess I'm going to have to entertain you with a few rope tricks to keep you from snooping. Any minute now you're going to find my magazines and my inflatable girlfriend."

Mel grinned. "Now *that* I can handle. I'm used to that stuff. It's the Wally-and-the-Beav business that makes me uncomfortable."

Denny looked up from his rope. "You know Wally?"

"No, I—never mind. Where do you want me?"

"On the bed. I need some room."

Mel plopped onto the bed and turned over on her stomach to watch him. He uncoiled the rope and looked up with a grin. "There's not enough room in here to show you anything really impressive, but I can—"

"Denny," Mel said suddenly. She was staring at the rope and ideas were clicking. "Do you love adventure?"

He frowned at her. "It depends. What kind?"

"The kind where we'll need a good rope and a darn good flashlight."

"No," he said, reading her mind. "You're not going. It's wet and it's dangerous."

"I have to," Mel said. "For my own peace of mind."

"The cave will probably be flooded, Mel. And if the troopers didn't find anything, we won't either."

Mel glanced at the shotgun in the corner by the door. "You don't have to go. I only want to know what he did with them, Denny. I have to see for myself. Maybe there'll be something on the ledge. A hair, a bit of cowhide, anything to prove I wasn't hallucinating."

"No," Denny repeated.

"I'll go with or without you," Mel told him. "You can't keep me here against my will."

"Yes," he said, "I can."

Mel looked at him and knew he meant it. "Please, Denny. This is important to me. I have to know. If I don't go now, I'll spend the rest of my life wondering how he did it. Can you understand that?"

Denny dropped his shoulders and looked at the ceiling. "Why do I have the feeling I'm going to be out of a job before this night is over?"

A guilty twinge gave Mel pause. "How much more money do you need for tuition?"

"I've got tuition," Denny told her. "I'm still shy on living expenses and transportation."

"You don't have to come with me," Mel repeated.

"I'm not letting you go by yourself."

"I don't want you to lose your job, Denny."

He turned his back on her. "Stay here while I go and find you some rain gear. And we're going to need a longer rope. I've got a good flashlight in the stable."

"Is there a car we can take?" Mel asked.

Denny paused at the door. "I'll see if I can borrow Grant's pickup."

"Wait," said Mel. "Are you going to tell him what you're borrowing it for?"

Denny's look was patient. "Don't move until I get back."

Mel didn't. She remained on the bed and found herself wondering if she really was crazy for wanting to go back into that godforsaken hole. One night of complete terror was enough for any homegrown Kansas girl, wasn't it? Why put herself through it again?

Because she had made a promise to Melanie Martin.

To her corpse, rather.

A promise was a promise, and Mel had promised to get the person who put all those horrible, puckered holes in Melanie's back. And in the cows. And the little coyote.

Flashes of those long hours in the cave caused Mel's stomach to begin quivering.

That's good, she told herself. Remember it all now so it won't jump you while you're down there. Because it will. If you're not prepared, the nightmare is going to hop on your back and ride you around until you start screaming.

She nearly screamed when Denny dropped a huge black rain slicker on the bed next to her. She hadn't heard him come in.

"Put it on and let's go," he said.

Mel got up and picked up the slicker. The sleeves were six inches too long, so she started rolling. "Did you get the keys from Grant?"

"Yes." Denny shrugged into his own slicker and put his rope back in the closet.

"What did you tell him?"

"That I was going into Marwell to see a girl."

Mel paused. "Who?"

Denny smiled at her. "Are you ready? We'll go out the back door. The guys are watching a porn video in the front room."

"Bet you'd be in there with them if I wasn't here," Mel said to him.

"Not if I could help it. It's one of Jay's discards. Besides, I prefer the act to the sight. Come on."

Mel stood back as he opened the door. "You kill me, Denny. Honestly. How did you get so smart? You always know just exactly what to say, don't you?"

"Shut up," he said.

Mel opened her mouth and then snapped it shut again as he

gave her arm a sharp tug. Denny pulled her down the hall after him and paused only a moment in the doorway to the front room. Mel glanced in, trying to see the television, and was quickly shoved away.

"I'll see you later, Grant," said Denny.

There was a low grunt in reply. Mel thought the video must be a good one to garner such attention. Once outside, she pulled away from Denny. "You don't have to be so pushy. And where's the shotgun? You forgot it, didn't you?"

"We won't need it," Denny told her.

"Says who?"

"Me." He turned his face to the sky. Only a few soft, drizzly drops were falling now. "One thing in our favor."

Mel looked around. "Where's the truck?"

"At the side of the house. We don't have a garage out here."

"Lead on," said Mel.

Denny led. He put her in the passenger side of an old GMC, then he ran to the stable and came back with a large flashlight and a thick coil of rope around one shoulder. Once behind the wheel of the truck, he turned to her.

"I wouldn't do this for just anyone, you know."

"I know," Mel said.


The rain ceased altogether as they reached the slope. Mel got out of the truck and took a deep breath. The darkness was complete. There were no stars to light the sky, no moon to guide even one footstep. Denny came to stand beside her.

"Can't we leave the headlights on?" she asked.

"No." He flicked the switch on the flashlight and handed it to her. "I'm not going to run down his battery."

Mel glanced at him. "That's thoughtful of you, considering that we're both virtually blind out here."

He ignored her. "Shine the light on the bumper so I can see what I'm doing. Are we close enough?"

"I think so." Mel tipped the light down. "See, there's the rope the cops used."

"They cut it?" Denny said in surprise. "Good rope doesn't come cheap."

"It does if your name is Guerin." Mel watched him knot his own rope around the bumper and found herself looking at his hands. Strong, sure, with a light touch. Good with ropes, horses . . . and women.

Mel, you're a slut, she thought.

"Okay." Denny straightened and spat on his palms. "I'll go down first to check out the water level. You light my way from the top, Mel, all right?"

She nodded and felt suddenly selfish for dragging him out here. If anything happened to him she would never forgive herself. She followed him to the cave entrance and felt her nerves begin to jangle as he dropped the length of rope into the hole. "Denny . . ."

"What?"

"Don't hurt yourself or anything."

His smile was crooked. "Just shine the light, Mel. And whatever you do, don't drop it. You said there was a ledge just below the entrance, right?"

"Right. It's a bit of a drop."

"Okay. Stay right there and listen for me."

Before Mel could say she would, Denny gripped the rope with both hands and dropped down into the hole. Mel quickly stepped forward and positioned the light down. She could see the top of his head, but no more. She heard no splash.

"Denny?" she called.

"I'm on the ledge," he shouted to her. "The water is almost even with it."

His voice sounded funny. Almost as if he . . . Then Mel remembered the dead coyotes. He was probably gagging from the smell. Her own nostrils pinched in sympathy.

"I don't think you should come down here," he called up to her.

Mel filled her lungs with clean air. "I don't want to," she mumbled. Louder, she said, "I'm coming down, Denny. Should I drop the light to you?"

"No," he said immediately. "I might not catch it. Just put it in the pocket of your slicker, beam up. The pockets are deep enough."

Mel did as he said. "Okay. I'm ready. Here I come."

"The walls are slick," Denny cautioned.

"No kidding," Mel said as she attempted to walk her way down. Upper body strength was not her greatest asset. The rope tried to chew its way through the skin of her palms as she struggled with the hand-over-hand method.

Finally she felt Denny's hands on her hips. Then she was standing on solid ground again. She kicked away the loose coils of rope at her feet and took the flashlight from her slicker pocket to shine it around them. She was amazed that he had heard her from above; the fast-moving water seemed deafening to her. When her light found the sunken corpse of a coyote she immediately jerked it away again.

"Can you . . . do something with them?" she asked.

"Like what?"

"I don't know. I was just asking."

"I'd rather not put them in the water," he said. "All the lead in them might hurt the cow ponds, I don't know. Mel, I don't know how you managed to stay down here as long as you did."

"I didn't have a choice," she muttered.

Denny's hand touched her arm. "We have to hurry. If it rains any more we'll be in trouble. Let me have the light."

Mel gave it to him and reached out to find his waist. She took a handful of his wet slicker and held on as he turned and began to examine the floor of the ledge. In the next moment she wished she hadn't grabbed hold of him, because when he slipped on the maggot-slick corpse of a coyote, his pinwheeling arm knocked her off the ledge and into the rushing water. Mel heard him shout, and then her ears filled with liquid and became blocked.

The water swept her along and slammed her into a jagged crevice where rock and water met. Her fingers clawed to gain a hold. The water kept going, but the rock stopped just above her. If she let go, she would be sucked under that overhang and taken wherever the water went. She struggled to pull her legs out, but the pressure was too great. It was all Mel could do to hang on. She thought she screamed Denny's name, but the water in her mouth made it unlikely. She coughed and tried again, but he was already there. Mel could hear him shouting at her.

"My boot! Grab it! It's right behind you!"

Mel couldn't see anything. She twisted her head and saw the beam of light just to her left. The flashlight was on the ledge in front of Denny. Around his wrists was the rope. Only his arms and shoulders were on the ledge, the rest of him was in the water. The muscles in his illuminated arm were taut.

"Take it!" he shouted.

I can't, thought Mel frantically. What if I miss? I can't see it. How am I supposed to grab it if I can't see the damned thing?

In the same moment Denny kicked her in the back of the head, Mel felt something touch her foot. Something slick, with a firmness that was somewhere in between rock and water. When the something seemed to tug, instinct and adrenaline made Mel kick away and twist around. She caught the hem of Denny's jeans and felt a bone in her little finger snap as she scrabbled for a hold on his boot. When the boot threatened to come off she went back to his jeans and literally pulled herself up his leg.

Denny was already pulling. Mel hugged his shin and swallowed water as he dragged them to the ledge. He kept pulling until she was completely out of the water. Then he collapsed on the ledge floor. Mel turned over on her side and began coughing. For long minutes they lay there, chests heaving, limbs trembling. Finally, Denny sat up and picked up the flash to shine it on her. "Are you all right?"

Mel nodded and pushed the light from her face. "I'm okay. I broke a finger, is all. It bent over backwards when I grabbed your boot. What about you?"

"I'll live. Are you sure you're okay? You hit that rock pretty hard." He moved the light slowly down her body.

When he came to her feet, he paused. Mel looked down and saw what he was looking at. She swallowed. A thick strand of brown hair was wrapped around her shoe. Mel closed her eyes before the milky patch of scalp dangling from her toe could form an image on her eyelids.

"Did you feel anything?" Denny asked quietly.

"Yes," Mel breathed. "Oh, I'm going to be sick."

Denny held her while she heaved. When she was finished he silently removed her shoe and unwound the hairs. He put them in his pocket and gave the shoe back to her.

"He probably put her in the water and weighted her down with something," Denny mused aloud. "Then, when the rain came and flooded the place, the pressure was too much for the weight. She got washed under there and became hung up on something."

"Or he put her there to begin with," Mel mumbled. "He could have shoved all of them under there, so if they dragged the water here they wouldn't find anything."

Denny nodded. "You're right. Are you ready to get the hell out of here?"

"Yes. I just don't know what to do once we're out. The sheriff will laugh and lock the door when he sees me coming."

"No, he won't," said Denny. "Because I'll be right there behind you."

Mel looked at him. "What about your job?"

"I can always get another one." He put the light on his face to show her his wink. "In Kansas City."

Mel squeezed his arm and felt around for the rope. "I don't know if I'm up to climbing out. My arms and my finger are doing some serious aching."

"I know what you mean." Denny guided her to stand just below the entrance. "Let me go first. When I get up, I'll pull you out. Here, take the light."

Thank God for big, strong farm boys, Mel thought as she

watched him ascend. Denny was tired, but his hands were still confident as he pulled himself up and out. Denny, she suddenly realized, was the type of person who would never falter. He was quick-thinking and clearheaded in a crisis, and he hadn't blinked an eyelash at the corpse business. He was really something, Mel thought.

"Ready?" he called down after several minutes.

Poor thing had to rest first, Mel told herself.

"I'm on my way." She put the flashlight in her pocket and grabbed the rope to begin to pull herself up. With his help, it took less than sixty seconds to reach the cave entrance. When the upper part of her torso was out, he dropped the rope and reached down to lift her the rest of the way.

"Thanks," she said. "That was much easier."

"I'm sure."

The voice clued her in right away. Without warning, Mel took the flashlight from her pocket and swung it as hard as she could. In the brief instant before it connected with his jaw, she saw Jay Guerin's cold black eyes. He fell back and away from her, giving her time to find Denny. Denny was a few feet away, lying face-down on the ground. When Mel swung the light back to Jay she saw a pistol in his hand. On the end was a silencer.

Mel screamed and rushed over to kick his wrist as he was sitting up. The pistol spun into the dark and Jay grunted in pain even as his other hand caught her by the heel and brought her to the ground. Before she could scramble away, his fist found her face.

Her head snapped back so hard Mel heard her spine give a disbelieving pop of protest.

Jay sat on her chest and delivered a furious succession of blows to her face and neck. With every breath he demanded to know why she was trying to ruin his life.

Mel felt the pain, heard the splat and crunch of each blow, and for a brief instant she thought she was back on a living-room rug in a bleary little house in KC. Her first husband was sitting on top of her and the fists just kept coming, over and over again.

But now the fists were claws around her throat.

"Know what I'm going to do?" Jay snarled as he began to squeeze. "I'm going to find the pistol, the one you stole from my collection in your paranoid state, and put it in your hand. Denny brought you out here and attacked you. You shot him. But not before he crushed your windpipe. That will explain everything, won't it?"

A terrible pressure was building inside Mel's head. She gave up the effort to pry away the hands at her neck and went in search of Denny's knife. When the tiny button clicked, she actually smiled at Jay.

Then she gave him the blade.

Jay's back arched and his fists flew up in the air as he cried out. Mel snatched the blade out and slid from beneath him. Holding the knife in front of her, she panted, "Come on. You want some more? I'll give it to you. I'll give you every inch, you sick bastard."

In the weak beam of the flashlight on the ground, Mel saw him on his knees, clutching at his side. The blood oozed black over his fingers.

Mel waited, breathless, while Jay decided on a course of action. When he staggered to his feet, she backed up. For a frightening moment, he lunged toward her; then he stumbled back and made his way to Grant's pickup.

"No!" Mel screamed, as his intentions dawned on her. "Don't take the truck!"

She leapt to her feet and ran toward the pickup. Jay started the engine, threw the truck into gear and kicked up dust as he floored the accelerator. Mel had to jump out of the way to keep from being hit. She rolled to a sitting position and shrieked in frustration as Jay sped off down the slope. Still making noises, Mel moved to collect the flashlight. Then she ran to where Denny lay. She turned him over slowly and opened his slicker. A large red stain covered his midsection.

"No," Mel moaned. "No, Denny, no. . . ."

Instinctively, she felt for a pulse. It was weak, but it was there.

Mel stood up, slipped out of her slicker and tore off her blouse. Denny's eyes opened when she pressed the fabric against the wound.

"Hurts," he whispered to her.

"I know," she choked. "I'm so sorry I got you into this. Please don't . . . Jay took the truck and . . . Denny, I don't know what to do."

"Whistle," he murmured.

"What?"

Denny's mouth twisted painfully. "How did . . . Jay get here?"

Mel's head lifted. She aimed the light in every direction. "I don't know. I don't see anything."

"Whistle," Denny repeated.

"You mean *whistle*?" Mel whistled. "Like that?"

"Louder."

"Okay." Mel whistled again, louder, and she wasn't surprised when Jay's tall palomino trotted up to them a second later. Denny had known.

Mel rushed to the horse and grabbed the reins to swing up in the saddle. "Keep applying pressure," she called to Denny. "I'll bring help as soon as I can."

Denny's eyes were already closing again. Mel swallowed a lump in her throat and kicked the horse hard.

The night seemed blacker than ever.

# 33

## SUNDAY, MAY 22, 10:30 P.M.

DAVID OPENED HIS eyes and was startled to find that he had actually slept. He decided he must have dozed off during Augusta's windy lecture on the genetic superiority of females. The fact that she was backed up by certain scientific evidence and the example of nearly the entire animal kingdom hadn't made her oration any more interesting. The Twinkie-punctuated ramblings of insane, genetically superior females had never held much appeal for David.

Particularly when he considered the fact that Augusta's genes were obviously less than superior. If the tape wasn't fastened to his mouth, he might have reminded her of this. As it was, his inability to contribute to the conversation had induced a soporific state just short of death by boredom. David was surprised she hadn't bludgeoned him awake.

His eyes rounded and his surprise became real when he turned his head and saw Jay Guerin sitting in a chair in front of the refrigerator. Jay's face was a pasty white. His right side was bright crimson.

Jay noticed David's stare and gave him a weary smile. "We don't bleed faster, just longer. I don't think it's fatal, but I did need to transfuse. The blade wasn't very big—I don't know where she got it—but it hurt like hell when it went in. Mel is a vicious little bitch, isn't she? For some reason she's out to get me."

David let his eyes do the talking. *I wonder why.*

"No." Jay shook his head. "I've never done anything to her. I don't know why she hates me so much. I can't stand it when women hate me for no reason. She doesn't even know me."

No past tense. That meant Mel was still among the living. David looked at the connecting door and then back to Jay again, questioning.

"Mother?" said Jay. "No, she doesn't know I'm here. She was taking one of her catnaps when I came in. She does that a half-dozen times a day. But yes, she'll be upset when she sees me." He paused to take a deep breath, and David saw pain ripple across his features as he let it out again. On the floor beneath the chair was a spattering of red. Jay was still dripping.

His voice became almost wistful. "Mother's anger is very different from mine. She can control herself and make every word and movement count. I can't do that. My anger controls me. Sometimes I think I'm one of my father's multiples. It's like another person takes over when I'm angry. Do you ever feel like that?"

David shook his head.

Jay ignored him. "It's like a fugue, but it's not a fugue because on a certain level I'm aware of what I'm doing. I just can't stop it. A part of me wants to stop, but that part isn't strong enough. Do you understand?"

David nodded.

Jay ignored him. "It doesn't take much to set me off, but it's definitely worse when I begin to feel trapped. Like one of those little wooden tops I used to play with, the kind you wrap the string around and then turn it loose with a flick of your wrist. That's what it's like when I become angry. I'm all bound up and wound up, and then I spin out of control. When I stop, I can't believe how fast or how far I went. Do you know what I mean?"

David didn't bother.

Jay didn't notice. "It would have been simple if Mel had been in Kate's room, like she said. But she wasn't. Mel was with Denny. When Grant told me Denny had borrowed his truck, I knew where they went. And I became angry.

"But you know something? Nothing will happen to me. Mother will see to that. The monster she gave birth to is still her little monster." Jay laughed, a dry, crackling sound, like the sound of his mother wadding up a bag of Doritos. "Oh, God, I really am losing it. I've been losing it for a long time, but I keep kidding myself. Mother must see that I am, Raleigh. She has to see."

David's pulse jumped as Jay suddenly lurched to his feet and moved unsteadily toward the wheelchair. His right hand looked sticky with blood. The rag he held against his side would never pass for white again.

"You are so lucky," Jay mumbled as he came to lean against the wheelchair. "So goddamned lucky and you don't even know it."

At the moment, David disagreed. His aching muscles tensed as Jay reached down with his left hand and tugged at the band of David's boxer shorts. He said, "You know what that is?"

David was perfectly still.

"It's something you take for granted," Jay said, his eyes growing red. "I can't. I lack the most basic part of the male anatomy, the part that makes you a man. You've never known this kind of pain, David Raleigh. You don't sit down to pee, and you've never squirmed at the idea of someone seeing you naked. You haven't cried because you know you'll never have a normal relationship with a woman. I won't ever know what it feels like to be *inside* a woman. That's why penetration is so important to me. I can't push myself inside a woman, but I can pierce flesh and know the same excitement as you. I can penetrate with death . . . metal death . . . and feel the same mindless pleasure. That's all it is, isn't it? Penetration of the flesh. Life and death."

David had to moisten his stare with a blink. In his mind, he was already forming the first paragraph of his story on Jay. When he realized what he was doing, he felt his funnybone bend and take a dip toward mild hysteria.

A story? Oh, no, son, I don't think so. You're not getting out of here, remember? Jay can do whatever he wants, tell you whatever he likes, because he knows you're not going anywhere. Your name might as well be Father Confessor right now.

Jay was still staring at David's penis. "Ted didn't know what to do with me. He thought a hobby, a new interest of some kind, would divert my attention from my abnormalities. I remember many a night when my grandfather would sit up with me and take my mind off the pain of a bleeding joint by telling me the history of a certain gun. He had no idea what he was doing. When he glorified the masculinity of guns, he couldn't realize what that meant to me. Even as a boy, I knew my life would never be normal. It was in the sympathetic eyes of the nurses who came to care for me, and it was in Ted's eyes. The hemophilia was nothing—it could be dealt with. My other problem was a different story, and I hated the pity I was subjected to."

Jay's eyes shifted then and he looked at David with bleak humor. "Today when a child is born with my problem there's a debate on whether to perform surgery and make the child into a girl. Can you imagine that?"

David couldn't. But he was beginning to understand Jay Guerin's madness.

Jay was rubbing his eyes. "All I want is for Mother to help me. She owes me that much. I know why I am the way I am, but I don't know how to stop it. I want to, Raleigh. I do. I want someone like Kate. Something happened to me the first time I saw her. It's hard to keep away from her, but I know I have to. At least until Mother helps me. She told Ted she would. She promised him the day she found him dying out there. I knew I had to give her some time to get over his death, but she's put me off long enough."

He looked up at a sound from Augusta's bedroom. He left David and walked back to the refrigerator, where he removed something and put it inside his shirt. From a box on the counter he removed a plastic-wrapped syringe. When he came back to David, his breathing was heavy.

"Don't say anything to her yet. I've got to find some place to hide for a while. From everyone."

Try under your mother's bed, David silently told him. It worked for me.

Jay unlocked the door leading to the hall. Then he paused and glanced back at David. "I don't dislike you, Raleigh. I don't know why she has you here, but I'm sorry she's doing this to you. In a house full of doctors, I think you're the only one here who might understand me."

David watched him leave. As the door closed he breathed in and wondered what that said about him.

He decided he didn't want to know.

Within minutes, Augusta opened the connecting door and lumbered into the room. She moved automatically toward the refrigerator and then stopped. A squeal emerged from either her nose or her mouth. She came to David and dug her nails into his arm. "Where did all this blood come from? Has Jay been in here?"

David blinked and feigned incomprehension.

Augusta pointed. "It's all over the floor in front of the refrigerator. What's happened to him? Has he been injured?"

The tape made it difficult to answer. David only looked at her.

Augusta slapped him and her eyes seemed to sink even farther into her fleshy face.

"You think it's funny, do you? My son is hurt and bleeding and you think it's funny? I'll show you funny. Oh, yes. I'll share my favorite form of entertainment and show you something really funny."

She moved behind his chair and wheeled him to the connecting door. She was still mumbling as she opened the door and pushed him into her bedroom. She turned the chair until David was facing the screen on the wall.

He held his breath as he watched her climb onto the bed and

pick up a slender microphone beside the control panel. Her normally dull eyes were shining as she flicked the first switch. "You're going to love this, David."

David looked at the screen and sucked in air through his broken nose when he saw Kate. She was in his room, on his bed. There was a light on somewhere, the bathroom, he guessed, because he could see her face pressed deep into his pillow, with the tiniest hint of a smile on her lips. She looked like a slumbering nymph made of silver, gold, and ivory. He wished he was there on the sheets with her.

Augusta flicked another switch. "It's dream time, Kate. By my calculations, you've just started another REM episode. Let's see if a few suggestions can change your dream scenario." To David, Augusta whispered, "This is nothing new, you know. I studied this years ago. Watch now, and learn something."

David made a noise against the tape.

Augusta snickered at him. "Kate? You're ready now. You're going in. You're going to a place you know very well. It's your sister's barn, Kate. Remember your sister's dark, musty old barn? That's where you are right now, and you can't see very well, but you can smell the hay and the wood and the heavy odor of animals."

Unbelievably, David saw Kate's eyes begin to shift beneath her lids. His heart began to pound against the ropes that bound his chest.


At certain moments in his life, David Raleigh had allowed himself to wonder at his seeming inability to care deeply for others. When he arrived home from his tour to find his parents dead and his past in ashes, it had been easier to hide from his brother than to show him the emotionless stranger who visited those fresh graves. David loved his parents, but he felt it was pointless to mourn for them. Bryan, the doctor, would have thought something was wrong with him. David would have agreed.

There were times when he wondered if something might have

been left out of him, some mystical component integral to the emotional makeup of human beings. The something that made them sob in despair, laugh with pure joy, and love and hate enough to kill. David wondered if his fascination with human motivation sprang from this void in himself. If by exposing himself to human emotion at its most powerful and intense levels, he was in some way compensating for his own lack of feelings. He had never known what novelists called "raw" passion, had never deeply hated, loved, or experienced anything but the most superficial emotions.

But he understood them. He could view them with the unbiased eye and categorize them as they came into being. That was how it went with his writing. That was how it was with Bryan. That was how it had been with Julia.

It was different with Augusta. The antipathy he experienced upon meeting her was magnified a thousandfold as he listened to her coo and murmur into her microphone. Where before he had only thought about leaping up and strangling her, he knew if it were not for the ropes binding him now he would do it. His fingers itched to bury themselves in the folds of her throat. The sweat that seeped out of his pores was poisoned with bloodlust. He wanted to kill this woman. He wanted to bathe himself in her blood and spit on her corpse.

Augusta was watching him. "Not having fun yet? Just wait." She returned her attention to the screen. "Only a few more stalls in the barn to explore, Kate. They're waiting for you. You can see the light. The smell is growing stronger now. The smell of animals. You can hear them moving about."

On the screen, Kate's eye movements quickened.

"You're moving toward the last stall, Kate. You have to, because he is waiting for you there, and he has a surprise for you. You're walking toward that light, walking, and then you see him. He's smiling at you. He's so glad to see you. Your sister's husband is always glad to see you."

Kate began to quiver. A frown appeared between her brows. David felt the flesh on his lips begin to tear as he strained at the tape on his mouth. He bucked against the wheelchair and heard Augusta chuckle at his rage.

"Your sister's husband has a friend with him, Kate, a big black dog, and you know what's going to happen. You know it and you dread it. You'd do almost anything to escape what he's going to do to you. You want to die. You want to curl up in a ball and just die rather than go through this again. The first chance you get, you're going to run away from him. You're going to run for the nearest window and break through, Kate. It's the only way to escape this nightmare you're having. You can already hear the glass breaking. It's the sound of freedom, the freedom you'll know once you're away from those awful, ugly hands, and that dog's hot, hot breath. The window, Kate. Run for the window and break through. It's the only way to escape."

David watched helplessly as Kate moaned and pushed feebly away from the pillow. Her chest was rising and falling in rapid succession. Her eyes darted wildly behind her lids.

"The window," Augusta murmured. "The window is freedom. He'll never touch you again if you can just reach that window. It's there. You can see it. You have to get up and run to that window. If you don't, you know what's going to happen. The big bad man is going to spread your little legs and—"

Kate shot up from the mattress and fell on the floor in a tangle of bedclothes as she tried to escape. Her mouth was open, her pupils dilated as she looked wildly about the room.

For a window, David guessed.

In the next second Bryan entered the room and his face creased with worry when he saw Kate in a tangle on the floor. Augusta cursed loudly and flicked a switch. David heard his brother's voice.

". . . crazy when I couldn't find you. You're leaving right now. Jay shot Denny and tried to kill Mel. I want you out of here. Come on. I'll help you carry your things downstairs. Are you all right?"

Kate only blinked at him. Bryan pulled her off the floor and pushed her toward the door. His mouth was working again, but David couldn't hear his words over the noise Augusta was making. She was screaming for Jay.

# 34

## MONDAY, MAY 23, 12:00 A.M.

PART OF KATE'S mind was still in her nightmare as she followed Bryan into the elevator. The voice in her mind had been forceful with intent, insistent to the point of command. Kate found herself still battling the urge to run mindlessly away, and the idea of encountering a window made her cringe. This had been like no dream she had ever known. Neither was the voice one she recognized. She hoped. She hoped there were no new voices inside her. No old ghosts come to haunt her again. Please, no, she begged as the elevator descended.

Then she stopped herself. She put a mental foot on the fear and held it down. I'm well, she told herself with the same force the voice had used. *I am well.*

Her flesh prickled as the elevator doors opened.

Bryan noticed and said, "I know it's unbelievable. But Jay might be desperate now, and I want you out of harm's way. The cook has agreed to take you into town and leave you at the hospital with Mel. I'll come as soon as I can. Dr. Guerin and I are going to stay with the patients until the police can arrive and find Jay."

Kate gave her head a small shake in an attempt to clear her mind. "Is Mel all right?"

Bryan's brow furrowed. "According to a fellow named Tim, her face was badly beaten. Other than that, she's apparently all right. It seems at first Grant didn't believe her about Jay, and, well, you know Mel. She dragged him out to his truck and showed him some blood, then she got in and took off without him. Grant borrowed Tim's motorcycle and went after her. Just before I came upstairs, Russell heard from Grant on the citizen's band and learned they were taking Denny to the hospital."

"How do you know Jay is still here?" asked Kate.

"Because all the vehicles and the horses are accounted for," Bryan said grimly. "And because of that."

Kate's gaze followed his pointing finger to the tiled floor. They were following a spotted trail of blood that began at the front door.

"Bryan?" a voice called, and Bryan and Kate turned to see Russell Guerin standing at the entrance to the hall. He seemed to have aged twenty years since Kate had last seen him. His shoulders were stooped, and his legs appeared unstable. There was a pleading in his dark eyes as he beckoned to Bryan.

"Can you come and . . . I can't control them anymore. They're all turning against me. She's gotten to all of them and made them hate me. Would you please come and help?"

Kate and Bryan traded a glance. *She?*

"Please," said Guerin. "Now."

"Go on," Bryan breathed to Kate. "Sandy's car is just outside the kitchen entrance. She said she would be right out. Leave the heavier bags here and I'll bring them when I come."

Kate took a last look at the enfeebled Dr. Guerin and told Bryan to be careful. He nodded absently and pushed her toward the door. Once outside, Kate walked briskly along the side of the house and rounded the damp brick corner to reach the kitchen entrance. She inhaled deeply of the rain-moistened air and tried to purge her mind of the last vestiges of the nightmare she had suffered in David's room. Everything connected with this house was a nightmare. Fear, anger, and pain seemed to be at the core of every brick.

"We should have listened to Mel the first day," Kate murmured aloud as she reached the dimly lighted kitchen entrance.

An old Volvo was the only car in the vicinity, so Kate guessed it belonged to Sandy, the cook. Kate moved to stand beside the car and wait where she could see the kitchen door. A terrible smell hung in the air and she soon realized it came from the row of garbage pails to the right of the small porch. Kate jumped at a sudden noise from the direction of the pails. A cat? she wondered uneasily. Or something bigger?

When she heard more sounds she leaped onto the porch and knocked on the back door. "Sandy, it's Kate Berquist. May I come in and wait inside?"

A rustling noise made her suck in her breath. Then Kate heard something that made her head swivel.

"Sweetheart."

Kate looked around until she saw a large bird sitting on the lid of one of the garbage pails. "Frank?" she whispered.

"Sweetheart," Frank repeated.

The door opened and Sandy peered outside. "Oh, it's you. I'll be right with you, honey. You want to wait in here?"

"No," said Kate abruptly. "I'm fine right here. Take all the time you need."

Sandy nodded and disappeared again, leaving the door open. Kate left the porch and approached the shivering parrot. Had he somehow escaped his cage before David's departure? No, Kate thought. David would never leave his Frank behind. He would have—

Kate stopped and her eyes rounded as the realization struck her. If Frank was still here, then David was still here.

"Frank," Kate said in a low voice. "Where is David?"

"Oprah," Frank mourned.

"David," Kate repeated urgently. "Where is David?"

"Bud," Frank tried.

Kate gritted her teeth in frustration. "We'll have Bud and Oprah when we find David, Frank. Where is David?"

The parrot hopped onto her arm with a flutter of wings. Its claws bit into her flesh.

Frank wasn't going to help her, Kate realized. And she was silly to think he could. He was nothing but a terrified parrot with no Bud, no Oprah, and no David.

Kate shifted the claws on her arm and stepped back to gaze at the house. Lights on the third floor caught her attention and she frowned as the memory of a conversation with David came back to her. She could feel his breath warm and tickling against her ear as he warned her that their conversation was being monitored.

The voice in her dream. If Augusta Guerin could listen, could she perhaps also speak?

"Frank," she said. "Is David in the house? Is he somewhere upstairs?"

The parrot began to squawk in agitation.

It could have meant anything, but Kate wasn't going anywhere until she found out. Carrying Frank with her, she hurried around the house to the front entrance. As quietly as possible, she opened the door and poked her head inside to look around. The main room appeared to be empty. Kate crept to the bar and shook Frank off her arm. Then she opened a beer and poured some in a small glass.

"Stay right here," she softly told him. "I'll come back for you as soon as I can. And try to be quiet."

Frank ruffled his feathers and clicked around on the bar a moment before turning his attention to the beer.

Kate left him and hurried to the stairs. She didn't have much time; any moment now the cook would discover her missing and run to tell Bryan.

When she reached the third floor she looked to her right and suddenly wondered if Jay was hiding in his gun room. It wasn't likely, she decided. That would be the first place to look for him.

Don't let me run into him up here, she silently prayed as she turned left and moved quickly down the hall.

There were so many doors to choose from. As on the second floor, there were three on the left and three on the right. Kate opened the first door on her left and found Jay's bedroom. She knew it was Jay's room from the framed pictures of guns on the walls and the two-foot stack of gun magazines on a low table just inside the door. Above the bed hung a pair of what looked like flintlock rifles. Kate backed out, closed the door, and turned to the first room on her right.

The second she twisted the knob she heard a voice. She paused to listen and finally determined that the sounds came from the next room on the right. Kate eased the door open and held her breath at seeing the contents of the room she entered. It appeared to be a small lab of some kind. As she glanced around she spied a connecting door that was slightly ajar. The voice she heard came from there.

Noiselessly, Kate moved across the room to the door and peered through the opening.

Her breathing stopped. David was in a wheelchair at the foot of a large bed. His face was swollen, purplish, and streaked with brownish stains that caked his neck down to his chest. A patch of white tape covered his mouth.

Beyond him stood a tearful Russell Guerin. Kate couldn't see who he was talking to, but there was only one person it could be.

"I don't know why you're doing this, Augusta," said Guerin. "You have everything. You have—"

"What's wrong, Russell?" a flat voice asked. "Is your little empire crumbling around your ears? How does it feel? How does complete and total failure feel? It's not pleasant, is it?"

"Hurting people," Guerin sobbed. "Why not hurt me? Why did you have to hurt them?"

"It was an experiment, Russell. I wanted to see if I could. Think of the applications. Think of the acclaim I will receive. *Me*, Russell, not you. It's my turn this time, dear. I've made some amazing discoveries here. You simply would not believe the discoveries I have made. And oh, no, I'm not going to tell you what they are. There was a time when I told you everything, I know, but it was all for nothing, wasn't it? Nothing for me, plenty for you. All at my father's expense. Well, it's time to pay, Russell. Time to pay for your neglect of me and my work."

"What neglect?" Guerin shouted at her. "You didn't want me. You haven't wanted me since the day Jay was born. And you sabotaged your own career, Augusta. I had nothing to do with it. You gave up everything when we moved here. And after your father died you had to blame someone, so you blamed me. For the death of your doting Daddy, for the guilt you feel over Jay, for everything!"

Kate expected a similar outburst from the unseen Augusta, but all she heard was a low, sinister laugh.

"An off-the-cuff psychoanalysis, Russell? Or was it an attempt at rationalization? You don't know anything about guilt, dear. Let me tell you what our son, yours and mine, has been up to lately. Remember the gun Natalie allegedly stole from his collection? Let me tell you how she really came across that pistol."

Kate blanched as Augusta went on talking, but her reaction was nothing compared to Russell Guerin's. His hands began to quiver and his lips contorted into a silent gasp of horror. Kate was about to move away from the door to find a weapon of some sort when she saw Guerin clutch his chest suddenly and stagger backward. His features stiffened with pain and he slowly crumpled to the floor. The unseen Augusta began to laugh.

Unable to stop herself, Kate shoved open the door and rushed into the room. "Call an ambulance," she ordered as Guerin slid to the floor. "He's having a heart attack."

With only a glance at David's startled face, Kate moved in to work on Dr. Guerin. She positioned him and began chest massage, and her frantic efforts at CPR brought nothing but a continuing roar of laughter from Augusta. The woman was laughing so hard she was hiccoughing.

Kate worked until her arms ached, but Russell Guerin had no desire to be rescued from death. His eyes went closed and it soon became obvious that he had no more will and no intentions of coming back. Kate finally stopped and let her arms fall numbly to her sides as she rose. She walked slowly to the bed, where the enormous Augusta Guerin was wiping her cheeks, still quivering with mirth. The dark, sunken eyes and powdered fleshy jowls caught Kate's stare and held it. She said, "Mrs. Guerin, you are a pathetic, despicable woman."

Augusta stopped wiping and looked at her. She opened her large mouth, but before she could speak, Kate stepped forward and slapped her hard. Augusta's eyes rounded and Kate struck her again, even harder this time. Then Kate turned to the console and ripped the microphone wire from its connection. She reached behind the console and ripped out every wire she could find while Augusta watched, dumbstruck.

Then Kate spied a plate on the floor beside the bed. A knife, fork, and a litter of steak bones rested on top of the plate. Kate bent down and collected the knife. The fork she kicked under the bed.

"I'm going to free David now," she said and she leaned close to Augusta. "If you try to stop me, I will kill you. Do you understand me?"

Augusta gave a mute nod and Kate turned away from her. As she reached the end of the bed, a strong hand suddenly clamped itself around her ankle and pulled. Her gaze met David's in a look of shock, and she had time to think: *under the bed,* before she fell face forward. Her head connected with the edge of the bed frame, and though her hands flew out to catch her, her bones seemed to turn to rubber the moment she reached the floor. She inhaled lint on the carpet, and then she wasn't aware of anything.

# 35

## MONDAY, MAY 23, 1:00 A.M.

MEL COUNTED EACH tick of the hospital clock until she thought she would go mad. Her face hurt. Her entire body ached. She hated the green surgery blouse the desk nurse had given her to wear. She wished the doctor would come.

Across the room from her sat Grant, Tim, and one other hand from the ranch. Though Grant had finally believed her, he insisted on blaming Mel for what had happened to his brother. Mel couldn't disagree with him. Occasionally she would look up and find one of them staring at her. They all blamed her. She was a no-good busybody who had caused nothing but trouble since the day of her arrival. Rather than ponder the mystery of their buddy Jay's behavior, they chose to dwell on the lesbian's culpability. It was understandable. Not acceptable, but understandable. They were males, after all.

So was Denny. But he was different.

He was special.

With a low groan of frustration, Mel rose from her chair and walked toward the door.

"Get me some coffee," Grant ordered.

"Me, too," said Tim.

Mel gave them the finger and kept walking. She heard chairs scrape behind her, but no one came.

Bunch of rednecks, she thought as she made her way down the hall to the elevator. She went to the small cafeteria and purchased coffee for herself. When she came back she stood just outside the waiting room door and sipped at the hot liquid. Within minutes, a doctor approached. He ignored her sudden, gurgled questions and stepped inside the waiting room.

"Which one of you gentlemen is Mel?"

"That's me," said Mel from behind him. The doctor turned, gave her a slow once-over, then looked to the other men as if for confirmation. Mel hated him for that. She hated every inch of his little green-clad body. Where was the doctor she had had? She wanted him to be the one to say whatever this worried-looking idiot had come to say.

"How is he?" Mel blurted.

"Disgustingly healthy. I wish I could patent those stomach muscles of his and sell them. He bled a lot, but there was no major organ damage. Things look good, but I'll be keeping him under close observation, regardless. At the moment he wants to see you."

"He's awake?" Mel asked in disbelief.

The man in green nodded. "He came out of it so fast it made me wonder if he was ever under. And he came out yelling. Would you care to follow me?"

"Wait a minute," said Grant. "I'm the next-of-kin here. She's nobody."

"At the moment," said the doctor, "she is who he wants to see. He's agitated right now, and if I do as he asks I'm hoping he'll calm down. I have the patient's interests at heart here, not yours."

"Why don't you sedate him?" Grant complained.

The doctor ignored him and guided Mel out of the room. As they walked down the hall toward post-op Mel said, "Why didn't you sedate him?"

"A patient's mental state makes a world of difference. If I

sedated him now he would still be agitated when he awakened, and we don't need that. The happier he is, the faster he'll get well."

Mel's initial dislike of the doctor began to change to admiration. He led her into post-op then, and she saw Denny. He was so pale and looked so tired that Mel's eyes welled up.

"Thank God," Denny said when he saw her. "I thought you'd already left."

"I wouldn't do that," Mel said. "I told you I wouldn't do that." She went to the bed and gripped the hand he extended.

Denny's eyes narrowed as he looked at her swollen face. "Did Jay do that to you?"

Mel nodded. "But it's not as bad as what he did to you. Why don't you get some rest. I'll come back later."

"No," Denny said quickly. "You won't come back because you'll be leaving. I wanted to tell you not to blame yourself. I know you do, but you shouldn't. I went out there of my own free will. Nobody made me go."

Mel looked at him, looked at the matted blond hair and the white gauze covering his midsection. She looked at the hand wrapped around hers and noted how strong it was, even now. "Denny, I don't know a woman on earth who deserves a man like you. I do blame myself. And with good reason. I don't know how to make it up to you."

Denny's fingers tightened. "I have a suggestion, if you care to hear it. But first tell me what kind of car you drive back in the city."

Mel frowned. "A blue 'eighty-eight Corolla. Why?"

"That'll do," Denny said. "Give me six months of your life and we'll call it even."

"What?"

"Six months. A trial period. If things don't work out, I'll move out and find my own place."

"What?" Mel repeated. "You mean live with me for six months? And drive my car?"

"I can drop you off at work before I go to my classes," Denny told her. "And after you help me find a job, I can buy my own car."

Mel leaned back. "Now wait a minute. You want a car, a place to stay, and a job out of me?" She heard a throat clearing behind her and she glanced over her shoulder in time to see the doctor leave the room.

Denny's smile was weak. "That's not all I want, of course. But it'll do for starters."

"You realize I don't live anywhere near a horse," Mel told him. "In fact, I don't even have a lawn. What I have is gravel and a yucca plant."

"That's fine with me," said Denny.

Mel stared at him. "I have to think about this, Denny. This is a big decision."

"There's nothing to think about, Mel. Either you want me or you don't. If I have to call in all my cards, I'll do it. Who found you the day you came out of the cave? Who believed you when everyone else laughed? Who pulled you out of the water down there tonight and took a bullet for his trouble?"

Mel turned away. "Manipulation and blackmail."

Denny grinned and squeezed her hand again. "Tell me now, because I'm ready to take that shot they offered."

She looked back at him. "Are you in pain?"

"I've been shot and had surgery, Mel. Of course I'm in pain."

"Smart guy," she murmured. Then she stood up and leaned over him to kiss his brow. "Let's talk about this when you're not delirious."

"Three months," he said.

"I might be crazy in two," she responded.

Denny smiled. "You're already crazy. You're crazy about me. You just don't know it yet."

"I'll leave my home phone number with you," she promised.

"I already have it," Denny said with a sheepish grin.

"How?" asked Mel.

"The phone book in Guerin's office . . . Melvina."

"Don't call me that, Denny. I hate it."

"Excuse me," the doctor said from the door. "There's an emergency long-distance phone call at the main desk for Mel Kierkes. Would that be you?"

Mel nodded. Long-distance? She looked at Denny and gave a shrug. "Who knows? Listen, if we leave in the morning before you're awake I'll call you the minute I get home. Don't flirt with any of the nurses and don't try any rope tricks with the I.V. tubes. Okay?"

Denny nodded. "Kiss me again."

Mel did. To the doctor she said, "He's ready for a shot now."

The doctor looked relieved. As she left the room, Mel heard Denny say, "She's something, isn't she?"

It made her smile as she walked down the corridor to find the phone.

Seconds later she said, "Rosalie? As in Mrs. Guerin's Rosalie?" into the receiver she held.

"Yes," the caller snuffled. "I couldn't do it. I just couldn't go through with it."

"Through with what? Where are you, Rosalie?"

"A restaurant. Colorado, I think. I called the house and Dr. Raleigh told me you were at the hospital. I couldn't tell him about his brother. I just couldn't."

"David? What about him?" Mel demanded. "Rosalie, try to make sense, would you?"

Rosalie tried. "It was me on the bus, Miss Kierkes. I took Mrs. Guerin's car and left it at the bus station. She paid me to do it. She paid me a lot. I thought I could go through with it. I thought I could just go away and forget everything, but I can't. She said she would have me hunted down if I talked, but I don't care."

"What about David?" Mel pressed. "What has she done with him?"

"I helped her move him to the third floor. She has him tied in a wheelchair. I think she's going to hurt him."

"What?" Mel whispered. "Which room, Rosalie? Where on the third floor?"

"The room beside Mrs. Guerin's. The first door to your right when you enter the hall. It's like a little hospital lab. She stores blood and food there."

"Blood?" Mel said.

"Yes, blood. The money wasn't worth it, Miss Kierkes. You can't offer money to your conscience."

"Thank God you have one, Rosalie," said Mel. She hung up the phone and raced in the direction of the waiting room to find Grant—until she remembered that the keys to his truck were still in her jeans pocket. Mel skidded to a halt and did a quick U-turn in the hall. To hell with Grant, she thought as she ran toward the hospital exit.

# 36

## MONDAY, MAY 23, 1:45 A.M.

DAVID VOWED TO himself that he would never do anything for Bryan again as Augusta and a pistol-toting Jay removed him from the wheelchair and placed him on a padded gurney. He thought of hitting Jay and making a break for it, but his stiff, sore muscles refused to obey even the simplest commands. The biting ropes were soon replaced with leather straps as Augusta bound him to the gurney. His backside felt better, and it was good to stretch his legs out again, even though parts of him were still completely numb.

"Why are we doing this?" the still white and bleeding Jay asked his mother. "The night you brought him up here you said you would explain everything later. I think it's time you told me why he's here."

"Because he has B-negative blood," Augusta said.

David saw Jay frown and shake his head. "So? What difference does that . . . Never mind. I'm going to check on Kate again."

"She's fine," Augusta snapped.

"I'm going to check," Jay said firmly. "She may be frightened."

"I doubt it," muttered Augusta. "You saw what she did to me."

"No, I didn't. I told you, I was unconscious until the fork hit me. She wouldn't do what you said she did. Kate isn't like that. She couldn't hurt anyone."

"For him she could." Augusta looked at David.

Jay paused. "What do you mean?"

His mother smiled and lifted her brows. "She's in love with him, Jay. Didn't you know that?"

Jay slowly shook his head. "No. Kate wouldn't love him. When I come back I need to transfuse again. I'm getting dizzy."

Augusta watched him go, then she turned to look at David. "See how disoriented he becomes? *He* has B-negative blood. And I think a whole blood transfusion is just what he needs right now. Your blood can save his life." She paused and smiled again.

"Remember the article you wrote on the Masai in Africa? The way they pierce the artery of a cow and mix the blood with milk in times of drought and migration? I was fascinated. Especially with the ceremonies they hold, and the warriors who drink the blood of lions to gain strength and courage. In passing, and in pun, you happened to mention that you had B-negative blood. Do you remember?"

David remembered. He had joked with the Masai and told them the B stood for "bad."

"I kept a close eye on you after that," Augusta continued. "Your blood isn't exactly rare, but people like you are. I remembered the story on the Masai when I read about your wife's suicide. I thought, wouldn't it be wonderful if Jay could drink the blood of that lion? Only symbolically, of course. Then came the waiting for another story to track you down. I waited and waited and then my dear recently departed Russell practically dropped you in my lap. Or your brother, rather. I negotiated for *you*."

"Mother?" Jay said from the door. "I'm getting very dizzy. You'll have to help me transfuse. I don't think I can do it myself."

Augusta immediately abandoned David. "Of course, my love. Come and sit in David's wheelchair. How was Kate?"

"Trying to get free. She had one hand loose. There are three police cars downstairs, Mother. I went to my room and saw them through the window. Waltman is with them. He knows I come up to the third floor to transfuse. What are we going to do?"

"They won't come in here," Augusta said imperiously.

"Yes, they will," Jay argued in a weary voice. "And you can't just leave Dad on the floor in there."

"Why not?" Augusta asked. "He died of natural causes. And it's your fault the police are here. I told you to leave that Kierkes woman alone."

Jay slumped down into the wheelchair. "Just help me transfuse, would you? I don't need to hear . . . about it right . . ." His eyes closed and his head tilted back. The pistol in his hand fell to the floor.

Augusta went to him and lifted one eyelid. "Poor thing. We're going to have to hurry, David. Make a fist please."

She asked him that every time, but it seemed to make no difference in the amount of tries it took her to find a vein.

On Jay, she seemed to hit a vein the first try. David thought about the police downstairs. That was good. They would come up here. They would have to if they were looking for Jay. She couldn't drain David before the search party reached the third floor.

And Jay didn't need *all* David's blood. He needed only a few pints, which would probably leave David with at least one, gauging from the bags Augusta had filled that day.

He couldn't watch it leaving his body. He could look at anyone else's blood, and he had on many occasions, but this was infinitely more personal.

David tried counting seconds in his head, tried making the seconds into minutes to keep from wondering what was taking the police so long. They were certainly taking their time about getting up to the third floor.

Then he thought about Kate. Keep working on that rope,

sweetheart, he told her. You throw me a curveball every time, I swear. I do believe you would have carved a steak out of Augusta if one ounce of fat had jiggled at the wrong moment.

Augusta was afraid of you, Kate. I didn't imagine that. She was afraid. Why, I don't know. The look on her fat face when you slapped her. That was something. It's probably been years since anyone dared to slap Augusta Guerin's face, if ever at all.

I hope you're working on that rope, Kate. I am definitely starting to feel the loss of my vital fluids. I haven't eaten in ages, and those police won't be packing any orange juice and Oreos when they get here. I'll need a transfusion myself, just as soon as you can arrange—

A noise to the right made him open his eyes. Jay had regained consciousness, and he was staring in horror at the red tube in his arm. "Mother, what are you doing? Are you trying to kill me?"

"No, no, no," Augusta assured him. "David's blood type is the same as yours, Jay. Everything will be fine. Just sit back and try to relax. This is the treatment I promised you. You can think of this as our first session. David's blood will help you."

"What?" Jay stared at her. "What did you say?"

Augusta exhaled through her nose. "I said this is your first session. You wanted me to help, so I'm helping you."

"Not this way!" Jay cried. He ripped the tape, needle, and tube from his arm and lunged from the chair.

David's blood kept pumping through the torn tube . . . onto the floor.

"*Therapy,* Mother!" a now red-faced Jay shouted. "I wanted you to help me through therapy!"

Augusta seemed not all bothered by his outburst. "But this *is* therapy, Jay. Component, no, *whole* blood therapy. And this is *David's* blood."

Jay's laugh was hoarse and disbelieving. "You're crazier than I am. You are. All this time I've believed every word you've said to me, done everything you asked of me, and you're sicker than I am. I should have known. I should have known when you started the blood-drinking and the out-of-body-experience bullshit. But like always, you made me believe you had a perfectly logical reason for doing such a . . . Damn you, Mother, you were never going to help me at all. All those promises, and this is what I . . . *nothing.* I'm never going to be . . . never have . . . you've ruined things for me and Kate and now . . . damn you, damn you . . ." He was sobbing now, making hysterical noises as he reeled into the adjoining room.

David craned his head and felt sudden fear. No, he thought. Don't touch her, Jay. Don't hurt Kate because you're mad at your mother.

Within seconds Jay was back, holding the steak knife in his hand. His face was wet with tears. He said, "I'm going to help one of us, Mother." Then he turned the knife and swiftly sawed open his left wrist.

David squeezed his eyes shut when he saw the bright spurt of blood.

Augusta cried out and stumbled to one thick knee as she tried to rush toward her son. "No! Jay, no! This will help! I promise you! David's blood will . . . *no!*"

David opened his eyes and saw Jay switch the knife to his left hand and awkwardly slice open the other wrist. An incredible arc of blood spattered the rising, still screaming Augusta. David's vision was growing darker, but he thought he saw Mel enter the room. Then he thought he had only imagined it. He couldn't hang on anymore. His blood was a pool on the floor and he had the sudden urge to go swimming. As he slid into the dark depths, he heard the sound of a gunshot.

# 37

## MONDAY, MAY 23, 2:15 A.M.

KATE DROPPED THE pistol and Mel snatched it up again. She grabbed the hem of Augusta's gown and rubbed furiously at the trigger and the grip. "No fingerprints," she said as she stooped to place the pistol in Augusta's still twitching hand. She paused and looked. "Right in the eye. What a mess."

Kate wasn't listening; she was using her fingers to clamp off the tube attached to David's arm.

"Uh-oh," Mel said suddenly. "Was she right-handed or left-handed? No, wait. Her controls were on the right, so she had to be right-handed."

"Right," Jay whispered from the floor. "She used her right hand."

Mel left the dead woman and moved to stand over the blood-soaked Jay. He was looking at Kate.

"Mother . . . dead?" he asked.

"Yes," Mel told him.

Jay made a sound that might have been a laugh and lifted his arm above his head to soak his face with blood. He closed his eyes.

Mel watched him until the arm fell, then she bent down to feel for a pulse at his neck.

It stopped under her fingertips.

Mel took her hand away and went to Kate. The blue in Kate's irises was swallowed by her pupils as she stared down at David. His skin was gray. Mel felt his pulse and found it unsteady.

"Bryan," Kate whispered. "We need him. He has the same type blood as David."

"Are you sure?" Mel asked.

"I heard her say David is B-negative. Bryan is, too. Get him, Mel."

Mel turned away, then she quickly turned back. "Kate, listen to me. What happened here—it doesn't leave this room. Do you hear me? Jay bugged out and cut himself and Augusta went crazy and shot herself with the pistol. That's what I saw when I came in, all right? You were still in the bedroom or wherever, okay? You weren't anywhere near that pistol. Have you got that?"

Kate nodded. "Hurry, Mel. I'm going to lose him."

"No, you won't." Mel spun and rushed from the room. Just outside the door she collided with two adrenalized deputies. As one, they demanded to know where the gunshot had come from.

Mel pointed. "In there. Double suicide." She rushed on without pause, muttering to herself about the efficacy of the Greenwood County deputies. Just minutes ago they had only glanced at her when she raced through the main room and dived into the elevator.

She met Bryan in the hall. "Mel!" he exclaimed. "Where's Kate? Is she up here?"

"Yes. So is David." In a garbled rush Mel told him two people were dead and his brother needed his blood.

Bryan's skin paled with shock, and as she tugged him along with her Mel tried to be more coherent. Before she was finished, he was rolling up his sleeve. The worried look of concern in his eyes told Mel all she needed to know about Bryan Raleigh's feelings for his brother.

The discovery of a third corpse in the bedroom was as much a surprise to Mel as it was to the deputies. She told them she didn't know anything about Dr. Guerin's death. All she had seen was the double suicide. (She hadn't seen Kate rise up from the floor like an angel of death and put the pistol right in Augusta Guerin's fat, startled face . . . )

Kate managed to look away from David long enough to explain Guerin's death and to corroborate Mel's double-suicide tale. Mel had been worried about that. Kate had looked out of it when Mel told her what to say. She still looked out of it, though she sounded convincing enough to the deputy called Waltman.

The deputies looked even more confused. Like they didn't know what to believe. Mel felt almost sorry for the poor, bewildered fools. Three dead, red, rich people and one transfusion taking place under their noses. The one named Waltman looked a bit nauseous as he called for an ambulance and the boys from the morgue. He looked like he wanted to wipe the blood off his shoes pretty bad. If she remembered correctly, Denny had said that Waltman was Jay's buddy.

Friends are always the last to know, she thought bitterly.

Which made her think of something else. When the ambulance attendants arrived to take over the transfusing, Mel took the worried Kate aside. "How are you, Kate? Are you all right?"

"I'm fine," Kate told her. "What about you? Does your face hurt?"

"Not now." Mel gripped her hand. "I have to ask you something. After I ask, we'll never bring up the subject again, all right?"

Kate nodded. Her pupils had contracted some, but her gaze never strayed from David for very long.

Mel lowered her voice. "Just out of curiosity, why exactly did you kill Mrs. Guerin?"

Kate looked away. "I had to."

"You had to. Okay." Mel wasn't sure what that meant. "She had you tied up or something, right?"

"Yes. Jay freed me before he came in here."

"I see. So you came in, saw the blood, and I guess you picked up the pistol—"

"She knew it was going to happen."

Mel frowned. "She did?"

"Yes," said Kate. Then she blinked. Her eyes filled. "If you're worried about this, about me, please don't."

Mel sighed in relief and put an arm around her. "I'm not worried, Katie. I won't pretend I understand what you mean by saying you had to, and that she knew, but if you say so, then I believe you. Besides, she nearly killed David. Right?"

Kate nodded and wiped her eyes. After a long moment she looked at Mel and said, "Thank you for doing what you did. For not telling the police."

Mel shrugged. "It was instinct."

# 38

## MONDAY, MAY 23, 1:00 P.M.

"YOU CAN HAVE it, I'm finished," David said to the hovering Kate. "What time do we leave?"

Kate held his plate and looked at the half-eaten sandwich. "We can't leave until the sheriff has affidavits from everyone, including you."

"I'll give it right now," David told her.

"You can't. They just left for the cave. Why don't you try to sleep some more? You should have stayed in the hospital longer."

David frowned. "I'm sure you have better things to do than play nursemaid today."

Kate ignored him and put the plate on his nightstand while she carried a corner of bread crust to Frank's cage.

"He won't eat that," David told her.

"He's eaten worse lately," Kate said. "A lot worse."

David pulled the sheet from the bed and wrapped it around his waist so he could get out of bed. He went to the dresser and then to the closet before he remembered.

"Did anyone find my clothes?"

She shook her head. "Would you like me to ask for donations from the remaining ranch hands?"

"Remaining?" David said.

"Most of them left this morning," Kate explained.

David couldn't blame them. He left the closet and moved to the window. The sun was shining brightly. Not a cloud in sight. He turned back to Kate. "Run across the hall and bring me some of Bryan's things."

"His clothes are packed. His bags are downstairs."

"Then go downstairs. Where are the shorts I had on a few hours ago?"

Kate fed Frank another piece of crust. "In the bathroom. I rinsed them out, but they're still stained." She dusted the crumbs from her hands. "If you're finished being a grouch and expressing your token male annoyance at female concern, then maybe you'd like to talk about where we're going from here."

"I'd *like* to find some pants," David said from the window.

"David," said Kate. "I need to know. Please talk to me."

He didn't look at her. "Tell me what happened last night. After I blacked out."

"I already did."

"The truth?"

Her voice was small. "I'll go downstairs and see if Bryan will let me go through his bags. I'm sure he'll have something you can wear."

David turned. "Kate."

She paused with her back to him. "What?"

"Come here and look at me."

"No. Your face looks awful."

"It never looked that good to begin with. Come here."

"No," she repeated. "I don't want to be badgered with questions about last night. I don't want to talk about it ever again. You'll have to write your precious story without input from me."

David eyed the stiff set of her spine. He left the window and moved to stand behind her. "Turn around and look at me."

Kate remained still. "Leave me alone, David."

David reached around and turned her so she was facing him. "I said look at me."

"All right." Her gaze lifted defiantly to meet his.

"Tell me the truth about what happened last night."

Kate put her hands up as if to push against his chest. "I'm not going to tell you anything."

"You should, because our future together is going to rest on your answer," David told her. "The right answer. Now tell me the truth. Who picked up that pistol last night? I know it wasn't Augusta."

"You really are a heartless bastard," Kate breathed.

"Right. Now tell me."

"David, please don't."

His stare was relentless. "Tell me."

Kate shoved him away from her. "It was me. *Me,* David. Mel took the pistol out of my hands and put it in Augusta's hand. Now leave me alone."

He came after her and put his hands on her arms to hold her in front of him. "Was it you who killed her, Kate? Was it you, or was it someone else?"

Kate was silent. Her eyes were suddenly round and dark with confusion. "What do you want from me?"

David cupped her face in his hands and kissed her deeply. Then he released her to return to the bed. He sat down and lifted his legs up to prop himself against the headboard. He leaned his head back and closed his eyes.

Kate stood where she was, her limbs trembling. "You're as despicable as she was, David. You're cruel and selfish and manipulative. You try to—"

"Are you really well?" David interrupted. "Do you remember putting that pistol in Augusta's face, *in her eye,* and squeezing the trigger? Was it you, Kate, or was it someone a little more aggressive?"

"It was me," Kate said. "So you can stop testing me. Are you trying to make me angry enough or hurt enough to see another persona emerge?"

"What makes you so sure one didn't? What makes you so sure it *was* you who killed her?"

Kate said nothing.

It didn't matter. David had an ending for his story. Not the one he would tell, but the ending the found the most satisfying. The mother of the bleeder, slain by a gentle, bloodless hand. Gentle until provoked, anyway. David could spend a lifetime trying to figure out the woman who stood before him. A lifetime full of surprises.

He slowly opened his eyes. She was still standing, still staring at him. He held a hand out to her.

"Another test?" she asked.

He nodded. "An important one. If you pass, we'll be together in more ways than one."

"And if I should fail?"

"Will you?"

They looked at each other for some time. Then Kate stepped away from the door and approached the bed.

"We'll see, won't we?"